Acclaim for t[...] of CORN[...] and LAWRENCE BLOCK!

"*Into the Night* may well be the most important mystery novel of the year, a truly bravura performance by Woolrich and Block."
— *West Coast Review of Books*

"A potent distillation of Woolrich's darkest obsessions… good unclean fun."
— *Chicago Tribune*

"Nothing beats a tale of fatalistic dread by the supreme master of suspense, Cornell Woolrich. His novels and hundreds of short stories define the essence of noir."
— *New York Times*

"Block grabs you…and never lets go."
— *Elmore Leonard*

"Along with Raymond Chandler, Cornell Woolrich practically invented the genre of noir."
— *New York Newsday*

"[Block is the] one writer of mystery and detective fiction who comes close to replacing the irreplaceable John D. MacDonald."
— *Stephen King*

"Cornell Woolrich is *the* master of suspense. When he sets out to leave you panting, you can bet he will succeed."
— *Isaac Asimov*

He said, "There's no use standing here like this. We haven't anything to say to each other."

I said, "If you think I'm going to give you up without a fight, you better think twice."

"You already have," he said. "It's over and done with. There's nothing you can do about it." And he started to walk.

"Isn't there?" I called after him. "Isn't there? Watch. Watch and see." But he never even turned around again.

That brought the thing to a head. That got it going, that brush-off on the street. Love ended there. There wasn't any more love, only hate from then on. Hate, and figuring out how to hurt him.

I worked on it, steady. While I earned my feed singing, I worked on it. While other men made love to me, I kept working on it. I worked on it in the morning, and I worked on it in the afternoon, and I worked on it at night.

Finally, I thought I had a way.

Since I couldn't get at him himself, I decided maybe I could get at him through her...

INTO *the* NIGHT

by **Cornell Woolrich**
and **Lawrence Block**

A HARD CASE CRIME NOVEL

A HARD CASE CRIME BOOK
(HCC-163)
First Hard Case Crime edition: May 2024

Published by

Titan Books
A division of Titan Publishing Group Ltd
144 Southwark Street
London SE1 0UP

in collaboration with Winterfall LLC

Print edition ISBN 978-1-80336-699-9
E-book ISBN 978-1-80336-701-9

Design direction by Max Phillips
www.signalfoundry.com

Typeset by Swordsmith Productions

The name "Hard Case Crime" and the Hard Case Crime logo are trademarks of Winterfall LLC. Hard Case Crime books are selected and edited by Charles Ardai.

Printed and bound CPI Group (UK) Ltd, Croydon, CR0 4YY.

Visit us on the web at www.HardCaseCrime.com

INTO THE NIGHT

1

At first there was music. Popular songs played on her little radio, the volume pitched low enough to keep the music from interfering with her thoughts. Then, as the sky darkened outside her window, she got up, crossed the room, turned on a lamp, then changed her mind and switched it off again. And, while she was at it, switched off the radio as well.

Better to sit in the dark, Madeline thought. Better to sit in the dark, and in the silence.

That way, though, you had only your own thoughts for company. And her own thoughts were bad company these days. They were a whirlpool, a vortex, sucking her deep down within herself, making her see parts of herself she didn't wish to look at. It didn't do to see too clearly into the darkness, didn't do to listen too closely to those thoughts. That was why the whole world played the radio loud, and kept the lights burning. To keep the thoughts drowned out. To keep the darkness safely at bay.

But there came a time when you couldn't do that anymore.

How long did she sit there, motionless, her mind hewing its own paths, finding its own way through a maze of ill-formed thoughts? She never knew. There was a watch on her wrist but she never looked at it.

Finally, without even thinking about it, she got to her feet and walked to the closet. Enough light came through the open window so that she could do this without stumbling. And she knew this little room well enough, had lived here long enough, so that she could move through it in pitch-darkness, with her eyes clenched shut.

She stepped upon a box to reach the closet's highest shelf. There she reached into another box, groped until her hands found the soft bag with the hard object inside it. She drew it from the box, left the closet, returned to the chair where she had been sitting. And sat down again.

The velvet drawstring bag had once held a bottle of Canadian whiskey. Now it held something more immediately lethal.

A gun.

She loosened the drawstrings, removed the gun from the velvet bag. Its smell seemed to fill the room, a scent composed of the smell of metal and the smell of machine oil. She fancied, too, that she could detect the scent of gunpowder as well. Perhaps the gun had been fired since its last cleaning. More probably, though, the gunpowder smell had been supplied by her imagination. The gun had been her father's, and as far as Madeline knew, he had never fired it.

He hadn't needed to. He had killed himself slowly, and in a more socially acceptable, less scandalous way.

With the whiskey. Expensive Canadian whiskey at first, of the sort the velvet sack had once held. Then, toward the end, with cheap rye whiskey and cheaper California wine. Until one night, they told her, he had a seizure and died on the street.

He'd left the clothes he was wearing, and another few changes of clothing barely worth giving to the Salvation Army. He'd left a manila envelope of meaningless old letters and post-cards and newspaper clippings; she'd given up trying to make sense of them and dropped them down the incinerator long ago. And he'd left this gun, this revolver, as his sole real legacy to his sole daughter.

And here it was now, the metal cold in her hand, the smell of it oppressive in the little furnished room.

What a legacy! What a parting gift!

In case you ever want to kill someone, Madeline.

Or in case you ever want to kill yourself.

How strange that he'd kept it all those years while he treated himself to a slower, quieter death. You'd think, she thought, that he'd either have gotten rid of the gun or used it. But it had been in his room when he died, and, miracle of miracles, the cops who searched his room had delivered it to her instead of appropriating it for their own purposes. And so it was in her hands now, ready for her to do with it as she wished.

Her hands couldn't leave the thing alone. She passed it from hand to hand, curled her index finger around the trigger, caressed the hammer with her thumb. Holding the weapon at arm's length, she sighted at various objects across the room, aiming at the little radio, the lamp, the darkness at the far corner of the room. She took aim, felt the trigger trembling under her index finger like a living thing, but never gave the trigger that final squeeze that would transform fantasy into reality.

Why keep the thing? Why have it around the room where she lived?

Because it was all she had left of him, she thought, but decided that wasn't it. She had tossed his papers down the incinerator, had given his clothes away, without a second thought. She had kept the gun because—

Because she must have known she'd have a use for it.

Her blood ran cold at the thought. Was that it? Was her father's last gift to her to be the means of ending her own life?

Put it away, she told herself. Put it back in the sack, and in the morning, when night thoughts have been banished by sunlight, take it out and get rid of it. Drop it in a trash can or down a sewer. Get rid of it before it got rid of you.

Did it even work? Was it even loaded? For all she knew it

was empty of bullets, its firing mechanism long since rusted shut, the whole thing useful only as a paperweight. But she didn't think so. It seemed in her hands to give off a murderous energy, as if the capacity to destroy, to kill, existed in it as a palpable living entity.

She put the barrel in her mouth, tasted metal on her tongue.

Felt the trembling of the trigger.

She took the gun from her mouth and held it to her temple. She put the barrel into her ear, then held it to her throat so that it touched against a pulse point. Just squeeze the trigger, she thought, and in an instant there would be no pulse, no thoughts in the mind, nothing, nothing at all.

But why?

That, she thought, was the strangest part, because the question was unanswerable. Why kill herself? Because her life was empty, she thought. Because there was no reason *not* to kill herself. But was that ever a reason to do anything? By the same token, she could argue that she ought to go on living, if only because there was no reason *not* to go on living.

Reasons.

Did people ever have reasons for the things they did? Did they even need them? Life, after all, was not a problem in logic. You didn't get a prize for figuring it all out, and that was just as well, because no one ever figured it out. Whether or not there was a reason to go on living, some people went on living. Whether or not there was a reason to kill oneself, some people killed themselves.

Turn on a light, she thought savagely. Play some music. Sing along with the radio, sing at the top of your lungs if you want to. But get out of this mood and get through the night, and first thing in the morning you'll get rid of the gun.

No.

Somehow she could not put the gun back in the velvet bag. Thoughts flickered through her mind. Something she'd heard once, a rule of drama: If you showed a gun in the first act of a play, you had to make sure it was fired before the curtain at the end of the third act. And weren't there tribesmen somewhere who, having drawn their daggers, would not return them to their sheaths until they had drawn blood? In the absence of an enemy, they would nick their own thumbs rather than sheathe their weapons unblooded. Perhaps this was superstition, or perhaps it was to prevent them from brandishing their weapons too casually.

Again she found herself holding the gun to her temple.

Her life had no purpose.

It was hard to say how it had come to this. Perhaps her life had never had purpose. She had drifted through it, living in one place or another, working at one thing or another, without realizing the extent to which she was drifting. She had lived without a purpose, blissfully ignorant of the need for a purpose, and now she found herself confronted by the purposelessness of her existence and felt devastated by the confrontation.

You could live a short life or a long one. You could nip a purposeless life in the bud or let it spin itself out for seventy or eighty or a hundred years. Either way you died, and once you were dead it was as if you had never lived.

You were gone and that was the end of it.

Then why hurry it?

Or: then why delay it?

Play the radio, she told herself. Turn on some lights.

Instead, once more she brought the gun to her temple. Once more her thumb drew back the hammer. Once more her finger tightened on the trigger.

Did she *decide* to squeeze the trigger? Are these things decided? Her finger tightened on the trigger as it had done before, only this time it went on tightening, and she squeezed the trigger.

The hammer descended on an empty chamber.

Relief flooded through her, relief that expanded to fill her own body. She had been spared, she had been saved, and her life of a sudden felt infinitely precious. Even as she trembled at the narrowness of her escape, at the same time she thrilled to the excitement of being alive. A moment ago life had held no excitement, and now, suddenly, the mere fact that she was alive was exciting in and of itself.

She had survived. She had played out her hand, risking everything, and she had won.

She sprang to her feet. Tomorrow the old gun would go where it belonged—in the trash, down the sewer, wherever it could do no harm. She would not need it again. She had kept it, she knew now, for this very purpose—to stand on the very brink of death and be given her life back. She had taken a horrible chance, but it was a risk she need never run again.

She danced across the room, switched on the lamp, filled the room with its cheering glow. She turned on the little radio, let the room fill up with music. She moved gaily to the music, her feet as light now as her heart had been heavy mere moments ago.

And, dancing, she realized with a start that she was still holding the gun.

She stopped, stared at the thing in her hand. Very nearly the instrument of her destruction, it had instead been the means of her deliverance, and her feelings for the object were impossible to sort out. One thing, though, was quite certain. She didn't want to carry it around with her now.

She found the velvet bag, tucked the gun into it, drew the

drawstrings tight. And then, dancing again, caught up in the music and in her own joy in life, she slapped the gun down on a table. Perhaps she meant merely to set it down. Perhaps the rhythm of the music and the joy of her own life urge made her slam the gun down so dramatically.

The gun discharged upon impact.

The noise of the shot was enormous in the little room. She caught her breath at it, and her heart clutched in her chest. Even as the sound of the gunshot was dying out around her, she moved quickly and without thought to switch off the radio, so that the silence which followed the shot could be complete.

Where had the bullet gone?

She moved, frantically, to touch her hands to her own body, as if she could have been shot without realizing it. What irony, to fail in an attempt at suicide, then to shoot oneself by accident just minutes later. But the bullet had not struck her.

Yet there had been a bullet. The room reeked of cordite, and the velvet bag showed a black-edged hole where the bullet had torn its way out.

She looked for a bullet hole in the walls, for damage to anything within the room. She saw nothing.

Then, as if magnetically, her eyes were drawn to the open window.

She was gazing at the window when she heard someone moaning outside.

A woman, alone, sprawled on the pavement. A woman, young, moaning, sobbing, her head cradled now in Madeline's lap.

A woman, shot in the chest on the sidewalk across the street from Madeline's rooming house. Shot in the chest, bleeding, the blood streaming from the wound. Eyes trying to focus, a mouth trying to form words.

Around them, a crowd was forming. People cried out questions, supplied answers.

Who was she?

Why, she lived here in the neighborhood. Starr, her name was, Starr Barrett.

No, not Barrett, Bartlett—Starr Bartlett.

Who shot her?

Why, there had been a shot fired from a passing car. Some lunatic, some thrill killer, driving through a quiet neighborhood, rolling down his window and firing at random.

My God, here? In this neighborhood?

Hell, it could happen anywhere. All it takes is one madman with a gun and a grudge. That's all it takes and it can happen anywhere, and to anyone. You get some madman shooting from a window, some lunatic killing little kids, some maniac stabbing hitchhikers. Or someone like this, firing at random from a moving auto.

The voices were background music to Madeline. She barely heard them because they didn't know anything. There had been no shot from a passing car, although death had been as random, as capricious, in selecting this young woman.

Her gun, her father's gun. The gun had spared Madeline's life and taken this life instead. It was true—you couldn't return your weapon unblooded to its sheath. The gun you showed onstage had to be fired before the curtain fell.

Now the curtain had fallen, and a comedy had turned to a tragedy.

There was a siren, a police car on its way. But she barely heard it. She was looking down into the woman's eyes, and as she sought to see into them she saw the very life go out of them. The girl shuddered once in her arms and was still.

❖

The lamp was on, and the radio. Both stayed on all night as she sat in her room, waiting for them to come for her. It was only a matter of time, she thought, before the police came to her room and knocked on her door. When that happened, she would admit them and tell them what had happened. How she had tried to kill herself. How she had been spared, and how a woman across the street had been chosen by some unseen hand to die in her place.

How, more prosaically, she had acted thoughtlessly with a gun, and how a bullet had found its way through an open ground-floor window and into living flesh.

And then what would happen to her?

She didn't know. What she had done had not been murder in the technical sense of the word. It had, to be sure, been an accident. But this did not mean the law would not find her at fault. It had been a criminal accident, and there would certainly be some penalty she would have to pay for it. And that was fitting enough. She had deprived another woman of her life. Whatever penalty the law exacted would be no more than fair.

And so she waited for them to come. She had slipped away from the scene outside moments after the woman's life had slipped away. Gently she'd laid the woman's head on the pavement. The crowd had opened up for her as she stepped through it, closing again around the woman's body without taking note of Madeline. But someone surely had noticed her, and someone would say something to a policeman, and they would come to her door, if only to seek her testimony as a witness. Perhaps she had been there when the woman was shot. Perhaps she had seen the killer, or noted the license number of the car. Certainly she ought to be questioned, so that they might determine what she did or did not know.

The radio played on. Outside, the police cars came and went, the crowd dispersed. The gun, still wrapped in its velvet bag, remained on the table where she had flung it. From where she sat, she could see the ugly hole marked with powder burns where the bullet had exited.

If she had known the police were not to come, perhaps she might have turned the gun again on herself. But she fully expected their visit and was willing to leave the matter of her retribution up to them. Even when the sky lightened with dawn, she waited for them to appear.

But they did not appear.

For two days she waited. She did not leave the room. She did not eat or drink. It was impossible to say if she slept. She stayed in her chair, and there were times when her eyes were open and times when they were shut.

After two days, she knew the police were not going to come.

Starr Bartlett.

The dead woman. A name that breathed life, romance, even glamour. Starr Bartlett.

Madeline had listened for the name on the radio, expecting it from the tongue of every news announcer, but each report began and ended and the name didn't come. Just as the police didn't come. She learned no more from the newspapers she bought after she finally left her room. A murder in a different section of the city, a better-off section, would have made headlines, but here? In Madeline's little corner of the city, in Starr Bartlett's, death was not news. A gunshot was not news. It was commonplace, familiar. Dog bites man.

Madeline asked at the newsstand, at the grocer's, at the Greek luncheonette that dished up eggs and toast at all hours. Finally she asked the gray-haired woman reading the horoscopes in a chair outside the self-serve laundromat, and the woman, speaking hoarsely around the remnants of a cigarette she'd smoked nearly down to the filter, said yes, she'd known the dead woman, to say hello to while they waited for their wash-and-wear to spin dry.

Starr Bartlett had lived in a rooming house just two blocks from Madeline's own. She was young, in her twenties, and unmarried. She lived alone. And she had been struck down by a bullet which people said had been fired from a passing automobile. The woman's own son was on the force, and he'd told her the police were convinced that the murder was the work of a random killer, possibly committed in imitation of a series of killings which had taken place two months previously in a large city a thousand miles away, and which had had enough press coverage to prompt a deranged person to emerge as a copycat killer.

If he struck again, the woman's son told her with a comforting pat on the arm, they would surely get him.

The implication being that this particular case had reached a dead end, and that, if there were no more similar killings, the murderer would escape uncaught.

Well, there would be no more killings, not with that gun. Madeline placed it, velvet bag and all, inside a brown paper bag, and tucked the package into her purse. She took a long walk, and in its course she pushed the wrapped-up gun down a storm drain. It would most likely never be found; if it were, it would never be connected to her.

So she had gotten away with murder.

She thought about that a day or two later as she sat at the Greek's lunch counter sipping a cup of coffee. She had bought a paper and could search through it for coverage of the death of Starr Bartlett, but without even opening the paper she knew there was nothing. And unless she confessed, she thought, there would be nothing. Starr was dead and her death had become part of the great body of unsolved crimes in the city's files. There would be no stories because there was nothing to be said.

She saw those eyes, staring up at her. And the light going out of them, as the life went out of their owner.

"You all right, miss?"

She looked up. The counterman's face was a mask of concern.

"The look on your face," he said. "Like you were gonna faint, or something."

"No," she assured him. "No, I'm all right."

Should she confess?

She thought about it. If the police had come, she would have confessed in a minute. But when they failed to appear it was as if she was being told that her confession was not required or even desired.

But what did that mean? Did she go scot-free?

That seemed inappropriate. Perhaps nothing would be gained by her confession, but what would be gained by her escaping punishment altogether? Wasn't she in debt? Didn't she owe something?

To whom? To the police? To Society with a capital S?

No.

To Starr.

The thought, once it came to her, seemed unmistakably obvious. She, Madeline, had tried to kill herself. She had been unable to do so. She had killed Starr instead.

Starr had died for her.

Therefore, she would live for Starr.

But how?

Starr, she thought, I wanted to die because my life had no purpose. Now I can find a purpose in living for you, and you can go on living through me. But for God's sake, who are you? What kind of life did you have, Starr? Starr, I don't know you at all!

"I suppose I should rent her room," the landlady said. "I guess I will, soon as I get around to it. I been sort of waiting for someone to come for her things, but I guess that's not going to happen. I haven't had the heart to pack up her things and send them. Long as her room's the way she left it, it's as if she could come back to it anytime. Soon as I pack up her stuff and rent the room out to somebody else, well, it makes her death that much more real for me, if you know what I mean."

"I know what you mean," Madeline said.

"I suppose I'm being silly," the woman said. "If you want to see the room, I guess that's all right. I don't see who it would hurt. The police have been through it, looking for reasons why someone would kill her. Then I guess they decided no one had a reason to kill her, that she just got in the way of the bullet."

That was truer than anybody realized, Madeline thought.

"Right this way, then," the woman said.

A rooming house not unlike her own. The same cooking smells in the hallway, the kind of smells you got when cooking consisted mostly of heating up canned goods on hot plates. Creaking stairs. Walls that needed painting.

"You just can't keep up with an old building like this," the woman said defensively, although Madeline had said nothing. "One thing needs doing after another. You can't keep up with it, you know. Or else you'd have to raise the rents, and people can't pay but so much. I keep it clean, though, and I only rent to decent people."

They were at Starr's door. The woman knocked on it, then caught herself.

"I don't know why I'm knocking," she said. "Force of habit, I shouldn't wonder. I respect people's privacy, it's the way I was brought up."

She produced a key, turned it in the lock, opened the door. The room was smaller than Madeline's, but similarly finished. The closet door was open, showing clothing on the hooks and hangers. The bed was made, and there was some clothing piled on it.

"You see what I mean," the landlady said. "It's like the room was waiting for her to come back to it."

"Yes," Madeline breathed.

"It's hard to take in what happened to her. Shot down that way."

"Yes."

"As young as she was."

"It's tough to die when you're young," Madeline said. "Like a stray dog."

"That's just it," the woman said. "She deserved better of life She didn't deserve to die like a dog in the street, and that's exactly how she did die. And for what purpose? For what purpose?"

Madeline didn't say anything. For a long moment the two women stood there. Then the older woman cleared her throat, as if she were about to say something, and Madeline said, "Tell me about her."

"What is there to tell? She lived here. Not for very long, but I felt that I knew her better than I did."

"How do you mean?"

"I don't know exactly. We didn't talk much. She mostly kept to herself. I told all this to the police." She looked at Madeline. "Why do you have to know all this?"

"Just a sense I have. That she and I were alike. Young women, single, living alone in rooming houses in this neighborhood. It could as easily have been me out there, out for a walk, struck down by a stray bullet."

"You feel a kinship with her," the woman said.

"I guess that's it. I feel that…that our lives are bound up in one another, even though we never met and I never knew her. I feel as though I owe her something."

"What could you possibly owe her?"

A life, she thought. Starr gave her life for me. She did it unwittingly, she didn't choose to do it, but what difference does that make? She died for me, and I have to live for her.

But of course she couldn't say that to the woman.

"Understanding," she said thoughtfully. "I owe her understanding."

"I don't know what you mean."

"Maybe I don't know what I mean either. But I feel as though our lives touched one another, and I want to get to know that woman whose life touched mine."

The woman said nothing for a long moment. Madeline moved through the room, went to the window, looked out. She turned, put a hand on the bed as if to test the springs.

The woman said, "There was no one in her life."

"You mean she lived alone?"

"I mean more than that. I mean she was alone with herself, completely alone. She wouldn't let people get near her. I liked her, I felt good seeing her in the hallway or on the stairs, I'd always pass the time of day with her, but I never got anywhere near her. I don't think anybody did. I don't suppose anybody could."

"I see."

"I think she was sorrowful," the woman said. "She didn't

broadcast her sorrows but I think it was there all the same. I think something or somebody caused her deep pain, and I don't think she ever got over that pain."

"Maybe she would have," Madeline said. "If she'd had a longer life."

"Maybe," the woman said. And then, after a moment, "But you know, there are some kinds of pain you never get over."

"Yes," Madeline said. "I know."

"Well," the woman said. "If there's nothing else, I have things I ought to be doing. A house like this, there's always something that needs doing."

"Could I—"

"What?"

"I'd like to stay here."

The woman stared at her. "You want to rent her room? You want to live where she lived?"

It hadn't occurred to her, but now she allowed herself to entertain the thought. Could she move right into Starr's life that way?

The thought was not without a certain appeal, but it didn't really make sense. She didn't want to become Starr Bartlett, which was anyway impossible on the face of it. No, she wanted not to live *as* Starr but to live *for* her. To perform some service for Starr that the dead woman could not perform for herself.

But what service? What could that be, and how could she ever discover it?

"No," she said. "No, I don't want to rent the room. I think you should rent it to somebody, though. Clear it out and rent it. The way it is now, it's a tomb for an absent corpse."

"Yes," the woman said. "Yes, you're right."

"But in the meantime, I'd like to spend a little time here," she went on. "I'd just like to be alone here."

"Alone?"

"Well, virtually alone. Alone with Starr."

"You've had your sorrows too," the woman said pointedly. "Same as she did."

"Maybe."

"I guess it'd be all right for you to spend a little time here," the woman said. "I guess it wouldn't hurt anything. Except—"

"Except what?"

"I don't like to say it."

Madeline waited.

"Sometimes a person'll decide to...do away with theirselves. And rather than do it where they live, they'll take a room just for that purpose. That happened here once. A man came, no luggage, said it was being shipped, said he'd pay a week's rent in advance, and that very first night he took pills and died in his sleep." The woman avoided Madeline's eyes. "And you," she said, "wanting to see a dead woman's room, and wanting to be alone in it. I don't think you'd be wanting to do that, and I didn't want to say anything, but I was the one walked in on that man and discovered his body there. One look and I knew he wasn't sleeping. He didn't look anything like somebody who was sleeping. His face was so blue it was near to purple."

"How awful for you."

"They said he was sick with something that would have killed him before long. He wanted an easy death, and he came here to spare his loved ones the horror of finding him. But he evidently thought it was all right for a total stranger to have that same horror."

"I'm not going to kill myself," Madeline said gently.

"I know you're not. I shouldn't have said anything, but I... had to."

"I understand."

"You stay here as long as you like," the woman said. "I don't know what good it could do you, but it won't do anybody any harm, will it? Spend all the time you want. I left her room as she left it. I tidied up just a little. The police were through her things and they don't always take the time to be neat. There were some things they left on the floor that I straightened up and put on the bed there."

"I see."

"As if she wouldn't want her things left messy. As if she cares now what her room looks like. But she was neat, you know. She kept to herself and she kept her things neat. So it only seems right to keep them neat now."

"Yes."

"I think you're right, what you said before. Soon as I have the strength for it I'll pack up her things. Instead of waiting for somebody to come for them, I'll just ship them back home to her mother. And I'll rent this room out."

Madeline nodded.

"But for now," the woman said, "spend what time you want here. Maybe her spirit's here, or a trace of it. Maybe you can have some kind of contact with her. There's stranger things than that happening every day of the year."

Madeline stood there motionless for a long time after, just where she'd left her. Listening to the echoing, inside her heart, of something that she'd said just now. Heavy and hollow, cold and lonely, sad and blue.

Its tough to die when you're young. Like a stray dog.

I must remember, and remember, and remember that, by the hour, she told herself. By the hour and by the day and by the week; yes, even by the year, if it should become necessary. Until I have at least partly undone this terrible thing that I've done to her. This thing that, try as I will, can never again be wholly undone.

After a while she took off her clothes, as Starr would have, here, in this, her room. She went over and selected a night robe from the things the landlady had left on the bed. Maybe it was the very one Starr had worn for her last sleep, on her last night on earth. But then she saw that it couldn't very well be for it was freshly laundered and even mended a little in one place where it had frayed—unless the landlady had done that after her death (and why should she?).

She put it on and went and stood before the glass in it.

"Starr," she breathed, to the figure she saw in it. "Starr. I can see you now. And that's a form of living on."

She put out the light, moved over a chair, and sat down by the window, looking out. It was evening in the city, and evening in the sky. Below there were a thousand stars, above there were just as many. But the ones below were like human lives, just there for a night and then gone. The ones above were like human hopes and dreams, they glowed on there forever. And if one life failed and went out, then another came along and took up the hope, the dream, glowing there immutably above, glowing there forever.

As I am doing now, she thought. As I am doing now.

And peering at them, until they seemed to be reflected in the strained width, the glistening anxiety, of her eyes, she breathed softly, supplicatingly to them: You must have seen her sitting at this same window before me. You must have heard the heartbeats of her hopes and aspirations, clearly in the stillness of the night. Do *you* know what they were? Do *you*?

You open a valise—and a life comes back into view. A life that was already done with, locked up and put away. And as you spread it all about you in the room, on the bed, on the seats of chairs, wherever there is room, somehow you feel a little frightened at what you are doing, feel you have no right to do this. It's like trying to turn back the laws of nature and of God. Force a minor, two-by-four resurrection on something that was already at rest. You'd better watch out, you keep telling yourself; you'd better be careful.

A photograph of a man, torn in half, the diagonal edge ragged, exposing the grain of the paper beneath the silver coating. His face showing in close-up, but only from one cheek down. Who was he? What was he to her? Where was he now?

Smiling at her. Smiling at the lens that had taken him, but it must have been she behind that lens that day, for it was a special sort of smile that you don't give just to the lens of a camera. Warmer than that, closer than that; saying, You're over there and I'm over here. But you were over here with me a moment ago, and you'll be back again a moment from now. We won't be apart any longer than that; we weren't meant to be; we won't let ourselves be.

But torn, torn in half, with as much passion as it had been taken, as much hate as there had been its opposite in the photograph's creation. Torn by whom, and for what reason?

In the corner, beneath the tear, an inscription in slanting black ink:

"To my darling Starr, Vick."

Who are you, Vick?

Don't you even miss her? Don't you even know she's gone? The moment's over, don't you even wonder why she doesn't come across there, back to where you are?

Keep on smiling, Vick. Keep on smiling forever that way. You're smiling at empty space now, and you don't know it. You have no eyes any longer and cannot see. She's gone from behind the lens of the camera. You remain, but she is gone. Gone and she'll never come back. Would you keep on smiling if you knew that?

In some quiet place—it looked as if it had been taken in some quiet place—she could almost hear the girl's clear silvery voice ring out again.

"Stand still now, Vick. Move back a little. No, just a little; that's enough. Now smile for me. That's it."

Smile forever, Vick. As long as the glossy paper lasts.

You can stop smiling now, Vick, she's not there anymore. You're smiling at vacant space, Vick. There's a hole in the world, behind the camera where she was.

She propped the partial photo up and sat looking at it.

The sun was going down outside and the room was getting dark.

A patch of light lingered to the end, right there where she had the photo. Playing it up, making it stand out; making the image on it seem luminous.

Tell me, Vick, she pleaded. Tell me while you still can.

So little of you is left, but your lips remain.

You could still speak.

The light contracted, swirled to a closing pinpoint, went out; like an iris-out on a motion-picture screen.

The photo was dark now, blended into the surrounding darkness of the room.

II

The train rushed from night into oncoming day, as though it were speeding from the heart of an hours-long tunnel on toward its steadily brightening mouth, coming nearer, ever nearer, far down along the track. Then suddenly it was all light outside, the scoured-aluminum color of first daybreak.

Suddenly there was a landscape, where there hadn't been before. A tall brick stack went by, with a full-grown shadow already. Suddenly there was today, where there hadn't been before. Suddenly there was *now,* and the darkness had become *then.* The whimpering of a little baby in its mother's arms, somewhere here within this same railroad coach, was the new day starting. As young as that, as malleable, as unstoried yet.

She hadn't slept. She hadn't wanted to, she hadn't tired. Sleep was for the purposeless, an interruption between nothings, to make them more separately bearable.

Head back against the sloping chair all night. Eyes half-lidded against intrusion but never once altogether closed; just as they still were now. Journeying, journeying, question marks for telegraph poles along the right-of-way. Journeying not into tomorrow, journeying into yesterday. A yesterday twice removed, at that. Somebody else's yesterday. A yesterday you skipped, that never was, once—to you—today. Ghost yesterday.

The man came to the door and said the name of a town.

She rose and took her bag down, and the train died under her as her tread moved down its aisle. It was dead already, when she reached the platform. Steam veiled the opening to yesterday, the car door, as she stepped down through it. Then it thinned and went away again, and left her—yesterday.

So this was it.

She glanced down at the cindery gravel needling her feet, and up at where the sun rode high in the sky, sending down rays like a chemical bath or solution, bleaching the world. And over at a weighing machine, with a round mirror that showed only sky though it was sighted directly at her face. Probably because the glass was fitted into its frame unevenly.

And at a semidetached shingle hanging lengthwise over a passage entrance, that read "Baggage." And at a bench, of contour-curving green slats, set against the station wall, with no one on it. With only a folded newspaper on it, left behind by someone. And the shattered wrapping of a candy bar under it, like a little silver derelict ship, rocking lightly in the wind but never sailing forth across the cement platform sea.

So this was it.

Here once you stood, Starr. Waiting for the train that was taking you away. Maybe right where my foot is now, as I move it out a little; to where that crack is in the cement. Maybe you moved your foot out too, to that crack, and covered it for a moment, looking at it but thinking elsewhere. Who stood with you? Did you stand alone? Did Vick stand here by you, perhaps his hand upon your arm in defeated remonstrance; most certainly his eyes upon your face in unavailing plea?

What was he saying? You didn't hear? Perhaps if you had listened, you would be alive now, instead of dead, at the thousand-mile-away end of these tracks. Wouldn't it have been better to listen to stale, dull, homespun words of advice, and be alive today, than to throw them over your shoulder, and be dead today? You don't answer that, Starr. And I don't either. For I'm not sure what the answer is.

Did you look around you for the last time (perhaps over his shoulder, as his arms held you)? Turn your head, a little here, a little there, a little elsewhere, as I do now? See a mirror that doesn't reflect your face, a shingle reading "Baggage," a bench with no one on it? Were you glad? Were you heartsick? Were you frightened? Were you bold?

The bricks and pavings, serried cornices and building fronts, perspective-diminishing streets, of home.

You have come back, Starr.

There was a lunch counter inside the station. There always is, in every station. She went inside and across to it and sat down on a stool.

She hadn't eaten on the train. She hadn't wanted to then, she still didn't want to now. She didn't want food, she didn't want sleep. She had no time for distractions like that, she had a dream. She too had a dream now; bitterer, stronger, than any dream Starr'd ever had. But you had to pause, to swallow, to sleep, or you faltered.

There was a girl behind the counter. A single, thin stripe of turquoise-green bordered the cuffs, the collar, the pocket orifices, the upturned cap brim of her otherwise all-white garb.

"I want coffee."

"Anything else?"

"Coffee and nothing else," Madeline answered impatiently, as though she were bored even having to waste time with that.

The girl came back with it.

"Could I ask you a question?"

"I can't stop you," the girl said pertly.

"Have you lived here long?"

The girl gave her the look that meant, What's that to you. But she gave her the answer along with it, as well. "Always."

"Then did you know anyone named Starr Bartlett? Ever hear of anyone named Starr Bartlett?"

"Never heard the name." Local pride prompted her to add an oblique rebuke. "We're not so small here."

Madeline tasted her coffee. It wasn't good. Even if it had been good, it wouldn't have been good.

"How do you get to—how would *I* get to Forsythe Street?"

"There's a bus takes you. The driver will call it out for you, if you speak to him when you get on."

Madeline looked at her coffee-dulled spoon, then at the girl once again, hesitantly.

"Just one more."

"No, that's all right," the girl said, with equally formal politeness. Meaning, you haven't asked me anything I resent yet. When you do, you'll know it.

"Where would be a good place to stay? I'm by myself. Just came."

"Somebody like you—" The girl appraised her. The girl was a shrewd appraiser. "A girl who wants to mind her own business— the Dixon is respectable. Awfully dowdy, but respectable. The respectable places always are dowdy, did you ever notice?"

Then, unasked and perhaps unwitting, she gave an insight into her whole philosophy of life. "It's not the hotel anyway. It's the person in it."

Madeline put her money down, left her cup three-quarters full, got down from the stool.

The girl called to her a little brusquely.

"Your coffee's only ten."

"It's on the big sign there," Madeline agreed.

The girl separated the excess, guided it a distance along the counter, with a stubborn smile. "I didn't do anything to earn this."

"I asked you three questions, and you set up my coffee." She was really asking her why.

"I don't know; there's not the same kick in it. It's like taking something from yourself."

Madeline reclaimed the donation. She wanted the girl to enjoy herself; the job was dull enough.

No one answered the bell. After the first ring had gone unheeded a sufficient length of time, she rang a timorous second time. Then waited even longer, fearing to seem importunate, fearing to antagonize. And finally, fearful in the extreme, rang a third time. Still no one came.

She did not know what to do then. She could not summon up courage to ring any more. Either no one was in, in which case it was no use anyway, or else someone was in and did not wish to answer, in which case she would be antagonizing them, the very thing she did not want to do.

At last she turned and started down the stairs. She had not given up, she did not intend to give up, not if it meant she had to fold her coat on the floor outside the door and sit on it waiting, the rest of the day and all of the night. But what she intended to do at the moment was seek out and accost somebody outside on the street nearby, who might be able to give her some information. Even a child if possible—she had noticed some of them playing on the sidewalk before. In fact children were often the best sources of information, lacking in suspicion and reserve as they usually were.

Be all that as it might, she had only gone as far down as the landing below and was still within fair hearing distance, when she thought she heard the door open, and did hear, in this case without any doubt, a voice call out (rather hollowly due to the enclosed hall), "Hello? Was there somebody here just now?"

And then again (and she could tell it would be the last time, would not be repeated), "Hello?" She turned and ran back up the flight she has just descended, with utmost speed, so that she might not be cut off from the voice.

As her face, and then her body, sprang agilely up above the hall floor level, she saw that the door stood open. Not just aslant, but wide open, with light that was like incandescent smoke fuming out from it into the dim hall, which had no windows. And out in the middle of the hall, well away from the door, turning her head inquiringly first up this way, then down that, stood a woman no longer young. The woman who, somehow, she knew to be Starr Bartlett's mother.

It was strange that she could feel so sure at sight, because if she had formed any preconceptions of her, and she had of course, not one of them was accurately fulfilled. She was the opposite in almost everything Madeline had thought she would be.

She had thought she would be gray, not only gray of hair, but with an overall faded, gray aspect. The word "mother" was no doubt what had formed this image in her mind. Having lost her own at an early age, she had had no contemporary, day-to-day experience with one. To her they were all of one type, not individuals. Quite the contrary, the overall aspect of Starr's mother was dark. Everything about her was black. Her hair was the unlikely and unlifelike black of tar, so that almost certainly some sort of vegetable dye must have been applied to it to keep it that even. Perhaps its use initiated years before, and had now become merely a habit rather than a vanity. Her clothes were black without exception; not a fleck of color showed on her anywhere. But this of course would be because of Starr's passing. Her brows were heavily black. And in this case naturally so. They were almost like little tippets of black sealskin pasted

above her eyelids. And lastly her eyes were black. Black as shoe
buttons. But very mobile shoe buttons.

Madeline had thought that her figure would be ample, plump,
maternal. She was rail-thin, scrawny. That she would be slow-
moving, perhaps even impeded in gait. Her step was sprightly,
that could be seen at a glance; it was at the other end that the
advancing years had assailed her. She was acutely, cruelly
round-shouldered. So that, although she was of a fair height,
she was made to seem short, even stunted.

"Mrs. Bartlett?" Madeline whispered. She had to whisper
because of the alacrity with which she had bounded back up
the stairs.

"Yes," she said, turning the black eyes on her. They had great
sorrowing pleats under them, Madeline saw. "Did you want
me? Were you the one who rang?"

"Yes, I was," Madeline said.

They came a little nearer to one another now.

"Do I know you?" the older woman said.

"No, you don't," Madeline replied quietly.

She thought, it's not kind of me to prolong this. Tell her at
once, don't keep her waiting.

"I knew Starr," she said then.

Two emotions, primary emotions, swept over the older
woman's face, one right after the other. They were as obvious,
as vivid, as though they were two separate revolving gelatin
slides, each one throwing its light on her face in turn. First joy.
Just plain unadulterated joy. The name itself, the beloved name.
Someone who knew her. Someone who was a friend of hers.
Someone who could tell of her. Then grief. Just plain abysmal
grief. Not she herself, only someone who had known her. Not
she herself, only someone who could tell of her.

Her mouth opened. And open like that, its edges flickered,

fluttered, as if it were trying to close itself again. And her eyes hurt so. Showed such hurt within them, one should say.

"Come in," was all she said. And rather calmly. At least it was not tremulous.

Madeline went first, at her almost unnoticeable little gesture. She followed and closed the door after them both.

It was a small elbow-shaped apartment of two rooms. That is to say, the two rooms were not in a straight line with one another; one was at right angles to the other, leading off in a different direction. The first one was the only one she could see as she entered. It was clean, but far from tidy. There was no dust or litter, but there was far too much of everything in it. It was overcrowded. Or else perhaps, because it was a small room, it gave that impression.

"Sit down," Mrs. Bartlett said. "No, not in that one. This one's better. The spring's broken in that."

Madeline changed accordingly.

She kept thinking, She used to live here. This is where she lived. Here, where I am now. And because of me, she doesn't live here anymore. She doesn't live anywhere anymore. I did that. I. How can I face those black eyes looking at me right now? How can I look into them?

"You haven't given me your name," Mrs. Bartlett said, smiling at her. She rested her hand endearingly on Madeline's shoulder for a minute.

"Madeline Chalmers," Madeline said. "Murderess. Your daughter's murderess." But only the first part passed her lips.

"Did you know her long?" Mrs. Bartlett said. A jet cross at the base of her neck blinked in the reflected sunlight, as though it had just shed a tear.

"It seems longer—than it was. Much longer. A lifetime."

The answer, carefully chosen as it was, made no impression. Mrs. Bartlett had averted her head, suddenly, sharply. "Excuse

me a minute," she said in a racked voice. "I'll be right back."
She went through the doorway—it was an opening really, it had
no door—turned right, and went into the next room, the bedroom apparently. She'd gone in there to cry, Madeline knew.

She heard no sound, and tried not to, in case there had been
any. But there wasn't any.

It didn't make it easier for her, this temporary digression.
She tried to take her mind up, looking at little things. Little
things that really didn't interest her.

One of the lamps, because there was an insufficiency of out-
lets no doubt, had its cord hoisted and plugged into a socket in
the ceiling fixture. The wall, at least on the one side facing her,
was in two shades of green. Most of its surface a fading yel-
lowing green, like peas when they've begun to wither and dry
up. And then in the middle of this, an oblong patch of a much
darker green, looking as fresh as if it had just been dampened
with water. A vacant nail protruded from the middle of it,
giving the explanation. A picture had once hung there long ago,
and then been moved. Before the window there was a bril-
liantly bright stepladder. But not a real one, a phantom stepladder of firming sun motes, placed there as though for some
angel in domestic service to step up on and hang the curtains.
Its luminous slats were made by the openings in the fire-escape
platform outside the window above.

On the roof, visible only in a slanting diagonal that cut across
one upper corner of the window, a woman was hanging wash.
You could hear the pulley squeak querulously each time she
paid out more rope to herself, but not see her or the wash.

Mrs. Bartlett came back again. You could not tell she had
been crying.

"Let me get you something," she said. "I'm forgetting myself.
Would you like some coffee?"

"Nothing, please," Madeline begged her with utmost sincerity.

Almost with abhorrence. "I just came here to talk to you, really I did."

"You wouldn't refuse Starr's mother, now would you?" the other woman said winningly. "It won't take a minute. Then we can sit and talk." She went into a narrow little opening, almost like a crevice, over at the far side of the front door, and Madeline could hear water running, first resoundingly into the drumlike hollow of a porcelain sink, then smotheredly into tin or aluminum. Then she heard the pillow-soft fluff that ignited gas gives.

Mrs. Bartlett came back again. For the first time since she'd admitted her, she sat down with Madeline.

"You look tired," Madeline remarked compassionately.

"I don't sleep much anymore since she's gone," she said. "At nights, I mean. That's why I have to sleep when I can. I was napping when you rang, that's why it took me so long to open the door."

"I'm sorry," Madeline said contritely. "I would have come some other time."

"I'm glad you came when you did." She patted Madeline's arm and gave a little snuggle within her chair that was pure anticipation. "You haven't told me a word about her yet."

"I don't know where to begin," Madeline said. And it was true.

"Was she happy?"

"That," Madeline said with infinite slowness, "I don't know. Don't you?"

"She didn't tell me," Mrs. Bartlett said simply.

"Was she happy when she was here with you?"

"She was at first. Later on—I'm not so sure."

Madeline thought, There could be something there. But how to get it out?

"Did she have any particular—ambitions, that she ever spoke of to you?"

"All girls are ambitious. All young things are. Not to be ambitious is not to be young at all." She said it sadly.

"But any particular?" Madeline persisted.

"Yes," Mrs. Bartlett said. And then again, "Yes." And then she stopped as if mulling it over.

Madeline waited, breath held back.

"Wait a minute," cautioned Mrs. Bartlett, getting up. "I hear the coffee bumping." She went out to get it.

Madeline softly let her breath out, like a slow tire leak. Oh, damn this coffee break, she thought. Just when we seemed to be getting somewhere.

Mrs. Bartlett bustled with cups and saucers and spoons, and a glass holding little lumps of sugar (she kept them in a water tumbler in lieu of a bowl), and it was impossible to continue consecutively. Whatever ground had been on the point of being gained, which was the most she could say for it, was lost again for the time being.

Mrs. Bartlett sat there and sipped, and the black eyes watched Madeline over the rim of the tipped cup, but in a friendly, trusting manner.

I can't eat her bread, Madeline thought. Meaning the beverage. Her gorge rose. I'm a murderess. I can't sit here taking food and drink with her. I killed her daughter. It's inconceivable, abominable, to do this.

"Don't you like it?" Mrs. Bartlett asked ruefully.

Madeline forced some into her mouth. And that was all she could do.

"I think I understand," said Mrs. Bartlett softly, after a great while. For the first time since they'd met, she dropped her eyes, lowered them away from Madeline's face.

Madeline removed the saucer from below its cup, and let the mouthful of coffee she had already absorbed run back on it again. This wasn't just a gesture of sentimental delicacy. Her throat had closed up; she would have strangled on just one swallow of the blood-warm liquid. She set the cup and saucer aside.

Mrs. Bartlett moved, very tactfully, very inconspicuously now, and suddenly the cups were gone from sight.

When she came back, Madeline had moved to another chair and was briefly sheltering her eyes with the edge of her hand.

"You *are* a real friend," Mrs. Bartlett said in gentle admiration. "You are." And she said it a third time. "You *are.*"

"Yes," Madeline said with bitter mockery. "Yes. Oh, yes."

They were silent for a short while. Then abruptly Madeline turned around toward her—one shoulder had been turned away until now—and said. "You know how it happened, I suppose?"

The older woman seemed to shrink lower in her chair. Settle, like something deflating. "Yes, I know," she said. "They told me." And then she whispered, "A shot—on the street." Whispered it so low that Madeline couldn't hear the words at all. But she knew what they were, because those were the words that belonged in that place. And the lip movements imaged them, fitted them.

After a while Madeline started to ask her, "Did you—?" Then didn't know how to say it.

"Did I what?" prompted Mrs. Bartlett, eyes on the floor.

"Did you—go there, did you go in to the city, when they notified you? Did you—bring her back with you? Is she resting out here?"

"I couldn't go in myself," Mrs. Bartlett said, quite simply, eyes still downcast. "You see, I'm all alone here. I wasn't in any condition to—I had to take to my bed the first few days after I received the news."

Madeline winced.

"But Mr. Thalor, he's the funeral director, was very kind, he arranged everything, took charge of everything, for me. He had her brought back here, and saw about purchasing a plot. I didn't have enough money to buy one outright, but they're letting me pay for it on the installment plan, a little at a time."

Madeline couldn't repress a shudder.

"It sounds terrible, I know," Mrs. Bartlett admitted. "But what can you do, when death strikes suddenly like that, and you're not prepared for it? I'd always thought that I'd go first, and she'd take care of things like that for me. I never dreamed I'd—be the one to bury her." She knitted a tiny fist, white and fragile as an ivory carving, and pressed it just over one eye.

Madeline saw that she had reached the end of her fortitude for the present. There was nothing to do but wait for another time.

She rose to her feet, and said, "I hope I haven't—I didn't mean to hurt you like this."

The little clenched fist was before her lips now, stifling them, crushing them in. She nodded her head a little, but whether in forgiveness or just in acknowledgment of the apology, Madeline couldn't know.

"May I come again?" she asked. "May I talk to you some more?"

Again the muted figure nodded, but this time the meaning was plain.

As she passed by her on her way to the door, Madeline let her hand come to rest upon her shoulder for a moment, in the futile, only, consolation she could give her. The little fist opened, fluttered upward like a bird spreading its wings, came to rest upon the solacing hand.

From the doorway, as she softly drew the door closed after her, Madeline looked back. Other than that one little gesture, she hadn't moved, she hadn't turned her head to watch her go. Madeline could only see her from the back, the light making a sort of blurry, soft focus about the outline of her head, sitting there, still there. Feeling only, breathing only. Life in death. Or death in life.

There are two deaths I am responsible for, Madeline told herself accusingly, and not just one. This one too. The death of a heart.

When she approached the little five-story apartment building the next day, Madeline was at first startled and then somewhat uneasy to see the familiar black-garbed figure of Mrs. Bartlett standing waiting in the shade of the green canvas door canopy, which extended out to the edge of the sidewalk. It was obvious by the way she kept turning every so often, first to look up the street in one direction, then down it in another, that she was waiting for someone to come along. And Madeline knew that someone must be herself. The shortest way from her own hotel had brought her along the opposite side of the street, she knew the older woman had not yet observed her (there was an almost unbroken line of cars parked along that side, screening her), and for a moment she had an impulse to turn around and go back again before she had been noticed.

Why was she waiting for her like that, hatted, out before the house? Was she taking her somewhere with her? Did she want her to meet other relatives, other members of the family? But hadn't that been Madeline's very purpose in seeking her out in the first place, to establish leads through her, other contacts? Then why the skittishness, why the timidity?

She forced herself to swerve diagonally across the street toward her, and as Mrs. Bartlett saw her emerge from between two of the parked cars, she came out to the edge of the walk to greet her, and tilted her face an almost imperceptible trifle, as if permissive of a kiss. Madeline placed her lips against her forehead.

"I'm so glad you came early," Mrs. Bartlett murmured. "I forgot to ask you yesterday where I could reach you."

Madeline then told her, seeing no need for concealment.

"I did so want you to come with me," the older woman went on. "I knew you'd want to too."

"Where, Mrs. Bartlett?" At once, instinctively, she was frightened for a minute into taut, sudden, wary evasiveness.

"Call me Charlotte."

"Where?"

"Why, to eleven o'clock mass, of course. It's just around the corner from here. We'll be just in time."

The killer praying for the slain. Oh, I can't. Yet this has been done before. Before, many times over. The murderer praying for the murdered. But oh, I can't. I can't go in there with her.

She stood rigid, rooted to the spot. Mrs. Bartlett took a step forward, then turned, and seeing that she had not moved in company with her, extended her hand—she was still only an arm's length in advance—and gently took Madeline's hand in her own, then went on once more. Unresistant, Madeline glided along after her. Almost like a sleepwalker guided by someone who is awake.

They turned the corner still with this strange link of hands and came up to the church. Curved gray stone steps led up to its entrance apron, and from the carved niches on either side the blank stone eyes of saints looked sightlessly out upon the world.

The touch of the first step against her toe seemed to wake Madeline from her trancelike passivity, as though a switch had been flicked, turning off some flow of compulsive current, and she disengaged her hand and balked there, Mrs. Bartlett one step higher than she.

"I can't go in here. Don't ask me to."

Mrs. Bartlett's eyes were calm and unreproachful; above all else they seemed to hold an infinite understanding, the wisdom of old age. "Is it because of the creed? Is it because you're of a different faith? Why, then we'll go to your church. God's houses are all God's houses. Unitarian, Baptist—"

She thought: A killer is a killer in any denomination.

"I'll go with you, and pray beside you," the woman continued. "In my own way, but to the same God. And I'm sure both of our prayers will reach Him just the same. He is just one God, not a segregated God."

Madeline averted her face, the way one does who is afraid of receiving a blow, of being struck. Not only turned it away, but turned it downward at the same time. Every slantwise line of her body, straining away from the church entrance, expressed aversion. Not the aversion of disgust, the aversion of fear. She began trembling violently all over, so that Mrs. Bartlett's hand, upon her arm, trembled by transference.

"I'll wait for you outside," she said in a muffled voice. "I'll wait here on the steps."

Mrs. Bartlett was looking at her curiously. She released her hold upon her. "I'll say two prayers, then," she said quietly. "One for her, and one—for you."

She turned and went slowly up the steps, and opened the door, and went in. It closed soundlessly after her, on its own massive springs.

Madeline stood there waiting, never moving. One foot on one step, the other on the next one down, in a position as of arrested entrance.

The door opened as some latecomers entered, and the music swelled out like a paean, then dimmed into a drone again. She turned her head, and caught a glimpse of taper beads twinkling like golden tears streaming down a wall, as if seen at the end of a long violet-dim tunnel. Then the door closed again, and the world was shut in two, this world and the other world.

At last the mass ended and the people came out, the women and children in their bright dresses, like flowers spilling down the steps all around her. Then when they'd all dispersed and the street was quiet once again, Mrs. Bartlett stood there alone at the top of the steps, last of all to come out.

She came down them slowly and turned aside, and though her eyes were on Madeline there was no recognition in them. Madeline wheeled and fell in beside her, but all the way back they were like two strangers who do not know one another yet unaccountably continue to walk abreast. The close communion of their walk to church was gone, had been destroyed.

When they reached the apartment house, Mrs. Bartlett entered first as her age entitled her to do, but she noticeably did not hold the door for Madeline, who had to catch and hold it in order to be able to make her way in. At the upstairs door, when Mrs. Bartlett took out her bunch of keys, her hand quivered so that she couldn't manage to insert the right one in the lock. They jangled loudly in the silence of the hall. But when Madeline reached out to try to take them, in order to do it for her, she snatched them back out of her reach with an abruptness that almost suggested animosity.

When she finally had the door open, Mrs. Bartlett stepped in, but then turned around and faced Madeline coldly, standing there in such a way that Madeline could not enter herself. He face was gray with pain, pitted with it, the texture of a pumice stone.

"Why do you want to come in here? I have no more children."

Madeline drew in her breath, sharp and cold as a razor cutting her throat as it went down.

"I had only the one. Find someone else's house now to bring sorrow into."

Madeline kept silent.

"You're the one," the bereaved woman went on. "You did it. I knew it when you wouldn't come into the church with me."

And little by little she began to close the door between them, still speaking as it narrowed.

"You did it. You."

The door closed.

Madeline's body gave a half roll-around of despair that brought her shoulders back against the wall, to one side of the doorway. She hung her head.

After a while she straightened, turned again, and knocked softly, entreatingly, on the door.

There was no answer.

After a while she went away.

At eleven the next morning the door opened and Mrs. Bartlett came out trundling a small wheeled shopping cart behind her. She saw Madeline standing there waiting, but didn't speak.

When she returned over an hour later, the small cart was filled with the purchases of her shopping tour. She saw Madeline still there, but didn't speak.

The door closed after her.

At about noon the next day the door opened again, and she came out again. She saw Madeline standing there waiting again, but didn't speak. When she came back some time later, she was holding a dry-cleaning garment of some kind protected by a plastic bag. She was holding it by a wire hanger whose hook protruded from one end of the plastic bag, and it was hard for her to hold it up clear of the floor and at the same time get out her door key.

Madeline stepped forward and unobtrusively took it from her hand and held it for her, while she brought out her key and unlocked the door. Then, just as unobtrusively, Madeline handed it back to her. She went inside with it.

The door stayed open behind her.

After a while Madeline timidly went in after her and closed it behind her.

Mrs. Bartlett had set two cups out on the table.

"I married when I was very young. Seventeen. We had nothing but misfortunes, almost from the day of our marriage. When I look back now sometimes, it almost seems like an omen.

"We had a little baby boy first, before Starr. Then we lost him, when he was about five years old."

"He died?" Madeline asked.

"No," she said. "Or, if he did, we never knew."

"I don't understand."

"He just disappeared one day. Disappeared from the face of the earth. We never saw him again. One minute he was playing in front of the door, in full sight. The next minute there wasn't a sign of him. I don't know if some degenerate enticed him away, and then got rid of him. If he'd simply been lost, he would have been found again eventually. No child stays lost indefinitely. The police worked on it for months. Months and months. They finally came to me about a year later. It must have been fully a year. Over a year. By that time I'd got used to living with it. They told me there was only one conclusion they could come to. He was no longer alive, or he would have been found before then.

They told me he must have been killed right away, within the first day or two, before the hue and cry had got fully started. And his body disposed of in some way so that it never turned up again. A child that age has such a small body," she said wanly. "You could almost hide it in a woodburning stove or a canful of ashes. Or roll it down an open sewer."

Madeline shivered and bit the back of her own hand. God, there isn't anything on the face of the earth more hideous than child murder! Adult murder is a clean, upright thing by comparison.

"I didn't give up hope even then. What mother does? But the weeks became months, and the months—Bennett, my husband, saw that I was brooding, eating my heart out, and he finally suggested that we have another. I guess to take my mind off it, give me a new lease on life. I refused point-blank. I didn't want to go through that a second time, the fear of losing it just as you've grown attached to it, learned to love it. I told him I wouldn't know a minute's piece if I had another child, after what had happened to the first one. It would be bad for the child, and worse for me. Nothing he could say would prevail upon me.

"Well, I suppose this is a rather delicate and personal matter to discuss, but so many years have gone by it's no longer very important. I don't know how he did it, but I suddenly found that I was carrying a child again. I even went to a doctor, to ask him to do something about it, but he talked me out of it. And Starr was born nine months later."

Poor Starr, Madeline thought poignantly. Even her own mother didn't want her.

"And after that?"

"It drove a wedge between us, it drove us apart. It wasn't anyone's fault, the marriage had just been ill-starred. Some marriages are. There was a long period of—I don't know what word to use. Tolerance. Indifference. Then in later years he started to drink. I guess he'd grown embittered. It's a terrible thing to see a man drink himself to death right before your eyes. The falls on the floor. The vomiting. The bodily indecencies. I kept the child from seeing as much of it as I could. Kept her in her room under lock and key. I mean, once he'd come back home at nights. But children are smart. They know things, they can sense them.

"And then—I suppose this is a dreadful thing to say, but God in His infinite mercy was kind. Kind to him and kind to me and kind to his child. He lay stupefied in a doorway all one bitter below-zero night, unable to get up and walk, and he died of exposure."

And was God good to Starr too? Madeline wondered iconoclastically. Carrying her off at twenty-two, after giving her such a childhood!

"When Starr was small, did you worry and dread a repetition of the first child's disappearance, as you had expected you would?"

"No, strangely enough, I didn't," Charlotte said. "I went to my priest, and he played a great part in relieving my mind. He said, in effect, that lightning never strikes twice, and it was almost outside the bounds of possibility that such a thing should happen a second time to the same family, the same parents. I saw what good sense this made, and from that time on I lost all my fears."

"Are you sure you have no objection?" Madeline asked, before untying the slender packet Charlotte had handed her.

"No, go ahead; you're welcome to read them if you want to," Charlotte invited. "There isn't anything of consequence in them;

just the typical letter a girl away from home sends home."

Then she added pensively, "I suppose it's foolish to keep letters—especially after the writer is gone."

"But we all do at one time or another," Madeline reminded her.

"You'll have to turn them upside down if you want to read them in order," Charlotte pointed out. "The early ones are at the bottom, the later ones at the top."

It may help me to know her better, Madeline thought defensively, and knew she was lying to herself. She wasn't trying to know Starr better; she was simply prying, trying to ferret out evidence, almost the way a detective would have. She was uneasily aware there was a big difference between questioning Charlotte conversationally and reading Starr's private letters, letters written to someone else. At least there was to her own mind, which was what counted. It was like seeing someone undressed.

She took them over beside a window and sat down there, to read them in more privacy. Charlotte remained where she'd been, silently looking down at the backs of her own hands, as if reliving in memory the time she'd first read them herself.

Madeline didn't read each one through from start to finish; she didn't have to. Her eyes would skim down the page and pick out a key phrase. Sometimes the whole gist of the letter, its importance to her purpose, was expressed in that key phrase.

...very tired from the trip. And of course a little homesick. Missed you and the town I grew up in. The first night in a new city you always feel strange...

...getting used to it now. Getting to feel at home...

...girl I work with insisted on dragging me to this party with her. I really didn't want to go, but I gave in so that she

wouldn't think I was unfriendly and standoffish. There was a man named Herrick there. Seemed like a very nice person. Brought me home afterward, just to the door. Asked if he could give me a ring. I lied and said I had no phone. I don't want to become involved with anyone yet, that can wait...

...I nearly fell over when I answered it and it turned out to be he. That girl where I work gave him my number, it seems. Wait'll I get hold of her, I'll give her a good talking to...

...the more I try to discourage him, the less I seem to succeed. The situation is becoming more than I can handle...

...It turns out he's married. It's true, he told it to me of his own free will, but that doesn't make it any better. I said a firm goodbye to him, and told him not to try to see me anymore...

...It hurt more than I realized it would. I must have gotten in far deeper than I was aware of...

...when he said who it was, I wouldn't open the door, so he slid a paper underneath it. I picked it up and looked at it, and it was a copy of the final divorce decree, his and hers. Uncontested. I thought it over for a while. Then I opened the door. Suddenly we were in each other's arms. I'd never realized it until that minute, but I'd been in love with him for a long time past...

...We were married yesterday...

...The longer I know him, the more I love him. It's like a dream come true. I love him so much that sometimes I'm afraid something will happen, some unkind fate will punish us for daring to be so happy. It seems too good to last...

...A year and a half yesterday. Eighteen months. Our yearly-and-a-half anniversary, is that how you say it? He gave me a gold charm bracelet. Each year you're supposed to

add another charm, until it's all complete. The first one says "I love you " How can the ones that are to be added improve on that? I gave him a lighter with his initials on it. We had champagne cocktails in the apartment, just the two of us alone by ourselves. Then we went out and had a Chinese dinner. Then afterward we went to a big musical show. As we were working our way out through the crowded lobby after the curtain came down, he wanted to take me to one of these big nightclub places, for a windup. I said, "Vick, don't use up all our money in one night. I know you love me. You don't have to prove it this expensively." All he said was—and he gave me that look that just melts my heart like a snowball in an oven—"Won't you let me prove it? Just this one night. Won't you let me prove it? Please, huh?" That little-boy look, that husband look, that lover look. I couldn't hold out, I couldn't. I threw my arms around him right there in all the crowd, and hung from his neck with my feet lifted clear of the ground, and kissed him about eighteen times. "There's only one Vick, there's only one you," I said close to his ear. "And that," he said, "is because there's only one Starr…"

Madeline refolded the letter and closed her eyes.

That rings true, she reflected. That can't be faked, that can't be made up. The very ink it was written with still glows this long after. They were desperately in love, madly in love, truly in love.

It was the last of the letters. There were no more after that.

"But the first wife didn't take it lying down. She was a singer. Worked in clubs. A roughneck, know what I mean? She did something to them that completely destroyed the marriage. Completely destroyed it."

"What?"

"I never knew what. Starr wouldn't say what."

"Did Starr ever meet her? Did she know her at all?"

"I asked her that myself. She said, 'I never set eyes on her in my life.' Those were her words. 'I never set eyes on her in my life.' Then she said, 'She called up just once. Just once, one o'clock one morning. Just one little phone call, but it wrecked my life, ruined my happiness, opened wide the gates of hell and pushed me through.' "

Madeline stared at her, intently, fearfully, wonderingly.

"As *I* stared at *her*," Charlotte said, reading the look.

"Did she say anything else?"

"Only this. 'I'd like to get even with her.' She rounded her small fist, held it clenched like this—and brought it back against her own face, between her eyes. 'I'd like to get even with her,' she said. 'But what could I ever do to her that could equal what she did to me? There can be only one of such a thing in this world, only one, never two.' "

Charlotte came to the door and her face lighted up when she saw Madeline. She was beginning to be fond of her, Madeline guessed, in spite of their connection—or somehow, perhaps, even because of it. They were both victims of unlucky chance, in a fashion that only another victim of a lightning strike could appreciate.

They kissed one another lightly on the cheeks.

"Come in," Charlotte said. "I'll fix you up a little lunch. It's so nice to have someone to eat with, and not be alone."

"No," Madeline protested. "I came to take you out. It's such a lovely day. Have you seen it yet?"

Charlotte nodded. "It really is. I could tell from the windows."

"Let's take a walk in that restful little park you have not far away from here—"

"Lakeside?"

"—and sit in the sun awhile and chat. Then I'll buy you whatever you feel like having, in a restaurant or tearoom. You'll see what an enjoyable way it will be to pass part of the day."

"You're spoiling me," Charlotte said wistfully.

Madeline shook her head slightly to herself while she stood waiting, partly in and partly out of the doorway. She couldn't help feeling a little disloyal, a little secretive. And yet, she told herself, there was nothing in this to harm Charlotte or be to her detriment. On the contrary, she was only trying to carry out her own daughter's wishes, trying to fulfill them. That should make her approve, that should make her feel content, if she were to know.

Charlotte came back with simply a hat and a handbag added to her basic dress.

"Make sure it's locked tight," Madeline reminded her protectively as she pulled the door shut after her.

They walked down the sun-glowing street together, the girl and the older woman, like mother and daughter. Like Starr herself might have, in a day that was gone now.

Madeline sighed a little. Starr. Always Starr. Why was I born with such an oversensitized conscience, she thought. Those that aren't, how much easier they have it.

They entered the park and, slackening still further their already leisurely pace, strolled down one of the long, winding, paved walks. The greenery was absolutely incredible, its hues heightened almost above nature by the clearness of the air and the brilliance of the sun. The grass was like emeralds, and even had a sparkle to it (from being recently wetted down, she supposed). The leaves on the trees were like little slivers and disks of wafer-thin dark green jade, and under each tree lay a pool of sapphire shadow. It looked like an artificially colored picture postcard of a park, and not a real one, on such a jeweled day as this.

"Cities, and their parks, still can be beautiful at times, even nowadays," Madeline remarked.

"I used to come here and play when I was a child myself, many times. My mother would bring me."

They came past a small lake with ducks swimming on it. The water flashed and dazzled like highly polished silver. Even the plumage of the ungainly little fowl glinted like burnished bronze and green-gold.

Madeline had seen her opening in the last remark.

"I suppose Starr did too, afterward."

"Yes, I brought her as often as I could. And the cycle repeated itself. Strange thing, life."

But now she's dead, so she herself will never be able to bring a little girl of her own here to play, in *her* turn.

Charlotte turned toward her quite unexpectedly and said, "I know what you were thinking just then."

Madeline didn't try to deny it. She simply nodded and said, "Yes, I was."

They came to a bench and Madeline said, "How about sitting here? Will this do?"

They both sat down.

Madeline took out cigarettes and offered one to her companion.

"It's been years since I've tried one," Charlotte said. "But I think I will have one for a change, as long as it's all right with you."

"I want to talk to you a little more about Starr," Madeline said. "That is, if it doesn't bother you."

"It doesn't now anymore," Charlotte said. "Not since you've been here. Before that it used to hurt even to think about her. Now it seems to help me, to ease me, if I talk about her."

Madeline wasted no further time on preliminaries. "When she went back to the city, when she left you the last time, do you think she intended to—rejoin her husband, effect a reconciliation to him?" She completed dropping her midget cloisonné-enamel lighter back inside her bag.

Charlotte looked up at her in considerable surprise.

"Why do you hesitate about answering? You're not sure, is that it?"

"I am sure," Charlotte said, and looked the other way.

"You're sure she was not going back to him?"

"I'm sure she was *not* going back to him. Not in the way that you mean."

"Oh, I see," Madeline said briefly, hoping that enough impetus had been given the conversation by now for the rest of it to come more or less by itself without having to dig at it too much.

It did but a little reluctantly.

"I asked her that question myself, when she started her packing the night before she was to leave. It was a natural one for a mother to ask a married daughter who's been estranged from her husband, don't you think?"

Madeline nodded, trying not to break in.

"She stopped what she was doing and looked at me. I'll never forget that look as long as I live. It was a terrible look. I'd never seen such a look on her face before. Not on anyone else's either. It was grim, it was deadly with hate. Her eyes were pulled back tight at the corners, and they were hard as rocks. Her mouth was drawn out too, into a thin, bitter line. And even her nostrils, I could see them pulsing in and out with her breaths. I repeat, it was the most terrible look I'd ever seen.

"And then she said—and even her voice wasn't the same— 'I'm going to look him up, all right. I'm going to look him up if it's the last thing I do. I'm going to look him up, you can count on it.'

"I didn't understand, just as I see you don't now, what she meant. I knew by the terrible, almost maddened look I've just been telling you about, she didn't mean reconciliation, she didn't mean forgiveness, she didn't mean love. Even the way she'd said it. She didn't say, 'I'm going back *to* him.' She didn't say 'I'm going back *with* him.' She kept hammering on the words 'look him up,' as though that was where the threat or the implication of whatever she intended doing lay."

Charlotte was holding her cigarette in the way of a woman unaccustomed to smoking, two fingers hooked around the extreme back end of it. She threw it down on the walk and stepped it out.

"Have him arrested, perhaps, have him taken into court. Or even put in jail?"

Charlotte shook her head, very quietly, very slowly. "More than that."

"What more than that can a wife—?"

"She intended to kill him."

Madeline gave an involuntary start. "How can you be sure of that?"

"I have the gun," Charlotte said flatly.

"How did you know she had it?"

"I didn't. It came about quite accidentally. She finished her packing that night, and we didn't talk about it anymore. I didn't want to see that look on her face anymore. I didn't want to bring it back. The next day she went out for a short while to do some last-minute shopping before she took the train. I came across some handkerchiefs of hers that I'd given her a helping hand with by washing and pressing. I'd forgotten to give them back to her the night before in time to go into the valise, and evidently she'd forgotten I still had them.

"I went into her room with them. The valise was locked and ready to go, but she'd left her keys on her dresser top. No reason for her not to. I'd never been the prying sort of mother that noses into a girl's belongings, even when she was younger. I opened it and started to spread the handkerchiefs out evenly all over the top of it. While I was doing this I felt something hard and heavy under one of the layers of clothing. I exposed it, and it was a gun."

A little of the fear and worry came back to her face, Madeline could see, even this long after.

"I was afraid to leave it in there. I kept seeing that look on her face the night before. I didn't want her to do it, to get into trouble. Her whole life would be worthless from then on, ruined. No matter what he'd done to her. I took it out and rearranged the valise, and relocked it. Put the keys back where I'd found them.

"I didn't know what to do with it. I knew if she missed it in time, before she got on the train, she'd look high and low for it. I didn't want her to get it back. Finally I thought of a place that might very well not occur to her. The refrigerator in the kitchen was very old, and there was a space between the back of it and the wall. I slipped it down inside there. The part that you hold, the handle, was a little bit thicker than the rest of it, so it didn't drop all the way down, it got caught and stayed where it was, near the top."

"Did she miss it?"

"No, she never reopened the valise again. The last-minute things she'd bought, she took with her in an extra shopping bag. There wasn't any more room in the valise for them, anyway."

She breathed heavily. "We kissed goodbye, and she took the train. That was the last time in this world I ever saw her. I never even heard from her again by mail. The next thing I knew she was dead. It must have happened right after she got back, within the next day or two."

Then she added, "She wouldn't even let me come to the

train with her, I remember that. She said she didn't want me to see her off. That alone showed she fully intended to do—what I've told you. We said goodbye right at the door of the apartment, upstairs. And then I watched the light inside the little pane of glass in the elevator door slowly going down. Like a life going out."

Two very small girls came pedaling by, holding hands, sharing a single pair of roller skates between the two of them. One went down, nearly pulling the other one after her. The fallen one's face began to work, in the preliminary stages of having a good hearty cry, but her skate-mate, like a very small-sized mother, assiduously helped her up again, patted her hair smooth, and tugged at the bottom of her dress to straighten it out. The cry never developed. They went swinging down the path again, blithe as ever.

"Cute," remarked Charlotte parenthetically, glancing after them.

At least they don't have our problems, Madeline thought.

"What did you do with it afterward?" she asked.

"Nothing. I didn't know what to do, I was afraid to tell anyone I had it. I was afraid to go to the police and report it, because that would link her to it. How could I explain having it in the first place? I couldn't say I'd found it, it could still be traced back to her. I was afraid to cover it up in a paper bag and just drop it into some trash can along the street. Somebody else might have found it and been tempted into doing something bad with it. Later, after her death, a repairman was coming to look at the refrigerator one day, and I was worried he might catch sight of it, so I took it out from behind there and put it into an empty shoe box, and hid that on the floor at the back of the closet. It's been there ever since.

"I can show it to you when we go back.

"Every time I go to the closet to get something out I see it, and I don't like to. It does something to me. One night I even dreamed about it. It came out of the closet by itself."

"I'll take it off your hands," Madeline said, lost in thought.

That evening she sat down at the little table-desk in her hotel room. It was a desk, really, only by grace of two shallow drawers holding hotel stationery, telegram blanks, a pad of printed laundry lists, and a large sheet of green blotting paper that covered its entire surface. She placed her handbag on top of this and opened it. She took out the revolver that Charlotte had turned over to her with unfeigned relief a little while ago, and examined it curiously.

She didn't know anything about revolvers, only that they could kill (and who should know that better than she?). She couldn't identify the caliber of this one, other than that it was fairly small. The typical kind that a woman or girl would buy and carry. But small or not, it could take away a life. It was nickel-plated, at least she supposed the gleaming silvery finish to be nickel plating, and its grip was either bone or ivory, which of the two she wasn't sure.

She put it down to one side on the blotting-paper surface and left it there for the moment. She unzipped one of the inner compartments of her handbag and took out a small, inexpensive pocket notebook, the kind that can be bought at any five-and-dime or stationery store. Its two-by-four pages bore ruled blue lines across them, as further indication of its low cost. On the cover was stamped, with unintentional irony, the single word "Memo."

But inside there was almost nothing written yet, only one brief phrase:

1. *To get even with a woman.*

She took a metal pencil with an ink cylinder in it from the handbag and ejected the point with a little click. Then she held it poised, but didn't write (as if once she wrote, what she wrote would be irrevocable, and she would be held fast to it). She thought of that line in the *Rubaiyat* that goes: "The moving finger writes, and, having writ, moves on/Nor all your piety and wit/Shall lure it back to cancel half a line/Nor all your tears wash out a word of it."

She looked at the gun, she looked at the pencil, she looked at the page between the two of them that was still blank but for the single phrase. It was a little like signing a death warrant.

She sat there for long moments, motionless. So still the ticking of her little traveling clock on the bureau could be plainly heard in the hush of her heart and her mind, the debating hush.

Once she wrote, she must obey it, follow it through to the end, for she was that way, and nothing could make her other than what she was.

Suddenly the pencil dipped to the paper, and the numeral "2" came out.

    1. *To get even with a woman.*
    2.

She stopped it again. She clasped her two hands, the pencil still caught between their multiple fingers, and brought them up before her mouth and held them there like that, pressed against her lips as if she were whispering to them.

The medicine I take to cure my illness is the illness itself repeated a second time, she thought. But have I the right to do this? *She* had hate for him, I have none. How can I have, I don't even know him. Have barely even seen him. Only his smile in a torn photograph.

I promised her. I pledged it to her. You cannot break faith with the dead, or they will arise to accuse you.

Suddenly the pencil struck the paper, rippled along in a quick, staccato line, rolled free and unfingered two or three times over. It was done.

    1. *To get even with a woman.*
    2. *To kill a man.*

III

Madeline first saw her one night at a place called the Intime. She was the singer there. She had a small combo of three backing her up, piano, traps, and bass. She was the singer there, and she was good.

> *"Oh-h-h-h-h-h-h,*
> *There's a lull in my life,*
> *Since you have gone away*
> *There is no night, there is no day…"*

There was a sort of narrow platform or balcony running along one side of the room just a little above head level, and she was on it, hands on railing, looking down on the listeners. A pencil spotlight from the other side of the room measured off her face with the exactitude of a white mask, leaving not a sixteenth of an inch of light over, leaving her throat and shoulders and arms and dress in smoky brown dusk.

Singing of love, of love lost. There was that utter velvet hush that means complete command of the listeners.

Couples side by side, holding hands, heads nestled on shoulders, believing it, drinking it in, living it. No one in the place was too much over thirty. It was for the young. The operator had had a good idea there, and Madeline caught on at once what it must have been.

People with a lot of money to spend on their night life go to one of the big flashy clubs with their dance floors, chorus lines, and twenty-piece bands. People with no money to spend on their night life go to the bar on the corner and watch TV with their neighborhood friends around them. But there is an in-between group that doesn't fall into either category. The young engaged couples and the young married pairs, still wrapped in rosy mists of love, still believing in it, still wanting to hear it sung. This place was for them and the buck or two they had to spend; Madeline could see them all around her, stars in their eyes, cheek pressed to cheek, dreaming their dreams. They'd come back again and they'd bring their friends, others of their own kind: the young-and-in-love. Mr. Operator had a built-in patronage. Young Mr. and Mrs. Tomorrow. Yes, he had a good gimmick there.

Throughout the song and the two or three that followed, she kept thinking, But this isn't enough. How do I get to know her? Get to really know her? Send her a fan note, saying I admire her, want to meet her? That's only good for a smile, a hand-shake, a few polite phrases, and then I'm expected to be on my way again. When men want to meet a performer, they became stage-door Johnnies. That's what I'll do she decided. Become something on that order, but with a slightly different purpose in mind. I'll become a stage-door Jenny.

She waited just long enough to gauge the applause. It wasn't thunderous, it wasn't crashing, it wasn't that kind of place. But it was warm and friendly, like soft summer rain belting a tin shed. They liked her, which is always half the battle.

From the outside the place was so inconspicuous you could easily have missed it. There was no canopy, no doorman, no conveyor belt of arriving or departing taxis. There was a very modest neon in handwriting script that spelled "Intime" over the door and to one side a sandwich board on an easel that simply said "Adelaide Nelson, song-stylist," and had her photo-graph on it and the name of the combo, "The Partners Three."

After a few minutes of standing about uncertainly in front of the place, she got a cab by forfeit, so to speak. One drove up, unloaded, and she got in and sat down before the seat was even cool.

The driver finally glanced around inquiringly, after waiting for her to give the destination of her own accord.

"I'm waiting for someone to come out," she told him, "so just stand awhile. Do you see that vacant slot up past the car just ahead of us? See if you can slide in there; that'll leave the entrance clear."

He did so, with a dexterity and sleekness only a professional cabman could have shown. That took her out of the direct line of Adelaide Nelson's vision when she would come out. She tested for range of visibility on several people who came out ahead, and found she could see them perfectly at that distance by looking through the rear window with a half turn of her head.

The driver smoked and toted up his logbook.

She just sat watching and waiting.

"Turn out the light," she said suddenly.

Adelaide Nelson had a fur scarf slanted carelessly over one shoulder, and no hat. Madeline got a perfect look at her. She had the same wait Madeline had had. At one point she even started up toward the cab Madeline was in, although its dome light was plainly off. Madeline cowered back into a corner. Before the woman could reach Madeline's cab, another one came gliding by, and she hailed and stepped into that instead.

Madeline said, "See that cab that woman just got into right in back of us? Just follow that the rest of the way from here."

"One of those things," he said noncommittally.

"You don't have to crowd it, but don't lose it either."

He was one of those rhythm drivers. He'd learned to time himself and space himself so that he took each light just before it changed, didn't have to stop once.

The lead cab got blocked off by a transverse bus at one crossing and lost the light, so he had to let himself lose it too and stay back in company with it. After that, the beat was lost and neither one of them got across a single light without stopping. But they both stayed together on the same block each time.

The pilot cab finally stopped, Adelaide Nelson got out, transacted her fare, and went inside a building under a long dark green sidewalk canopy.

"What's the number on that?" Madeline asked, peering closely at it.

"Two-twenty."

She'd already made it out for herself by that time.

"All right, now you can keep going." She gave him her own address, the residential hotel where she'd taken a room.

"That was it?" he asked blankly.

"That was it."

She knew more was coming. It did.

"She take your fellow away from you, is that the angle?"

"I don't have any fellow to take. And if I did, and he took that easy, she could keep him."

The papier-mâché briefcase she'd bought in Woolworth's. The musical score sheets she'd bought at a music store. The notes on the score sheets were her own. Poor things but her own, she'd reflected as she set them down, and that wasn't kidding.

She knew piano, in a very circumscribed, lesson-a-week-at-the-age-of-twelve sort of way. And she could hum, who can't? And she knew that in a lyric the end word on every second line has to rhyme with the end word two lines before, but the in-between lines don't have to. Which is about as far as some songs go, anyway. But she wasn't interested in salability, just plausibility. Getting to know a woman.

The door opened, and they were close to each other for the first time.

At such point-blank range, Adelaide's makeup was a caricature. But it wasn't individual personal makeup, it was performing makeup, Madeline realized, so that had to be allowed for. A pair of artificial eyelashes, superimposed on her own with no regard for nature, stuck out all around her eyes like rays in a charcoal drawing of the sun. A bouquet in which alcohol and floral essence strove for mastery was distinguishable for several yards around on all sides of her. Her hair was frizzy to the point of kinkiness, and the color of ginger. Combing it must have been like trying to comb a bramble bush. She had a pair of untrue blue eyes, which probably deepened almost to green when she hated. She probably hated a lot. She had on some sort of a hip-length quilted coat and a pair of quarter-thigh-length shorts, both white. Her feet were bare, and her toenails, Madeline noted, were painted gold.

There was something defiant about her as she stood there; not specifically toward Madeline, toward the world in general. Don't touch me or I'll claw you; an air like that.

"You the one?" she said. "I thought you were a man, the way the note read."

"I thought I stood a better chance that way," Madeline admitted.

"You did," Adelaide told her bluntly. "Come on in anyway," she added gruffly, "and let's see what your stuff is like."

She flung herself backward into a chair, but from the side, so that one leg caught over its arm and remained that way, cocked out at an angle from her body. She began to riff through the score sheets. She did remarkable things with a mouthful of smoke; protruded her underlip and sent it up in a jet so perpendicular that it actually stirred her hair a little where it overhung her forehead on that side.

"Not bad for a title," she remarked, and repeated it aloud. "'Have a Heart (Take Mine).'"

She got up and went over to the piano. Leaning over it standing up, she took one finger and started to tap out the notes on the keyboard. She shook her head dizzily, as if to clear it of the disharmony, and started over again. Shook her head again and stopped.

"What've you got here?" she growled. "This stuff doesn't even jell."

A sudden thought occurred to her. "Maybe I'm holding it upside down," she remarked, and reversed it on the music rack. Then she turned it back again. "No, the clef signs are all pointing this way."

She gave Madeline a long, skeptical stare. "Didja ever study composition?" she demanded.

"Not exactly," Madeline said. "All my friends say it comes naturally to me."

"Oh it does?" Adelaide snapped. "Well, take my tip and send it right straight back again. I don't know what it is you're getting, but it sure isn't music. I think it's the Morse code in Slovakian."

"What do you mean?"

"I mean you don't know the least thing about music," Adelaide snapped. "You think all you have to do is throw a handful of notes on the page and they come out a song. That's not the way it works, any more than you can throw paint on a canvas and get the 'Mona Lisa.'"

"I worked hard on that song," Madeline protested.

"Oh yeah? The way it looks to me, you don't know what hard

work is. I knew a man once who was a physics teacher. He said
there's a formula for work. I said sure, two parts elbow grease
and one part sweat. But he told me the formula and it stuck.
You know what it is?"

Madeline waited.

"Force times distance. In other words, it's not just how hard
you push something. It's also how far you move it. If you push
with all your strength against a wall, and it doesn't move an
inch, you haven't performed any work And this"— she bran-
dished the score sheets—"this doesn't move anything. It certainly doesn't move me."

"I don't understand," Madeline said. "When you talk about
walls—"

"You're beating your head against one," Adelaide said briskly,
"if you expect to get anywhere with this. And you're wasting my
time."

It's your song, Madeline told herself. You've got your whole
life tied up in it and this woman just told you it's no good. This
is your chance. If you can't win her with the song, win her with
the way you feel about it.

She willed her face to sag in disappointment. "I'm very sorry,"
she said stiffly, reaching to gather the score sheets and take
them from Adelaide. "I certainly had no intention of wasting
your time."

She walked to the door, turned the knob, drew it open. She
turned, looking on the verge of tears. "Thanks anyway," she
managed, her voice breaking on the second word, and then she
was through the door and drawing it shut behind her.

A moment or two passed. She heard the knob start to work
around, as the door was about to open once more. She quickly
planted her forearm against the wall and buried her face in it,
in an attitude of crushed, heartbroken youthful despondency.

She even made her shoulders quiver a little, as if with sound-less sobs.

The door opened, and she knew Adelaide was standing watching her.

"Kid." Adelaide's husky voice softened a little. At least, insofar as it was capable of softening. "Sorry I was so rough on you, kid. Forget about it, and come on back in. I won't buy your songs, but I'll buy you a drink on the house. It's a lonely, dreary Tuesday afternoon."

Madeline slowly prepared to unearth her face and turn it, giving herself time to form a timid, tremulous smile on it. But underneath she was exultant. She was In.

Women can often form friendships with one another far more easily and far more quickly than men can. For one thing, their egos are less brittle, less ready to take offense and bridle at some misconstrued word or action. Once the pact is a fact, has been accepted, they are less inclined to stand on their dignity with one another, they show far less reserve toward one another. That is because a number of the precipitant factors producing this are lacking. They are seldom if ever financially jealous of one another per se, and by the same token are apt to be more trustworthy financially with regard to one another. The throat-cutting urge of business is lacking.

It was pity that opened Adelaide to the possibility of friend-ship with Madeline, pity combined with the guilt she felt over her outburst. But pity and guilt can only sustain a relationship for a certain amount of time before the object of pity becomes the object of resentment for having burdened the other party with an unpleasant emotion. In this case, the two women moved quickly past the stage of pity and guilt to the foundation of a deeper relationship.

Madeline realized, as she came to know Adelaide, that she filled a need the other woman had for a friend. She was some-one to talk to, someone to confide in. At the same time, she was someone to lead and to instruct, someone to whom Adelaide could feel superior.

"Call me Dell," she told Madeline early on. "What's Adelaide, anyway? A city in Australia. I bet you've never been to Australia."

"You're right."

"Neither have I, but I've been enough places to know I don't have to go there. You know why? Because all places are the same. Or, even if they're different, I'm the same person wher-ever I go. And the life I'd find there would be the same life I fall into wherever I go. There'd be the same kind of men, even if they spoke with different accents. They'd want the same thing from a girl and offer the same thing in return as they do here. I'd be singing the same songs and hearing the same line of crap from everybody I met."

"You sound bitter," Madeline offered.

"Do I? That's good news. You're better off being bitter than sweet. If you're sweet, the world's full of people looking to eat you up. When you're bitter enough, they take one taste and walk away."

"And that's what you want?"

"That's how I stay alive," Dell said.

While friendship softened Dell's attitude toward Madeline, it didn't make her change her mind about the music Madeline had written. "These aren't songs," she said flatly. "From the looks of what you've done, you don't know anything about putting a melody line together, let alone figuring out the chords. If you had a great sense of melody, you could get somebody else to work out the chords and do up a lead sheet, but I don't see any of that here. Why are you so hipped on writing songs, anyway?"

"It just feels like something I have to do."

"Yeah," Dell said. "Well, I can understand what that feels like. Anything that gets in your blood that way, it's hard to find a way to say no to it. If you're lucky, the desire and the talent come in the same package. But some unlucky people get the one without the other. Of course, if you get the talent and not the desire, it's not necessarily the worst thing in the world. I knew a girl, I swear she had a voice like an angel. Unbelievable pipes. And not just the raw material. Her phrasing, her timing, everything was right about her. Everything but one thing."

"What was that?"

"She didn't have the desire. She didn't care about it. She could have been a headliner right off the bat, and she probably could have made it big. Records, television, maybe even the movies. She had that kind of talent. But without the drive she didn't put up with the crap that's part of the business, and you know what happened to her?"

"What?"

"She met a real nice guy and married him, and the only singing she does now is to her husband and her kids, and she's living in a house in the suburbs and happy as a clam. Doesn't sound so bad, does it?"

"I guess not."

"That's what happens when you got the talent and not the drive. When it's the other way around, you got a lifetime of disappointment. Well, what the hell—that's what you get when you've got the drive *and* the talent, too, because this is a business where even the winners lose most of the time. But at least there are a few victories along the way, something to keep your hopes up."

"And I don't have any talent?"

"Not in the music department. But I'll tell you something, much as I hate to encourage you—"

"What?"

"Some of your lyrics aren't so bad. None of 'em really work, because a lyric can't exist in a vacuum. A lyric's not a poem, it's the verbal part of a song, and it has to be suited to a melody. A really good lyric, even when it's all by itself, has a melody locked up inside it waiting for a composer to find it and yank it out. You don't have lyrics in that sense, but you've got bits and pieces that show a certain flair."

"Like what?"

Dell thumbed through Madeline's papers. "Well, like this," she said. " 'You and I together all alone, in a little country of our own, where the population's only two.' That's just a fragment, but there's something about it I like. But that doesn't mean it's a lyric yet."

"Maybe I can work on it."

"Maybe you can, but I don't know why you'd want to bother. When you stop to think about it, all songs say the same thing. They all tell you love's wonderful, one way or another. Some say it hurts and some say it's a picnic, but they all think it's what makes the world go round. You think the world needs to hear that message again?"

It was funny, she thought, how quickly Dell sought to erase the sensitive side of herself. She couldn't say a nice word about a partial lyric without wiping it out with a bitter sarcastic comment in the next breath. What Madeline came to realize was that there were two Dells. The worldly cynical brassy Dell was onstage most of the time, but there was always the other Dell waiting in the wings.

The other Dell was quieter, less forceful. And this other Dell spoke so seldom, spoke so little, that you wanted to hear every word she said. She was dead, had been killed off, would never be alive, and you wanted to know as much about her as you could.

"There was Johnny Black. He wrote the biggest hit of its day, 'Dardanella.' They took it away from him. Or at least, moved in on it, cut in on it. To get it published, he had to let them tinker, rearrange a note or two. All to get their split. You know that long, mournful wail that starts up in the verse, and then dies down again? And then starts up, and then dies down again. Every time I hear it, I think it's Johnny Black, moaning in his grave because they cut his heart out.

"There was Byron Gay. He died dead broke. Twenty years after he was gone, somebody dug up one of his numbers. It was called 'Oh!' Just 'Oh!' Probably the shortest song title on record. It made twenty-five thousand dollars in one season. It couldn't have happened to a nicer corpse.

"It's a tough business. A bitch of a tough business. Don't let yourself be hooked into it. Marry, and have a school bus full of kids. You strike me as more that type."

And then at another time, in self-contradiction, she would say: "It has its moments of sudden inspiration, too, that make all the rest of it worthwhile, I guess.

"Like the struggling young songwriter who got caught in a rainstorm on the streets of New York one day. He ducked into the nearest hotel lobby to get in out of the wet, and while he was sitting there waiting it out, he overheard a wife say to her husband, 'Hasn't it let up? Can't we leave yet?' The husband turned around from the window he was looking out of and said, 'In just a few more minutes. Wait till the sun shines, Nellie.'

"Or the time Rodgers and Hart were in a near car collision in Paris, and one of the girls with them put her hand over her rib cage and gasped, 'My heart stood still!' "

In all of us, Madeline thought broodingly, there are two. The one we might have been, the one we are.

There was a shrewd side to Dell, as there is to many women who appear at first sight to live by frivolity alone. It was more than just shrewdness, she had an excellent business head. Granting her original premise of getting something for nothing (and is that so foreign to business?), she took it the rest of the way from there with an acumen that would have met with the approval of any board of directors.

Showing off a solitaire one day, breathing on it lovingly, then frictioning it against her sleeve to polish it, she remarked idly, "This has about two weeks to go."

"What d'you mean? You give them back?" Madeline asked in surprise.

Dell arched her eyebrows in rebuke. "Be sensible," she admonished her. "Only the weak in the head do that.

"That old song Carol Channing used to sing," she went on. "'Diamonds Are a Girl's Best Friend,' that's the bunk. Not so. You can hoard them for twenty years, and what have you got? Still diamonds. They're beautiful, but they don't work for you. And anything that doesn't work for you isn't really beautiful at all, is it? Put it this way: AT&T pays three point six a year. Diamonds pay exactly oh point oh a year. Diamonds don't feed the kitty.

"So here's what I do. I have a sort of special personal friend—" She interrupted herself to laugh at herself. "Well, he'd have to be a special personal friend, wouldn't he?—who comes up with a piece of this stuff every now and then. On special occasions. Like Christmas, like a birthday. I give it a run of about two months, and then when he's good and used to seeing it on me and doesn't pay any more attention to it, I take it off display. I take it down to a diamond broker I know, he puts it up for sale, takes his commission, and I collect the balance. I take a beating every time, but I don't mind that. For instance, a piece worth two thousand, I'm glad to take twelve hundred for. You never can get back the full price. Then I take my twelve hundred, which is now all clear, to another special friend I have, this one's an investment broker, and he buys me a hunk of U.S. Steel or General Motors or some other blue chip with it. I put it away and forget about it, and it starts working for me from then on. So when I wind up someday with too much rust in my pipes to go on singing, and when the men don't turn up anymore with the diamonds, I'll have enough money coming in to keep body and soul together."

"You've got it figured out," Madeline said admiringly.

"You've got to, the way life is. You know that song Billie Holiday sang? 'God Bless the Child Who's Got His Own.' God, it tears me up, the way she sang that song. She didn't just sing it, you know. She wrote it. She wasn't a songwriter, nobody who sings like that should have to do anything but sing, but she wrote that song. And before she wrote it, she did something else."

"What?"

"She lived it. 'God bless the child who's got his own.' You can't wait for other people to give it to you, you can't live on crusts of bread from other people's sandwiches. 'God bless the child who's got his own.' If you don't take care of yourself, you're always going to be the kid outside the candy store, nose against the glass, looking in, wondering why everybody else has got the candy and all you've got is a cold nose and an appetite."

Later, she asked Dell how her gentleman friend would feel if he knew she sold his gifts.

"Take it from me," Dell said, "he doesn't *want* to know. Because if he knew, he'd think he had to be upset about it, but why should he? He gives me diamonds because he can't give me money because that would give our relationship a name neither of us wants it to have. But what's a diamond beside money disguised as beauty? He could give me fake jewelry and it would look the same when I wore it. Diamonds are an acceptable way for him to give me money, and if I invest that money instead of wearing it, all I'm being is smart. But he wouldn't like it if he knew, because it would mean looking at something he doesn't want to see."

"And God bless the child," Madeline said.

"Amen to that. You know how to write a song? Start off with a feeling—your own feeling, not one you got secondhand from a song. Something you feel as deeply as Lady Day felt that song. Then write a lyric that's so good it's got the melody curled right up inside it."

"I'd have a better chance," Madeline said, "if I had a piano. That's why my melodies are so bad. I'm trying to hear the notes in my head. If I had a piano, I could sound them out, write down the melodies that I hear instead of guessing at them."

"So save your pennies and buy yourself a piano."

"I haven't got enough pennies. And even if I did, I don't have room for a piano. I was thinking—"

"Oh?"

"There's plenty of time when you're not here," she said. "If I could come here when you're out, not all the time but whenever I've got something I want to work out on the piano all by myself. If I did that, I think I could come up with some lead sheets that wouldn't look like the Morse code in Slovakian."

"Was that what I called your song? Yeah, I guess it was."

"And if I came up with something decent, you'd get first crack at it. Since you'd be helping me with it, you could even be coauthor, in case the song turned out to be a big hit and other singers covered it."

Dell shook her head. "I thought I was good at building castles in the air," she said. "You not only build them, you turn around and start renting out rooms. Here you haven't even written the song yet and you've got it on the Top Forty and the two of us splitting the royalties. What is it you want, exactly? I hope you're not looking to move in here because I don't want roommates."

"Just a key to the apartment," Madeline said. "I'd call first, to make sure you weren't home."

"I should hope so. The last thing I need is somebody walking in at the wrong moment."

"I'd be very careful," Madeline said dutifully.

"All right, it's a deal," Dell said. "You can have my duplicate key. On one condition. Anything missing it's understood you take direct personal responsibility for and make good on it."

"I agree," Madeline said.

"Here's the key, then." Dell went over to her dressing table, opened a drawer, took the key out, and tossed it into Madeline's lap.

"I'm not Santa Claus," she let her know. "I might get a good workable song out of this yet, at that. For peanuts."

After a good thorough wall-to-wall casing on the occasion of her first two visits in Dell's absence, which revealed very little or nothing that she didn't already know, she didn't bother going there with any great regularity anymore. Paradoxically, and against all expectation, she found she stood to learn a great deal more when Dell was present, sousing and chattering away, than from her muted—and carefully sterilized—surroundings when she was absent. They had nothing to tell, no voice in which to tell it. What could they show her? A double strip of purple stamps in a desk drawer, a bottle of amber Chanel on a dressing-table top. A jigger of aspirin on a medicine cabinet shelf. A quart of the ubiquitous Canadian Club in the refrigerator, along with a six-pack of Heineken for those who were tapering off. Even her little blue booklet for telephone numbers, hanging by a loop beside the instrument itself, was chastely discreet. A liquor store. A music publisher. An all-night delicatessen, for those four-in-the-morning snacks—with whom? The place where she bought her shoes. Not a personal name in it.

Smart; she must have kept them all in her head.

People didn't seem to write to Dell to any very great extent. Not because they were afraid to, probably, as much as because the world in which she and they moved was too swift to wait for letters to catch up. A phone call said everything that needed to be said. Yesterday's keenness for a get-together, by the following day might already have cooled to disinterest, or somebody else might have come along in the meantime.

There were no photographs of the two principals in her present life, nor of her former husband either, the man who had later married Starr, but then this last wasn't to be wondered at. She'd probably torn them all up at the time of the debacle—as Starr herself, apparently, had torn up the one in her room when things unraveled later.

There was a whole row of medical bills, all from the same doctor. The first had just the amount. The second had "Please" added to it in handscript. The third bore an imploring "Third notice." The final one had the sum x-ed off, and the notation "How about tonight?" in its place.

"So that's how she took care of that," Madeline caught on with a sudden flash of wry insight.

She left little notes on the piano a couple of times after having been there. "Was here. Had workout. Mad." And one time, just to make it sound plausible, "Is 'The Blues I Get from You' a good title?"

The next day there was a curt answering note from Dell, left in the same place. "Can it. I don't do blues, remember? If you're going to work at my piano, do material I can use, at least!"

Madeline thumbed her nose at it.

Madeline knew a time would come when she'd start talking about her former husband, and that time came. If a woman loves a man, she is bound to talk about him sooner or later to her confidante. If a woman hates a man, she is equally bound to talk about him sooner or later. She wouldn't be a woman if she didn't. She wouldn't have loved, she wouldn't have hated, if she didn't.

Madeline bided her time, threw out no leads, dropped no hints, planted no verbal traps. It would be freer, fuller, if it came by itself. It came by itself.

She was browsing through sheets of music one day, looking for something new to break into her repertoire. She came to one and she started to hum her way through it. Then she broke off and put it down so sharply it almost amounted to slapping it against the piano top. Madeline looked up at the sound. She could make out the title on the cover, upside down, from where she was. "That Old Feeling."

"No good?" she asked.

"Too good," Dell said. "It's more than a song, it's an actual experience. I know, because I've been through it. I saw you last night and I got that old feeling." She turned to Madeline. "What the hell," she said. "You don't want to hear this."

"Yes, I do."

"Why? Just because I pick up some sheet music and get in a mood? That doesn't mean I have to tell you a sad story and bring us both down."

"Sometimes it helps to tell it to another person, whatever it is," Madeline said. "To get it off your own chest."

"And onto yours instead? What's the point?"

"That's what friends are for."

"Don't give me that," Dell snapped. "I don't know what friends are for, but it's not to listen to all the garbage people got locked up in their hearts. Maybe it's what psychiatrists are for, but not friends. So why should you listen? What's in it for you?"

Madeline shrugged. "Maybe I'll get a song out of it."

"A song?"

"Or an idea for a song."

"I told you," Dell said. "You don't get the good ideas by looking inside other people. You get 'em by looking inside yourself."

"Maybe looking inside other people, or listening to what's inside other people, is a way I can find out what's inside myself."

Dell thought about that. "Yeah," she said after a moment. "That makes sense. Well, I can stand it if you can. But I'm warning you, you might want to pick up a violin and accompany me. It's that kind of a story."

"Sad, huh?"

"It's the story of a marriage," Dell said. "There are two kinds of marriages. Bad ones and imaginary ones, because the real ones aren't good and the good ones aren't real." She shook her head. "I don't know where to start."

"How did the two of you meet?"

"We first met at the mail desk of the Eastland Hotel in Portland, Maine. We were both up there on our time off. All I wanted was my key. Instead, the clerk handed me a message. Before I even looked at it I said, 'This can't be for me, I don't know anyone in this town!' I was right. It was for some Swede named Miss Nilson and they'd put it in the wrong box. The 'i' was looped, looked like an 'e.'

"He smiled at me, and I let him. He began to talk, and I let him. I liked him almost from the minute he first began to talk.

Before we separated he said, 'Now you can't say you don't know anyone in this town anymore.'

"The next night he came over to me in the lobby, and took me into one of the lounges, and bought me a drink. The night after, he bought me dinner. When time was up, we came back to the city separately, but we had arranged to meet again after we returned, and we did. By that time, I was in love with him already. He wasn't in love with me, I see that now. I was the one way out in front all through the whole thing. But we both made the same mistake: we both mistook my love for him for a return love on his part. When he kissed me, he was only answering my kisses, not giving me originals. When he held me in his arms, he was only completing the half circle of my own embrace. On the strength of this illusion, we got married; he said the words, I put them into his mind.

"It was a bad risk from the start. I was safe only as long as he still hadn't come up with a love of his own. When he did, and it hit him, I was all screwed up.

"It hit him about two and a quarter years after we were married. Twenty-seven months; that would be about right. We got along very well, those first twenty-seven months. He didn't even know he didn't love me. For that matter, I even forgot about it myself, I was so taken up in loving him.

"I can't pinpoint exactly when she came along. I'm not that good. She didn't break one of those electronic beams that open or close a door, her arrival wasn't that precisely registered. But somewhere between the twenty-sixth and the twenty-eighth month she came along.

"The only thing I can't explain now is *how* I knew. There was some subtle change in him. I knew what it was then, and looking back now I know that I knew then, but I still can't say how I knew, any more than I could at the time.

"She was young, I knew that about her too. I saw him glance at a girl of eighteen or nineteen when I was with him on the street one day. He wasn't interested in her per se, it was a speculative look, so I knew that he must have been comparing her to this other one, and I knew by that that this other one must be around the same age, eighteen or nineteen. Even in a love affair, detective work can be brought into play.

"Pretty soon I knew everything about her, everything but her actual face and her actual name. I knew almost as soon as it happened when they had begun loving up together.

"I used to sit by the hour, thinking, Maybe there's still some way I could win him back. Maybe it's not too late even yet. It's happened before. It's happened to others. Why not to me?

"Yes, but how? I'd say to myself each time. How? I was never able to get past that 'how?'

"Then one night something happened that gave me an idea, and I thought I saw the way. I was sitting there alone, watching TV and yet not paying any attention to it, both at the same time, when the phone rang. It was a man, and he had the wrong number. He asked if Miss Somebody-or-other was there. I said, 'Nobody by that name lives here.' It turned out our two numbers were identical but for the two last digits, and even those were the same but in opposite order. He'd gotten them transposed, and gotten me by mistake. He excused himself and got off, and that's all there was to it.

"But I started to think about it, and the more I thought about it, the more I felt it might be the very thing I'd been looking for. Jealousy. Try jealousy. Patience hadn't worked, lack of opposition hadn't worked. If I raised hell and stormed at him, I'd only lose him all the quicker. But maybe jealousy would do the trick. Maybe if he felt that somebody else wanted me, even though he no longer did, I would look good to him again. Men were funny that way: what the other guy didn't want, they didn't want either; there must be something the matter with it. What the other guy wanted, they wanted too; there must be something good about it. They were like sheep. Or I suppose I should say, wolves.

"It took me almost a week to get up enough courage to try it. I thought about it all the time, but I still didn't do anything about it. I used to try to visualize his face on the night he would come home and find out I'd been carrying on behind his back. Stunned, first. Then angry. Maybe he'd even slap me. Maybe he'd swear me out, call me all those low-down names they call their women when they catch them cheating. I hoped so, how I hoped so. Anything, anything would be better than this indifference.

"On the day of the night that he would next be seeing her (and I told you, I was as sure of them as I was of my own birthdays) I went out and bought a few necessary props, I guess you might call them. Things I didn't habitually buy.

"I went into a cigar store and I asked the clerk for the name of a good, expensive brand of cigar.

"'Garcia y Vega,' he said. 'Twelve-fifty a box.'

"'I don't want a whole box,' I said. 'Just let me have two.'

"He put them into a small bag for me and remarked, 'Your husband's going to like these.'

"My husband, I said to myself, is *not* going to like these, is what I hope.

"From there I went into a package store and bought a half pint of bourbon, which was the smallest amount I could get. Since it wasn't intended for drinking, there was no use spending too much money on it.

"I tried to think of what else might conjure up a fictitious masculine presence, but nothing further would come readily to mind. I was determined to make this as realistic as possible, no holds barred.

"There was a little elderly man, well, I should say about sixty, on the late-afternoon to late-evening elevator shift in our building. All the others were youngsters. I went outside to the hall and rang for him, after he'd come on, and handed him the two cigars with one of the strangest requests I bet he'd ever had yet from a woman tenant.

"'Smoke these,' I said, 'but be sure you bring me back the butts. I want *both* butts back. And not too—er—soggy, if you can help it.'

"He did a very good job of covering up whatever surprise he must have felt. 'Will tomorrow be all right?' he asked. 'I'll smoke one when I get my coffee break at six, and I'll save the other for tonight when I get home—'

"'No, no, no!' I said quickly. 'I've got to have them *both* back, and no later than five-thirty. You'll have to work it out the best you can.'

"'It's kind of heavy smoking,' he said dubiously.

"I went inside and got the rest of the stage setting ready. I got out two highball glasses and poured about an inch of the whiskey in each one. Then I stood them side by side, very close together, on our knee-high refreshment table in the front room. Then I filled a big bowl with ice cubes, and ran hot water over them from the faucet, so they looked like they'd been slowly melting away for hours. Then I got hold of all the cushions in the room and scattered them all around that one particular place on the sofa opposite where the drinks were, throwing some on the floor, to make it look like there'd been quite a hot thing going on there.

"I went into the bedroom and I took particular pains with the bed. I pulled it all apart first, so that it looked like an earthquake had hit it. Then I telescoped the two pillows one on top of the other, and kept punching my hand into them until I had a big hollow in their centers. Then I got out a pair of my pink nylon underpants and shoved them down underneath between the sheets, but letting them show just enough. I mean, even beds that had had it happen didn't look that realistic.

"I disarranged my hair a little bit, but not to an extreme, because the first thing a woman will do is see to her hair, no matter how preoccupied she is or was. I put on more lipstick than I usually use, and then I took a Kleenex and purposely smeared it offside from one corner, as though I'd been wildly kissed. Then I took the whiskey bottle, and using it like you do toilet water, put a drop here and a drop there and a drop behind each ear. The rest I sprinkled all over the carpet, so that I had the room smelling like a distillery.

"The bell rang and Dave had brought back the two cigar stubs sitting atop an empty envelope. 'I kept one going on top a corner of the mailbox in the lobby,' he said, 'and the other on top a fire extinguisher on the fourteenth floor, and every time I had the car empty I'd step out and take a few puffs. But I feel kind of bilious. I never smoked two at once like that before.'

"I tipped him for his trouble and took the cigars. I balanced one on a tray beside the two whiskey glasses. I took the other one into the bedroom and put that in a tray right next to the bed. To get any closer it would have had to be *in* the bed.

"Then I sat down and waited. Waited for him to come home and be jealous. And be interested again in me.

"It would have been just the kind of luck I ran in not to have him come home at all, after I'd gone to all that trouble. He often stayed out like that on nights when he was seeing her; went straight from work to pick her up for dinner or whatever it was they had on, throwing me a terse 'Staying downtown tonight. Be back later on' by phone on his way over. He couldn't have made those messages more impersonal if he'd tried—he even left out the I's and You's. And never even a reason given anymore. I wasn't even worth lying to!

"But I got a break in this one small thing at least, if nothing else. A taxi stopped at the door and I saw him step out and come into the building.

"I stood up and got on cue for the curtain to rise.

"He put his key to the door and opened it, and I gave a startled little hitch, as if I'd been taken by surprise. 'Oh!' I said. 'I didn't expect you so soon.'

"'When *did* you expect me?' he said, with complete neutrality, complete disinterest.

"I saw that he had as little an eye for the room as he had for me, and he was going to miss the whole thing if I didn't point it up to him.

"I rounded my mouth, drew in my breath, clapped my hand over it, glanced over at the cigar butt, then quickly away from it, and tried to look confused. I thought I did a pretty good job. It wasn't an easy multiple play to make, all more or less at one time.

"He'd noticed the direction my eyes had taken, and he looked there himself, and finally spotted the debris of the rendezvous.

"I'm giving it to you just as it happened, blow by blow. If I had any pride I guess I'd lie a little, try to dress it up. But I didn't then and I don't now, not where he's concerned.

"He grinned at me. Not sarcastically, even. Not maliciously. Nothing like that. Grinned good-naturedly, amiably, almost the way he would have grinned at another man whom he'd caught in an embarrassing moment.

"'Who's your new friend?' he said. And then, starting to unfasten his necktie, he went on into the bedroom without wasting any more time on it.

"I heard him exclaim 'Wow!' in there. And there was laughter in his voice.

"'Glad you're happy,' he called out to me. 'Cause I'm happy too. This way we're all happy, the whole four of us.'

"And with that he started running the shower and taking a quick shave, so he could go right back to her again.

"I just stood there rooted; wilted and ashamed. And the blush that might have helped out when I did that bit of play-acting a few moments before was all over my face now when I didn't need it anymore. I could feel myself burning up with it.

"When he came out into the bedroom again and was changing over to a new shirt and necktie, he started to whistle. It wasn't bravado, it wasn't making fun of me, wasn't derision. It was completely natural. I could tell, I could tell by the sound of it. He probably didn't even know he was doing it at all. He'd already forgotten what he'd seen, it didn't mean anything to him, didn't exist.

"He was whistling his own happiness.

"He shrugged into his jacket, and he walked with a lilt and a bounce over to the door, and not a word passed between us, not a look, not a care. And the door closed after him.

"My head just went over, a notch at a time, lower, and lower, and lower, like something with a run-down spring.

"I was no good as a faithful wife. And I was no good even as an unfaithful wife."

She threw her arms wide apart, and there was indescribable pathos in her voice. "What the hell *was* I good for, anyway?

"He came back real late again, and got in next to me. I kept my face pressed to the pillow. He snapped on the bedside lamp for just a second, I guess to see what time it was. And that cold cigar butt was still there in the tray, where I'd put it.

"He put the light right out again, but in the dark I heard him give a chuckle, deep down in his throat."

＊

"I could tell when he'd been with her. A wife always can. The little signs, telltale little signs that give a man away, if you know what to look for. Tired, indolent, exhausted, all vitality spent; lying there like a log beside me, not even knowing I existed. A certain peaked expression, a hollowness in the cheeks and at the temples, that was gone again inside twenty-four hours. To come back once more inside forty-eight. Circles under the eyes, which I knew he hadn't gotten from me."

She smiled in retrospect. It was a sad smile, remembering a sad thing.

"What was the good of saying anything? Would that have stopped it? Has it ever stopped it yet? But I knew, I knew. Oh, how I knew. He might just as well have brought me photographs.

"First it was hit or miss, haphazard, like at the beginning of any affair. Then it went into a regular rhythm, almost like a married couple. Three times a week. Never missed. *They* were the married couple, and I was the outsider, living under his name.

"Why does it matter so much," she asked Madeline rhetorically, "that your husband is sleeping with another woman? I wondered then and I wonder now. He slept with other women before you met him, and you know he did, and that doesn't bother you. I guess because she's taking away something that is yours now, belongs to you. Before that, he was nobody's, it hurt nobody. And there's so much more than just the physical that you're being robbed of. The intimate, confidential things that are said at those times, and not at any other time. She's the recipient of them now, not you. The plans that are made at those times, the innermost thoughts that are revealed, the love names and love words that are spoken, all of them go to her now, not to you.

"You just stand there. A door has closed between you now. He's on one side, you're on the other. You can't get through. Not all the keys, not all the pounding with your hands, not all the hammers, not all the axes, can make it open or break it open.

"So what do you do? I'll tell you what you do. You live with it. Live with it as best you can. A few of us do away with ourselves. Not most of us, though. That's for high-strung young girls that are just beginning the game, have no inner resources yet to fall back on.

"Then one day he comes to you about it. *He* comes to you, you don't go to him.

"One day he comes to you. One night, rather. You're lying there awake, with the lights out. You're always lying awake with the lights out. He lies there, and he thinks. You lie there, and you think. But the two chains of thought don't mesh anymore like they used to.

"He says quietly, 'Dell, are you awake?'

"You say just as quietly, 'I'm awake, Vick.'

"'I want to talk to you.'

"Your heart starts going like the sweep hand of a watch. This is it. At last. Finally. Here it is.

"'The thing is,' he says, 'I don't know where to start.' What do you say to that? You don't say anything at all. You just lie there and let him work it out for himself. Half hoping he'll forget the whole thing.

"But he doesn't.

"He says, 'Dell, we've had some good times. Haven't we?'

"You don't answer. It's not the sort of question that requires an answer.

"'But something's changed,' he goes on. 'I don't know how to explain it. I'm not saying it's your fault. It's not your fault. If it's anybody's fault, it's my fault. But I don't know that anybody's ever at fault when this kind of thing happens. I don't think people have much choice. I think things happen and people can only go along with them.'

"Get to the point, you want to shout. Put a lid on your dime-store philosophy and get to the point. But instead you just lie there and wait for him to go on.

"'Dell, I can't live here anymore.'

"'Why not?'

"'Because we used to have something,' he says, 'and now it's gone.'

"'Not for me it isn't,' you say, hating yourself for saying it, for needing to say it. 'For me it's still the same.'

"'Dell, I'm going to move out.'

"'When?'

"'Now, if you want.'

"'That's crazy,' you say. 'It's the middle of the night. You don't want to leave now.'

"'Well, if you're sure you don't mind—'

"'Of course I don't mind.'

"'First thing in the morning, then.'

"So he takes off his clothes and comes to bed. And he lies on his side of the bed and you lie on your side, and you wish you could just fall asleep but of course you can't. And you wish you could stay on your own side of the bed but you can't do that either.

"So you curl up beside him. He can't sleep either, and you know what to do, how to touch him, and you get the response you want. He's unwilling at first. As if he's cheating her by being with you. But you know what you're doing and he can't help himself.

"And while it's going on, all you can think is that it's the last time, the last time.

"Afterward, he falls asleep. You try to sleep, and you can't, and after a while you give up trying. You get up and walk around the room, and then you come back and sit on the edge of the bed while your mind just spins like a top."

"He woke up. I still sat there, looking out the window, in the other room. He got out of bed and went into the bathroom and ran the water for his shower. I thought, This is probably the last time I'll ever hear him take a shower. And hit his chest, like he does. And snort, like he does, to clear the water out of his nostrils.

"I thought, What a funny thing to think, at a time like this. Or is it? Maybe it's the right thing to think at a time like this.

"He got dressed, and he came to the bedroom door a minute and looked in at me, before he was quite through, while he was measuring off the two sides of his necktie.

"'I won't come back tonight,' he said. 'I won't come back anymore. I'll send for my things instead, some time during the day.' And then he added, as though he were asking my permission, 'Okay?'

"'Okay,' I said. I still sat there.

"He said, 'You act more dead than alive.'

"I said dully, 'You would too.'

"He finished finally, and came out, set to go.

"I said, 'Are you sure you want to go through with this, Vick?'

"'Come on now,' he said reproachfully.

"It was the funniest parting I ever heard of.

"He said, 'What about money? You better tell me now.'

"'That isn't what I want,' I said. 'I can always get that. That's the easiest thing to get there is.'

"He went out and closed the door after him.

"I still sat there.

"He came out of the building doorway down below on the

street, and turned around and looked up at the window. He saw me looking down at him.

"He lifted his hat, tipped it way up high in parting salute to me. Then he stepped into a taxi the doorman had whistled up for him. The taxi drove off and my marriage was over.

"I never knew before what an insult it could be, how much it could hurt, how needling it could feel, to have your own husband exaggeratedly tip his hat to you like that.

"There was a bottle of goof pills in the medicine cabinet. I took them down. Then I brought a glass of water over. I sat down and kept switching from one to the other, until both were gone. The water tasted strange, but that was because I wasn't used to drinking water straight.

"I no sooner did it than I came to my senses with a bang. I yelled at myself. What am I doing *this* for? Why should I make it even easier on him than it is already? I'm gonna live! I'm gonna live so that I can get hunk with him, get square with him, screw him up but good! And I grabbed up the phone and hollered into it, 'Judas, Joseph, and Mary! Somebody send me a stomach pump up here quick, for the love of Pete!'"

"I met him on the street one day. It wasn't planned, it was quite by accident. It was the sort of thing happens to two people maybe once in ten years in a town the size of New York.

"He looked at me and recognized me. Of course he recognized me, why shouldn't he? I saw that he wasn't going to stop, so I did instead, and that more or less forced him to stop against his will.

"He looked good and happy, and that didn't make me feel good and happy.

"He said Well?

"I said Well?

"Then he said So?

"I said So?

"No great soundtrack of a conversation up to that point. But there were a thousand unspoken words in it. Hope and indifference and mockery and entreaty.

"Finally he said, 'There's no use standing here like this. We haven't anything to say to each other.'

"I said, 'If you think I'm going to give you up without a fight, you better think twice.'

"'You already have,' he said. 'It's over and done with. There's nothing you can do about it.' And he started to walk

"'Isn't there?' I called after him. 'Isn't there? Watch. Watch and see.' But he never even turned around again.

"That brought the thing to a head. That got it going, that brush-off on the street. Love ended there. There wasn't any more love, only hate from then on. Hate, and figuring out how to hurt him.

"I worked on it, steady. While I earned my feed singing, I worked on it. While other men made love to me, I kept working on it. I worked on it in the morning, and I worked on it in the afternoon, and I worked on it at night.

"Finally, I thought I had a way figured to frame him, pin something on him he didn't do. The details don't matter now anymore. But I needed some help. So I turned to this friend I had, who still had connections from the old days, even though he'd gone legit a long time ago, the way most of the smart ones have.

"To my surprise, he wouldn't have any part of it, and he talked me out of it and advised me to drop it. Those things always backfire, he said. They're never foolproof. You'll be the one to get hurt, Dell, not him. Let the guy go. Don't keep trying to get him back. He made a clean break of it. Let it stay that way. Leave him alone.

"That was the man's point of view, not the woman's. And I was wise to his little personal angle too; he was in love with me himself, and Vick had been too much competition for him. He'd had to take a backseat the whole time I was married to Vick. No wonder he liked it better this way, Vick safely out of the way.

"Well, I gave that particular project up as unfeasible, but I didn't quit for a minute. If he thought I'd quit trying, he didn't know me.

"Since I couldn't get at him himself, I decided maybe I could get at him through her. In fact the more I thought of it, the more I liked it. I decided this was the better way of the two. Do something to him, and he still had her to love him. Do something to her, and he didn't have anyone to love him. That hurt the more of the two ways.

"She had religion of a sort, more or less. I had ways of finding out things. I found out she always went to early morning mass on Sundays. Seven o'clock mass. He never went, and she never went herself any other time the week around. She always went to this same little neighborhood church, and to get to it she had to pass through this deserted side street. On early Sunday mornings it was practically dead, not a soul around. There was a new development going up, and the old buildings that were still standing had all been vacated and boarded up. I saw that for myself. You know how they do, whitewash X's marking the windowpanes. Then where the new construction was already well advanced, there was this long plank scaffolding to protect the sidewalk. Like they always put up, in case anything should fall from above. Walking along under it was almost like going through a long tunnel, it was so dim and walled in. And on Sunday morning no workmen would be around. She would be boxed in there, unable to advance, unable to retreat, if anyone caught her fairly in the middle of that confined place.

"Next I got hold of the addresses of a number of low-type dives or joints that were said to be hangouts for ex-cons and petty hoodlums and the like. For nearly a week straight each night after the show instead of going out on the town, I'd strip off the glitter, change to a plain black dress so I wouldn't attract attention, and put on a pair of dark glasses.

"Then I'd go to one of those places and hang around. Oh, there were plenty of passes made, but when they saw that wasn't the game, they gave up trying.

"Finally I made the sort of a contact I'd been looking for. Well, it was slow work. I had to be cagey. He had to be cagey. I had to build him up. He had to build me up. But after three meetings we were finally ready to get down to cases. In the meantime I'd had him checked thoroughly, knew where he was living, knew what his past record was, in fact knew much more than he knew I knew, so that he didn't stand a chance in the world of taking me.

"Once we understood each other, the rest of it went fast. It was just a matter of agreeing on a price.

"'I'm doing this for a friend,' I said.

"'Yeah,' he said, 'so am I.'

"'I got a friend who'd give anything if she knew somebody who'd let fly at a little twist that goes by a certain place every Sunday morning at six-thirty.'

"'Anything?' he said. 'How much is anything?'

"'Well, let's say five hundred.'

"'That ain't anything,' he said. 'That's a quarter of anything.'

"'I'd have to take that up with her,' I said.

"'Let fly?' he said. 'Let fly what?'

"'Well, the whole trouble with her is she's too pretty. Now, a fist or a rock ain't going to change that. It comes right back again after she heals. It's got to be something that *eats* its way in slow. Then she stays like that for good.'

"'Acid,' he lip-read knowingly.

"'Does *your* friend want to get it, or should *my* friend get it?'

"'My friend can get the right stuff. He knows where. No problem there.'

"'I'll call and find out about the "anything." '

"I went into a phone booth, counted out what I had brought with me, and came out to him again.

"'You get a thousand now, she says,' I told him. 'The baptism of fire comes off Sunday. You get five hundred more here, this same joint, this same table, on Monday.'

"'I'll check,' he said. He didn't even bother pretending the phone bit. He just went into the men's room, stayed a short while, came out again putting a comb into his pocket, and said, 'On Monday another thousand, and it's in the works.' Well, there *was* another phone in there (I imagine), if one wanted to be technical about it.

"'It's in the works,' I said. I gave him the first thousand under the table then and there.

"'What's this?' he asked, and read the little piece of paper I'd had on top of it.

"'That's the real name and present address of your "friend," ' I told him. 'I know he can change his address easy between now and Sunday, but the info about him can also follow him to the new place just as easy. He's done time in prison in the past. He's got a two-strike against him.'

"He looked at me a long time. Not sore or frightened, just admiring me, like.

"Then he showed the edges of his teeth a little. 'Smart,' he said.

"I agreed with him. 'Yes, she is. Very.'

"The thing would have come off perfect, without a hitch, only I started celebrating a little too early and a little too hard. I came home right after my Saturday night show and started drinking. My friend, the one I mentioned to you earlier, the one who'd talked me out of pinning something on my husband, was here in the apartment with me. I'd lift my glass each time and say something like, 'Here's to somebody I know that's not going to look so good to somebody else I know, around this same time tomorrow night.' And I started singing, 'What a difference a day makes, twen'y-four little hours'—and looping it up altogether.

"Last thing I remember was him going to use my phone and closing the door after him. But I didn't think anything of it, he was the kind of guy just as apt to make a phone call at three or four in the morning as at twelve in the afternoon.

"When I woke up, it was early afternoon. He was still around. We were making a long weekend of it. I yawned and stretched enjoyably and said, 'Well, it's all over with by now. I wonder how she likes the new face she's breaking in today? Above all, I wonder how *he* likes it. I bet he can't look at it without turning green around the gills himself.'

"'She's not breaking in any new face,' he told me. 'She's still wearing the same face she wore yesterday, and the day before, and she'll keep on wearing it.'

"I sat up sudden and wide awake. 'What do you know about it?' I asked sharply. 'How do you come in it?'

"He jiggled the hand he was holding a glass of tomato juice in, by way of stirring it up. 'I sent a couple of boys I know over there bright and early, five-thirty, six this morning, to look him up where he was posted waiting for her. They did what I'd told them to; took him with them a considerable distance out of town, beat the living jazz out of him, and told him if he ever showed his face around again they'd finish up on him.'

"'My good thousand dollars!" I squawked, and clapped my hand over my eyes.

"'Here's your thousand dollars,' he said, and took it out of his pocket and handed it back to me still in the envelope in which I'd originally given it to the guy. 'They found it still on him. Evidently doesn't trust banks or mattresses.

"'Next time you're willing to put up that much,' he added, 'why don't you put it into something more constructive?' "

"And then you gave up trying," Madeline prodded.

"You don't know me," Dell said meaningfully. "You don't know me at all."

God, I wouldn't want her down on me! Madeline thought.

"For the second time I switched. Just like I'd switched from him to her, at first, so now I gave up trying bodily harm. I saw that wouldn't work. I switched instead to character damage.

"I got me a private detective. I got him out of the fine-print ads in the back of a disreputable magazine. You know the type of thing. 'Do you feel unsure of your mate's loyalty? Call on us. Strictly confidential.'

"He was a darb. He didn't have an ethic to his name. I wouldn't have even minded that if he'd only been personally clean. He hadn't changed his shirt in a week and his socks in a month. You could've told which part of a room he was in even with the lights out. But I always say, Get a dirty guy to do a dirty job. A decent guy wouldn't have handled an assignment like that in the first place. See, it wasn't to save a marriage, protect it from an intruder, a third person. I was paying him to deliberately break up a perfectly good marriage, and not my own but somebody else's. That was what I was hiring him for.

"I laid it on the line to him. My fist looked like a head of cabbage, the way bunched greenbacks were coming out between all the fingers. No wonder they've got that nickname for it, cabbage.

"I told him the grubby industrial town she was born in. I said, I want you to go there, and I want you to stay there, until you've dug up something on her. Something that'll make her as sooty as the town is. If you can dig up something big, all the better. If you can only dig up something little, never mind, we'll blow it up into something big. Don't leave a stone un-turned—"

Just like I did, Madeline thought parenthetically, only in reverse. Mine was benevolent, hers was malevolent.

"It's on me, I said to him. The whole thing's on me. I'm footing the bill. I don't care if you stay there six months. I don't care how you pad your expense account. I'll pay for it. I don't care if you have a broad in your room every night, a case of Carstairs in your room every night. I'll pay for it. It's worth it to me. Just so long as you come up with something on her. I've never enjoyed spending my money half as much as I'll enjoy spending it now. Ask around. Dig up the kids she went to school with. Look up doctors. Maybe she had a miss once. Maybe there was syph in her family. In the old days, when it presented a problem. Or insanity, or a criminal record. Check on her birth certificate, they must have it on file there, find out what that can tell you.

"Get something on her. I don't care what it is, but *get something on her.*"

And even in the repetition, her voice was a terrible thing, a thing such as Madeline had never heard before. It wasn't a voice, it was hate incarnate.

She spoke more quietly again. "About three months after he went there, he rang me up one night long-distance. Reversed charges, of course. When I heard what he had to tell me, I was in ecstasy. I'd never expected anything like it in a million years. All I'd hoped for was to find a little mud that I could sling at her. Instead, he'd dug up an entire tar pit. I rolled over and over on the bed, carrying the phone with me up to my ear. Then when the wire started to pull up short, I rolled over and over back again the other way until it was freed again.

"It was like dropping some kind of a bomb in between them. It blew them so far apart they could never get back together again, not in this lifetime. I bet from then on if either one of them ever saw the other, they'd start running for dear life, they couldn't get away fast enough."

"But what?" Madeline asked. "What was it?"

Dell dropped her eyes, with self-satisfaction but also with guile. "That's as far as it goes," she said inflexibly. "Beyond that, we don't talk about it in this house."

One day the phone rang while Madeline was there. Dell got up and went inside to it. It was just past the doorway. Madeline went ahead tapping single notes and writing them down on the score sheet.

After a few intimately indistinct phrases, she heard Dell say, "A friend."

Then she added, "Of course a girl. What do you think I do, entertain men here behind your back? I wouldn't last long that way."

Then she went on, "What do you mean, how do you know it is?"

Then she concluded, "Because I say so, isn't that enough?"

Suddenly she called, "Mad, come here a minute." Madeline got up and went in there. Dell thrust the phone out toward her, but without relinquishing it. "Say hello into this," she instructed.

"Hello?" Madeline said uncertainly.

Dell immediately took it away again, so that Madeline had no chance to hear what was said in return. Madeline went back to the piano. "Satisfied?" Dell was saying. "You sure take a lot of convincing."

She rejoined Madeline a few moments later, poking her thumb resentfully over her shoulder. "That guy!" she steamed. "He sure gives me trouble. It's getting so I'm afraid to go out on the street with him anymore, for fear my agent might pass and tip his hat to me, or the club manager might go by and give me a hello, or I might get a nod from somebody who once worked the same spot with me ten years ago. That's all it takes, and I find myself explaining and trying to square myself all the rest of the evening. And then when I get all through he still doesn't believe me, anyway." She held one hand to the side of her face as though it hurt her there and took a few short steps this way and that. "I'd have to be quadruplets, and all four of us working on a double shift, to be able to crowd in all the cheating he gives me credit for."

Madeline just looked at her solemnly, taking the tirade in. She didn't ask who he was, and Dell didn't say. She had a fairly good idea Dell wouldn't have told her even if she had asked, and that was one of the principal reasons she hadn't.

A few weeks after that, just as she was about to put the key Dell had given her into the outside door of the apartment, she held back, thinking she heard a voice somewhere on the inside. She inclined her head toward the door, but the sound didn't repeat itself. But some cautious instinct made her put the key away and ring instead. She didn't want any possible third party to know she had a key to the apartment in her possession, although she couldn't have said why. In the final analysis it was no one's business but Dell's and her own.

Dell's voice asked who it was, from the other side of the

door. She sounded guarded, cautious, as though apprehensive about what the answer might be.

"Mad," Madeline said.

The door opened immediately. A look of strain was just leaving Dell's face and a look of relief coming on in its place. Nevertheless she lowered her voice conspiratorially. "I can't ask you in right now. Got one of my Big Moments in here with me. You understand, don't you?"

"Oh, sure. Perfectly all right. I'll drop around tomorrow instead."

"Do that."

Suddenly a man's voice cut in: "Who you talking to out there?"

"Just a friend," Dell answered without turning her head.

A larger hand than hers took hold of the door edge above where her own was resting, and pulled the door a little wider open. Then a man's face peered out at Madeline, a little to one side of Dell's and about a foot higher up.

Sometimes you see a face a dozen and one times, and then later on forget it. Sometimes you see a face just once, and then see it over and over to the end of your days in retrospect. This bodiless face looking out at her now from a doorway was to be like an eyeless mask, one of those twin masks representing comedy and tragedy in the theater, pinned to the curtain of her memory from then on.

It was a face that had been handsome once. Its handsomeness had worn thin now, but the configuration of it could still be detected beneath the layer of the years and the experiences. Dark, lustrous Mediterranean hair, and dark, lustrous Mediterranean eyes. A cleft in the chin that years of shaving seemed to have ground into a blue-tinged, marbleized, scooped-out hollow.

But the eyes showed no recognition whatever of Madeline as a person. Just the fact that she was a woman, and not a rival, not a trespasser. They didn't care if she was ugly or fair, tall or short, wide or narrow. They were the eyes of jealousy, of sheer possessiveness alone.

The face withdrew without having said a word to either of the two women. But its silence was a surly, not an appeased, one.

Then a moment after, from back within the apartment, his voice sounded in a growled order. "Well, come on back in here, whenever you get through exchanging cake recipes or whatever it is you're doing out there."

Dell said in a harassed whisper, "Never comes around in the afternoon like this. But never. Today's the first time."

Then she added hastily, "Well, I better get back in there before he cracks the whip over me some more."

Madeline went away. There's dynamite in it somewhere, she thought.

She got things piecemeal, but she kept getting them.

"What a beautiful bracelet."

"Ange gave me that."

Dell was already so lit she couldn't fasten the thing without resting her whole elbow on the dresser top and leaning on it to try to steady it.

"That the broker?"

"No, the broker's Walter. C'mere, see if you can do this for me."

Then another time, answering the phone she said, "Hello, Jack."

When she came back she gave Madeline a knowing smirk and pitched her thumb back over her shoulder in derision. "Ange, checking up on me. He didn't have anything to say, just wanted to see if he could catch me at anything."

"But I thought I heard you say Jack."

"That's his first name." Dell was too busy prodding ice into a glass to keep much of a guard on her tongue. "In the old outfit days they called him 'Little Angie.' "

"Oh, that's why you call him Ange sometimes. Does he like it when you call him that?"

"Why shouldn't he like it? That's his name." Dell sampled her new drink. Or rather, left the sample behind in the glass, and took the drink itself. "Jack d'Angelo."

Now she knew one of them.

During another of these matinee sessions she got "confidential" with Dell. That is to say, confidential on the subject of her finances.

"Dell, I was wondering. I have a little money put aside. Not as much as you get from some of the pieces of jewelry you sell. But I hate to leave it lying around in a savings bank. You only get a measly three and three-quarters. Would you advise me to put it into some of those stocks like you were telling me about?"

"Honey." Dell made a pass of dissuasion with the flat of her hand. "You can't touch them unless you've got a big wad of dough backing you up. The market's sky-high right now."

Madeline let her face droop disconsolately, as though she saw all hopes of ever attaining financial independence fading from view. "But are they all high? Aren't there some that are a little lower than others?"

Dell had that warm glow, of friend toward friend. And there was a touch of show-off in it too. Besides, love wasn't involved, so there was no danger.

"Wait a minute," she said generously. "I'm going to call Walter up and ask him. I'll let him think I want to know for myself."

The building had a downstairs switchboard, so she couldn't dial.

Madeline listened carefully.

"Cardinal seven, four two hundred."

Then, "Mr. Shiller, please."

Now she had the other one too.

She went back to her own place, asked for "Cardinal seven, four two hundred."

A voice answered, "Warren, Shiller, Davis and Norton, good afternoon."

She hung up. She cross-checked it with the directory, and that gave her his office address.

She sat down to write the letter. The letter of betrayal.

Why to him, why not to the other one? The other one would have seemed to be the likelier prospect, but in actuality was he? Maybe her psychology was turned inside out, but not the way she saw it.

He was insanely jealous. Right. He had lived by violence— or at least by illegality—at one time. Right. He had come up out of the underworld jungle, where punitive death was a commonplace. Right.

But when all this had been granted, that was when her reverse psychology entered into it. For these very reasons, he was the less likely candidate of the two. He had no influence, at least in respectable places, to see him through afterward. He had an unsavory past, there were all sorts of strikes against him. He wouldn't dare to jeopardize his hard-won legitimacy by stepping out of line.

Whereas the broker was secure, respected, had an impregnable background, probably had all sorts of powerful influence backing him up in high places, and because of this very immunity would be far the readier of the two to carry out whatever measures he felt this treachery to his ego and his love life demanded.

Or so believed Madeline, the theoretical but unpracticed.

So to him she wrote.

Letter number one: "Dear Mr. Shiller: This is not a poison-pen letter—" But it was. What else was it?

Letter number two: "Dear Mr. Shiller: I think as a friend you ought to be told—" But they weren't friends.

Letter number three: "Dear Mr. Shiller: I hate to see anyone sold out behind his back—" Sheer cant. What she was doing was sneakier than what Dell was doing.

Letter number last: "Dear Mr. Shiller: Some girls haven't even one man. Some girls, like Dell Nelson, have two going at the same time. It doesn't seem fair, does it?"

She went down to the stamp machine in the lobby, put a coin into it, and got out a stamp. She stuck it on the letter, she dropped the letter into the mail slot, and she even pounded all around the mail slot with the heels of her hands to make sure it settled down properly inside.

The getting-even was on the way.

Things started moving fast from that point on.

Dell called her up, and her voice was all unraveled with strain. This was around five in the afternoon, next day.

"I'm in a jam!" she said, as winded as though she'd run up and down a flight of stairs a half a dozen times.

"What's up?" Madeline asked, startled but not too startled. She hadn't expected it to start rolling quite this soon, that was all.

"I don't know. But I don't like the way he sounded. I guess I played both ends against the middle too long. That's where you come in. You've got to help me."

"*Me?* What can *I* do?"

"You've got to run interference for me."

"What does that mean?"

"You've got to come over here and stand by. There's no telling what he may do. He may bang me around unmercifully."

"Wait a minute," Madeline brought her up short. "This is your life. I can't come barging into it at the drop of a hat. You kept it pretty much to yourself all along. Now that you need help, suddenly it's an open book with a place mark left in it specially for me. Well, no thanks."

She couldn't resist asking at a tangent, "Which one of them was it?"

"Walter. Walter called me up. He was sore about something. I never heard him so sore before. Every time I tried to smooth his fur and say something nice to him, he'd come back at me and say, How many others do you tell that to?"

"Well, there was your out right there. Why didn't you just hang up and get rid of him that way?"

"I was afraid to. I didn't want to lose him altogether. Sometimes they never come back. There's a time to get huffy and hard-to-get, and there's a time to hold on tight."

"Well, what about the club, can't you duck him down there?"

"It's Monday. We don't have a show on Mondays."

"Oh, I forgot."

"He knows that, too."

"Well, maybe it won't be so bad," Madeline tried to console her.

She gave a wail of anticipatory misery. "It'll be plenty bad. He's one of these quiet ones. I know him."

"The surprising thing to me," Madeline philosophized, "isn't that it finally happened, but that it didn't happen long ago, the parlays you've been playing."

"Preaching isn't what I need now," Dell told her. "I need somebody here with me, I need somebody standing by me."

"Why don't you call the police, if you're that afraid of him,"

Madeline said with an edge of contempt in her voice.

"You don't do that when you've been what we have to each other. If he ever finds out I called a girlfriend, he'd find it easy enough to forgive that. But if he ever finds out I called the police, he'd never forgive that. You don't know the ropes, dear."

No, Madeline thought morosely. I guess I've never gone down for the count as often as you have.

She had triggered the whole thing, it was developing into what promised to be a perfectly beautiful mess, and now she was being asked to step in a second time and screen the potential victim's hide.

"You've got to come! You've got to! You're the one friend I have in this world. Look at all I've done for you. My door was always open to you. Drinks on the house. I let you use my piano."

Oh, shove your piano, Madeline thought parenthetically. An expression she had acquired from the very person she was now returning it to.

"I even got market tips from him for you. Are you going to go back on me now, when I need you?"

"Al-l-l right," Madeline drawled reluctantly. "I'll tell you what I'll do. I'll call you in about an hour's time. If he's acting ugly and you're finding him hard to handle, I'll hustle on over and bring you my moral support. If everything's under control, then you don't need me. How'll that be?"

She thought: Even if I get her out of it tonight, it'll catch up with her some other night, now that the seeds of suspicion have been planted, and the second time I won't be on hand to bail her out.

Dell almost yelped her gratitude. "Thanks, baby-honey! Oh, thanks! I knew I could count on you, I knew you wouldn't let me down. I'll do the same for you someday."

Who needs you? thought Madeline scornfully. I don't play men by the carload.

"Better than that. Y'know that stone-marten jaquette you admired, the one Ange gave me? It's yours, I'm giving it to you right now."

Madeline made a sound down within her throat that might have been taken for gratitude, but was actually ridicule.

"All right, I'll take a quick tub and get dressed. Call me in an hour. Well, make it quarter past, that'll give me more time to turn around."

"Don't get loaded," Madeline warned her bluntly. "It's important that you keep your head clear, and know what you're doing."

"Check," Dell said obediently. In two months flat, Madeline had gotten the upper hand on her. And by sheer personality impact alone. For she hadn't tried in any way, either actively or passively, to dominate her.

Six o'clock came. Now's when I promised I'd call her, Madeline thought, and I'm not doing it.

Half past, and she still hadn't called her. Why don't I just let it ride? Let her take her own medicine.

At quarter of seven she finally gave in, picked up the phone. "Emerson eight, eighteen hundred." Then when the downstairs switchboard answered, "Eighteen-A, please."

He came back and said, "There isn't any answer."

At seven the same routine. "Emerson eight, eighteen hundred…Eighteen-A, please."

"There isn't any answer."

At seven-fifteen, for the third time, "There isn't any answer."

After a moment or two of indecision, she went downstairs, outside to the street, got in a cab, and went over there to find out for herself what kind of a turn this had taken.

Dell's doorman was busy shepherding two tailcoats, a broad-tail and an ermine, into a cab. He had his back to her, so Madeline found her way in unaided. She punched the eighteen button in the self-service elevator, the door glided closed with the softness of a purr, and she rode up.

She got out and rang the doorbell. Nobody came to the door.

She rang again, with a jab of irritation sharpening the gesture. Still nobody came. First she wets me up with her tears for help, she thought resentfully, then she clams up and ignores me. Probably they've reconciled, and he took her out to dinner.

She took out the key Dell had given her and opened the door. She figured maybe Dell had left some sort of a note of explanation for her on the piano, like they'd used to do so often in the old songwriting days.

"Dell?" she called out.

There was no answer. There was no one in the place. There was no note either, on the piano or anywhere else.

Dell had had a rye on the rocks, or possibly five or possibly ten, at some indeterminate point between her getting-up time and her leaving the place. Only one glass had been used. She never changed glasses when drinking alone, why should she? Her own mouth germs couldn't affect her. But this seemed to prove he'd never shown up.

On the piano was a song sheet. Probably the last thing she'd looked at before going out. For some inscrutable reason, to the end of her days, for as long as she remembered having met and having known Dell Nelson, whenever she thought of her, this song title would flicker across the eyes of her mind. "Heaven Drops Its Curtain Down upon My Heart."

Madeline took a cursory look into the bedroom before leaving. The bra that Dell must have changed out of before her bath lay looped around one of the footposts of the bed. From where she stood she could glimpse a narrow triangular wedge of the bathroom, and in this a sliver of green-blue showed up, just above the rim of the tub. Dell had left in such a hurry she'd even forgotten to let her bathwater run out of the tub.

Madeline went over closer and looked inside. It lay there blue-green, smooth and motionless as ice, the warmth gradually going out of it into the air around.

She leaned forward and looked closer still.

Dell was still in it. Dead in it.

A cigarette, the last cigarette she had smoked, a woman's cigarette with a dab of red at the tip, still lay on the edge of the washbasin where she had parked it as she got in. A drop of water on the washbasin rim had stopped it from consuming itself past the quarter mark.

Her head was at the bottom, face upward. It could have fallen there, or it could have been pushed there, held down there. It could have been a heart attack, a skidding fall against the bottom of the tub, a dizzy spell from the combination of alcohol and hot water, resulting in self-drowning, or—a homicide. Madeline couldn't tell which it was.

She looked closely at the hands. They were still looped loosely over the edge of the tub; they hadn't gone down with the rest of her. They were caught on the turn of the rim by the wrists. Alongside of them were two small flecks of red on the enamel, about as much as a mosquito makes if you squeeze it, and a thin trickle of much paler red that had gone down into the water. The water itself showed no traces. Not enough blood had been spilled to stain it.

That told the story. It had been a murder. She'd been held under until she drowned.

Madeline got down on her heels and examined the hands exhaustively, from an inch away, without touching them. There were no marks on them anywhere, no scratches or nicks. She even looked at the undersides, the palms, by stretching out full length on the floor and putting her face up under them.

The blood was not Dell's. But underneath the tips of all ten nails, where a smidgin of white should have showed past the point where the nail enamel ended, there was instead a caked hairline of red. She'd clawed someone, either on the face or forearms or hands, in fighting for her life.

Madeline got to her feet and stood looking down at her. At the startled blue eyes, colder than ever now, staring up through the blue-green water. Adelaide Nelson had played the game her own way and lost it.

And yet which one of us ever yet won it? philosophized Madeline. It's a game you can't beat. If death doesn't take away your chips, as in this case, then old age comes along and cleans out your table stakes just as surely. Maybe she'd had the best of it at that. At least she'd gone out looking good. Still desirable enough to be killed for it.

A man should die bravely. A woman should die beautiful.

Reflex fear, which had been strangely held back until this point (possibly by the feverish excitement of the discovery), now came on fast and chilling. I have to get out of here, she told herself, big-eyed. What am I doing standing around here, lingering here, like this? Someone may walk in.

Her dread wasn't so much of being accused of the crime itself—in fact that didn't even occur to her—as of being inextricably enmeshed in it from then on, saddled with it past all endurance. Detained, questioned ad infinitum, and above all rendered publicly identifiable, to the frustration of any possible fulfillment of the mandate which still awaited carrying out.

She wanted no part either of it or in it.

She left the bathroom hurriedly, left it just as she'd found it, door wide, light on; moved across the bedroom like a swift, silent streak. Across the main room, eyes straying to this side, to that, in oddly nostalgic snapshots of farewell. No more oleander tree watered with highballs. No more notes left on the piano. Taps waiting to be played instead: *Heaven drops its curtain down upon my heart*.

She listened carefully a moment, then opened the door sparingly, and neatly sidestepped through it. The hall was empty. She closed the door after her. She didn't bother cleaning the knob. Somehow that seemed to belong more in books than in real life, she couldn't have said why. Anyway, there'd probably be a myriad of others touching it after her.

The indicator above the elevator was at rest. It was down at the street. She pushed and brought it up to her. Then she got in, and pushed "two," not the street. She was lucky, no one else got on during the entire sixteen-floor ride down. No one saw her riding that car.

She got out at two, and walked quietly down the stairs, which opened out onto the lobby, to one side of the elevator. She had noticed them many times, in her comings and goings. She stopped just out of sight, just before they made their final turnaround into view, and waited there for the chance to leave unseen. She determined not to move without it, not to accept anything less, not if she had to stand there two hours on end. Just one stray glimpse of her by someone, and it could backfire later on when least expected and involve her in disaster.

The setup was favorable, from her point of view. The callboard, on which incoming visitors were announced to the various apartments, was over on the other side of the lobby, away from the foot of the stairs. In performing his chore, the doorman had his back to her. However, she would have to time herself so that he didn't turn around too quickly and glimpse her as she went out the door (and consequently wonder where she had come from). It was a long entrance-lobby, and the distance she had to traverse was not inconsiderable.

He was outside on the street when she first came down. It was impossible to escape detection with him in that position. He had to be brought inside by some arrival and placed with his back to her.

A young man was the first arrival. The doorman came in with him. "Miss Fletcher," the young man said. "Mr. Larkin." Miss Fletcher promptly said to come up. A dinner date probably, and she was expecting him. He was noticeably carrying an orchid inside an isinglass box.

A single arrival was no good to her. It took too little time to announce him and left the doorman free again too soon.

A trio showed up, two men and a girl, to pick up the fourth member of their quartet. Madeline made an abortive move forward, then her courage froze and she backed up again. The doorman said the three names awfully fast. She would have been pinpointed less than halfway to her destination if she'd made the try.

But if you wait long enough for the right combination, you finally get it. If you wait for the right kind of weather, it finally comes along. If you work a safe long enough, it finally opens. If you bet on it enough, your horse finally comes in.

People came and people went. Even an elderly lady in a wheelchair was brought in by an attendant. Obviously a tenant, since she wasn't announced.

Then finally it paid off. A whole group of arrivals came in in a body. Actually there were not more than five or six, but they seemed to fill the lobby with a clamor of voices and restless movement and carefree laughter. They were all young, high teens or low twenties, and they were evidently all invitees to some dinner party or birthday party or engagement party, for most of the boys carried wrapped gifts.

The doorman was inundated. He disappeared in the middle of all of them, and Madeline, with the calm assurance of complete anonymity, stepped down off the stairs and glided across the lobby, not a hasty motion in her entire body.

Just as she passed through the door, she heard him direct them: "Seventeen-A, everybody." A shudder flickered down her spine. The party was being held underneath the apartment in which the corpse lay.

Sensible enough not to linger in front of the building to pick up a taxi, she walked briskly, with head lowered to lessen chances of recognition, to the nearest corner, and there made a play for one and got in.

Unless there's an unlucky star hanging over my head, she told herself, not a living soul saw me come into or go out of that building. And she superstitiously switched her middle finger across her index and kept them that way.

The first thing she did when she got back was take a drink, to try and steady up. She, who had scorned Dell's drinking. But this was therapy.

She couldn't bear the thought of sitting down at a table and eating, after what she had just seen. She kept walking back and forth, walking endlessly back and forth, sometimes pinching her eyes together, sometimes holding the side of her jaw as if she had a toothache. She had one, a toothache in her conscience.

It was more than just the sight of a dead body—even a friend's dead body—and she knew it. It came on slowly, but once it had started there was no stopping it.

I killed her. I killed her just as surely as if I was the one held her head under, instead of the man. He was only the instrument, I was the instigator. The blame for this death is on me.

So this is how I free myself from the burden of Starr's death. By taking on another, a worse killing. One that really *is* a murder. This is what I've accomplished. This is what I've done for myself.

Around ten—she didn't notice the actual time, but somewhere around ten—she took another drink. Then she resolutely put the bottle away and turned the glass upside down. It was bad for you, when you were undergoing an emotional crisis like this. It enlarged it, it blurred it, it kept you from thinking logically and plunged you into unrealistic melancholia. It was only good for physical shock, like after having seen Dell's body, but not for mental and metaphysical distresses.

The second drink did no good, but at least she finally stopped walking around and sat down. She could tell she was building up into another guilt complex such as she had experienced following Starr's death. Only this one promised to be far worse.

Dell was no good. The world won't miss her, she told herself. But I had no right to kill her. It wasn't for me to judge her, she answered herself.

This probably would have gone on all night, at increasing heat and at increasing pace, but a diversion suddenly occurred which stopped it short. Not only that, but eradicated it completely from her thoughts and from her system.

The buzzer at the door sounded, and when she went over and opened it, two men were standing out there.

"Miss Madeline Chalmers?" one said, and politely touched the edge of a finger to his hat brim.

One was average in height, the other a little better than average, and a good deal huskier in build as well. Both were the sort of people who, a moment after you had looked at them, you couldn't have told what they looked like. Perhaps a sort of professional invisibility, you might say.

"Yes, I am," she said tonelessly.

"We'd like to speak to you. May we come in?"

"Not now," she said unwillingly, and turned her head aside. "I'm very tired, and I can't see anyone right now."

"I'm afraid you'll have to, Miss Chalmers," he said, as polite as ever but with an added crispness. "This is police business." And he showed credentials.

As soon as this! passed through her mind. Not more than three hours ago—and already!

But the worst part of it was the way she could feel her own face pale, as she stepped aside and let them pass. Its whitening was almost a physical sensation, like a pulling back, a drawing tight, of the skin.

They saw it too. They must have, and that wasn't good.

She sat down on the middle section of the sofa. The larger one sat down at its end, facing her. The other one brought over a chair and sat down diagonally across from her. They formed an approximation of a small, intimate triangle. Only, she didn't find it cozy.

It began at once. In casual fashion, but at once, without preamble and from then on without letup. Every question impeccably polite. More polite than the average ballroom or dinner-table conversation.

"Do you know an Adelaide Nelson?"

"Yes, I do."

"How well do you know her?"

First hitch already, and only the second question.

"It's difficult to pinpoint a thing like that," she hedged.

"It shouldn't be. Do you know her well or don't you know her well?"

"I know her moderately well."

Watch your step now, she kept warning herself. Watch your step. One wrong word and you're in it up to your neck. These boys are experts.

"How long have you known her?"

"I first met her in September."

"About two and a half months, would that be about right?"

"About two and a half months, that would be about right."

"Have you ever been up in her apartment?"

"Yes, on a number of occasions."

"Frequently, would you say, or seldom?"

The doorman used to see me coming and going all the time. I wonder if they've gotten to him yet. What if I say seldom, and he says the other way around?

"In the beginning, quite often. Afterward it tapered." Which actually was the fact.

"Any particular reason why it should taper off? Did you grow cooler toward one another?"

"No-o," she said with cautious consideration. "It wasn't intentional. This just happens sometimes, in the course of human, human"—she couldn't find the word for a moment—"associations."

"How did you first come to meet Miss Nelson?"

"I looked her up." She told them about her songwriting aspirations. "The music publishers were no good. I thought if I could tie in with a performer, I might get somewhere."

"Did she string you along? Is that why you had to keep going back to see her repeatedly?"

What were they trying to do in this particular spot, build a grudge between Dell and herself?

"Not at all. You see, she was kind enough to let me have the use of her piano. I don't have one of my own to work on."

"And was she always there when you went over?"

The key! she thought in a panic. Here comes the key! My God, I've boxed myself in.

Another of those incriminating bleaches passed over her face. One of them reached out and held her arm a moment to steady her. It wasn't an encouraging hold and it wasn't a friendly one; it was a steadying one only. Like when you want to keep somebody up.

A flagrant lie was the safest, as risky as it was. It was her word against the doorman's. She couldn't afford to let them "place" her alone at the apartment. God knows what dangers might crop up out of that.

"Always. Without fail. You see, I never neglected to call up ahead of time to make sure she would be there. If she didn't answer, I didn't go."

"That brings up another point. When was the last time you were up to see her?"

They're coming to it now, she cautioned herself. Hang on.

"Let me see. Today's Monday. The last time I was over there was on Friday a week ago."

"You weren't up there today?"

"No."

"You didn't go up there at any time today?"

"No, I didn't."

Notice how they're pressing? she said to herself. This is very thin ice. It's the first time they've made me repeat a denial.

"Did the two of you speak with one another on the telephone?"

Here was a bad one. Did the hotel switchboard keep a record of incoming calls, if they were answered? Probably not, but one of the girls might remember that a woman had called her up. Dell's voice had been excited enough to attract attention.

She didn't want to bring the association up this close to the deadline. It was too dangerous. And deadline was the right word. She took a chance on an out-and-out lie instead. They couldn't prove that it had been Dell. They certainly hadn't tapped, because Dell had still been alive, and her calls hadn't yet become police business.

"No."

The large one said, like a huge but deadly silent tiger landing on its prey with all four paws, "Who was the woman who called you up at about five o'clock, approximately, this afternoon?"

With every word I sink in deeper, she thought, appalled. How the hell did they find out about it? Or hadn't they, was it just a shot in the dark? Either way, she had to stick to her lie, she was stuck with it now. She groped desperately. Hairdresser? They'd check. Relative? They'd check. Nurse in doctor's office? I haven't been to any doctor's office.

"A woman who used to go to the same church I did, a few years back. She lost her daughter, and I was kind to her at the time, and she's never forgotten it since. Today was the anniversary of the death. She's a Mrs. Bartlett." (How much more plausible than that can you get? she thought.)

They didn't press further on this. It's strange, she said to herself. Sometimes when there's nothing there, they dig and dig and dig. Then sometimes when there's something there just waiting to be dug up, they muff it. Maybe they're only human after all, and it's foolish to be so afraid of them.

"Did you ever meet any of Miss Nelson's other friends?"

"No. Not one."

"Did she ever discuss them with you?"

"No. She was extremely close-mouthed."

What were they fishing for there, she wondered, a jealousy motive on her part, over one of the men?

"Didn't you ever hear her even talk on the phone with any of them?"

"Once or twice the phone rang, but I didn't pay attention. The music covered it up."

"Did she ever show you any of her belongings?"

"She showed me a fur piece once. And some pieces of jewelry."

"Didn't you wonder who gave them to her?"

"It was none of my business," she said piously.

"Just for a moment, didn't you wish that you owned them, that they were yours?" the tiger one said craftily.

She jumped to her feet, infuriated, then abruptly sat down again, just as infuriated. "What are you implying?" she said in an anger-cracked voice. "That I had my eye on them? That I took something without permission? There's my clothes closet. Go over and look inside it. See for yourself."

To her utter complete consternation and then complete infuriation, he took her at her word and got up and did so.

When he came back, ignoring the blazing look she gave him, he said unconcernedly to his partner, "Not a fur in there."

But once she'd allowed herself to cool off sufficiently, she understood why he'd done it. He hadn't seriously expected to find anything in there. It was just a psychological trick, to jangle her, undermine her self-confidence, if possible. Put her on the defensive.

She felt by now as if their questioning had been going on forever. The strain was beginning to tell, particularly so soon after the not-yet-worn-off shock of finding the body. And she had an uneasy feeling she hadn't come through it as well as she might have. For one thing, by not asking from the beginning what had happened to Dell, which would have been the normal reaction of anybody placed in her situation. What had kept her from it, probably, was the guilty knowledge that she already knew, and the fear of letting this slip out in some way if she asked at all. It was too late now to do so with any degree of plausibility or grace.

They were at it again. The technique was to keep the person bouncing, and if possible off-balance. Somewhat like dribbling a basketball or swatting a punching bag this way and that.

"Did you leave the hotel at any time this evening?"

How could she say no? The elevator boy, the desk man, the man on door duty, had all seen her.

"I went out about seven."

"And where did you go?"

She had taken a taxi a few yards offside to the door. She took a chance on those few yards covering her up. Because a taxi meant a destination, you didn't take it without one.

"Nowhere. I went just for a walk. I needed some exercise and I needed some fresh air."

"Do you go for a walk every evening at about that time? Is that your custom?"

"No. Tonight was the first time."

"And where did you walk?" came from the tiger one, who by this time had become a personal enemy.

"On the street," she snapped.

The other one made a strangled sound down in his throat, and murmured half audibly, "One down on you, Smitts."

"And what street was that?" he asked dulcetly.

She recited six of them in a row. "Satisfactory?" she asked sarcastically.

"For a walk, yes," he said imperturbably. The implication, somewhere down deep, being, "If you had taken one, but you didn't."

"And you came back—"

"By around eight."

She knew why all this. That was the time slot that encompassed Dell's death.

"Had you had your dinner before or after?"

"Neither. I did without it tonight."

The tiger one purred, "Did something happen to make you lose your appetite?"

This time she couldn't hold back. "Not at the time. But it has now." And she left his partner out of the incinerating glare she sent him. He was making her very angry, which is a bad thing for a person under questioning to be.

Suddenly he got to his feet, and as if at a given signal the other one did too.

She let out a long, unconcealed sigh of relief, and let her head go limply back against the top of the sofa. The next thing she knew, he was saying, "I'm sorry, but we'll have to ask you to accompany us."

Her head jerked upright again. "But why?" she wailed almost tearfully. "Haven't I answered all your questions?"

"Yes," he said briefly.

"Haven't I answered them satisfactorily?"

"You would know more about that." Meaning, whether the answers were true or not.

The other one, standing by the door, said, "Coming, Smitts?" but she knew he meant it for her and not his partner.

"After Miss Chalmers," Smitts said pointedly, and brought up the rear.

She shuddered uncontrollably as she walked between them down the long carpeted hotel corridor, which seemed to stretch ahead for miles. "I feel terrible about this," she said in a fearful whisper. "I never was taken anywhere under police escort before."

"Weren't you?" Smitts said laconically.

The glass-prismed chandeliers, the offside mirrors, the offside needlepoint chairs. The offside desk, not meant for anything more serious than RSVPs and thank-you notes. You weren't supposed to walk along here with two detectives for company, involved in an act of violence. Going down to their place, at their order. You were supposed to walk along it in furs, with diamonds on your fingers and on your neck, owning the world. The only thing that hurt you, maybe a little corn because your Italian shoes are too tight.

And then, far too late, she finally asked, "What is it about? What's happened to her?"

"Shouldn't you have asked that before?"

"It could have been anything, how was I to know?" she said defensively. "She drinks a lot. Sometimes when a person's drunk they make all sorts of bad accusations against others."

"But when they're dead," he said, "they make the worst accusation of all."

"Dead?" she breathed, appalled, and only hoped she did it right.

"You'll never win an Academy Award." He gave her the look you give a cat that's come in out of the rain. It's all bedraggled, but you feel sorry for it, you have a heart. You even want to give it warm milk.

The transit from hotel to street to car was made fairly painlessly. No one looked at her a second time, or if they did, seemed to see only a pretty girl escorted by two young men in business suits. Detention was the last thought anybody would have connected with her graceful free-swinging arms.

The car was unmarked. Or at least, it definitely wasn't a piebald "Mickey Mouse" prowl car. Riding in it with them, she tried to analyze her feelings. Actual fear was minimal. But there was an uncomfortableness other than that. For the first time in her life she felt gauche, awkward, unsure of herself. That was probably because the initiative had gone over to them; she was no longer a free agent.

At the precinct house she was shown into an unoccupied room and asked, as politely as if she were a visitor or a guest, if she minded waiting there a minute. "We'll be right with you," one of them promised, and they both went out through a door ahead of the one they had entered by.

The room was depressing, but not particularly ominous or threatening. It was painted an ugly darkling green halfway up the walls, and the rest of the way up was just white plaster. Why the green stopped where it did was problematical. Either they'd run out of paint or they'd run out of money. Or someone had walked off with the painter's ladder. The window was of the old-fashioned proportions of the windows of sixty years ago: tall and narrow. Its glass was protected by a pattern of wire mesh embedded in it. The purpose of this she couldn't conjecture; certainly no one would be foolhardy enough to throw rocks at a police-station window, would they? It, the window, overlooked a backyard which it shared with a soot-blackened tenement backing up toward it from the other side. In some of the windows of this, people could be seen going about their daily lives without even a glance at the punitive place across the way, so used to it were they by a lifetime of propinquity. Which argued, at any rate, that suspects were not beaten or otherwise roughed up in these exposed rear rooms. And then again, did it? The tenement tenants might have even been immune to that.

Finally, the room had a number of scarred and scarified wooden chairs in it, ranged in a row against the wall, and a wooden table, likewise scarred, likewise scarified, cigarette burns galore scalloping its edges, and likewise back against the wall.

She turned her head, and a woman in uniform, a matron, had come into the room. She nodded pleasantly but impersonally to Madeline, sat down on one of the chairs, opened a narrow-spread paper, and lost herself in it.

Madeline could feel herself becoming highly nervous over her presence in the room. It seemed to predicate a rigorous forthcoming questioning, and perhaps even arrest, with the woman present to comply with regulations because the detainee was a woman herself.

As though she could read Madeline's thoughts, the matron murmured, gruffly but kindly, without even looking up from her paper, "Take it easy, snooks. Probably just routine. Be over with before you know it."

Suddenly as if she had found something she was looking for, she exclaimed: "Libra. That's me! Let's see what's in store for today."

But what was was never made known, because the door re-opened at this point, and Smitts and cohort came back in again, along with two others, one a man with bushy silver hair, who obviously upranked the rest of them. A full quorum was going to question her. One of them, though, was only a stenographer; she noticed he'd brought a pad with carbon inserts with him.

Unexpectedly she found herself being introduced to the captain, which took a good deal of the curse off the imminent questioning and lent her added confidence. A person in line for arrest isn't usually introduced formally to the arresting officer —or at least to his superior—beforehand.

"This is Miss Chalmers, Captain. Captain Barry."

He even held out his hand toward her, and when she'd placed her own in his, turned hers first on one side, then on the other, as if in friendly reluctance to part with it.

The table was shifted out from the wall just enough to give clearance on all sides of it, chairs were ranged, and they all sat down, including Madeline, who acted on a wordless nod from the smaller of the two who had been up to the hotel, the non-tiger one, and took one of the chairs. The top leaves of the stenographer's pad gave a preliminary rustle as he furled them back out of the way until he came to a blank space.

The matron remained obliviously against the wall, poring over her tabloid, lost to the world.

The damn thing started in all over again, only with three of them now, instead of two. (And the distance to a detention cell, she couldn't help reflecting ruefully, that much shorter than it had been.) Unavoidably, much of the ground covered had already been gone over at the hotel. This was no hazard in itself. She had an acute memory. And the three things she had to remember to stay away from still remained the same they had been before: possession of a key to Dell's apartment, knowledge of who the two men in her life were, and that final phone call for help an hour before her death.

The interrogation seemed endless. There were times when it proceeded like a fencing match, with her parrying their thrusts and deflecting everything they thew at her. There were times, too, when the three of them went through the motions of searching jointly for the truth.

The captain's eyes, when they caught hers, seemed to have a fatherly glint in them. I have a daughter your age at home, they seemed to say. And she knew it would be easy to relax into the embrace of those eyes, to let them put her entirely at ease, but somehow she sensed that was how he wanted her to react. She couldn't afford to let her guard down, no matter how warmly some man turned his eyes on her.

She steeled herself and went on playing her part.

A patrolman stuck his head in the door, said, "Captain Barry says Miss Chalmers can go home whenever she wishes."

She got to her feet at once, the current instant being the "whenever" of her wishes.

One of the men said, "Good night. Hope we haven't been too rough on you."

She knew she ought to answer. She didn't feel much like it, but reciprocal politeness is a habit hard to break. "Good night to you men too," she said without any warmth.

She closed the door after her. A moment later she reopened it and stuck her head back inside the room. "Did I leave my handbag over there by the table?" she asked them.

Smitts glanced down at the chair she'd just been occupying, gave his head a shake. "I didn't see one with you when we left the hotel. It's my impression you came away without it."

She backed a hand between her eyes. "What'll I do for taxi fare?" she blurted out without stopping to think. A moment later she realized the hotel desk could pay it for her easily enough.

But Smitts's teammate, who seemed to be a decent sort of person, had already reached down into his pocket. "I'll stake you," he offered.

To her surprise she saw Smitts slice the edge of his hand at him in dissuasion. She wondered why.

He turned around to her and said, "I'll drop you off, if you don't mind waiting for me a couple minutes outside by the sergeant's desk. I'm going off at twelve."

She would have preferred the offer to come from someone else, but the heat of battle had subsided now, and with it her grievance. She was too tired even to dislike him very heartily anymore.

She sat down on a bench out there. The desk sergeant looked her over curiously, then went back to his own concerns.

The "couple minutes" became ten, the ten, fifteen, the fifteen, twenty. She started to steam up again inside. She fidgeted, but she clung stubbornly to the bench. She kept hoping she could get some hint out of him as to where she really stood in the case. "Miss Chalmers can go home whenever she wishes" was too indefinite. She had to know: Was she in or was she out?

When he finally came outside to her at twelve-twenty, he put a worse finish to an already bad situation by clapping himself dismayedly on the forehead and exclaiming, "I clean forgot about you!"

"Obviously," she said coldly, getting to her feet. The cutting look she gave him, if he had passed a finger in front of her eyes he would have lacerated it badly.

They got into the same car she'd been brought down in, and this time she was able to make out clearly that it had no markings.

"The cap had us all in for a last-minute briefing," he remarked as he pushed off. "That's what held me up."

She wondered if it had had to do with her, and wondered if she asked him, would he answer. Before she could get up the nerve, a man with an itchy pedal foot in the adjoining lane started across the intersection before the light had changed.

"Wait for the light, bud. That's what it's there for," Smitts said in a low-register growl.

The man turned and looked at him. She held her breath for a minute, remembering there was no insignia on the car. Then the man looked forward again and glided off, this time permissibly. He didn't know what a close shave he'd had just then, she said to herself. One word spoken out of turn and...

When they reached the hotel, he got out on his side, closed the door, came around, and opened the one on her side. Before she'd caught on to the maneuver, he'd closed that one after her and they were both out of the car.

"All right if I come up for a minute?" he asked tentatively.

She turned swiftly and faced him. "Don't you think I've had enough for one day? Don't you think I'm tired? Didn't the captain send out word I could go home?"

"You are home," he said.

"Yes, but I want to be there alone, without any"—she looked him resentfully up and down—"supervision."

"I'm off duty."

"You're *never* off duty. You're trying to trip up someone even in your sleep, I bet."

"I'll only stay a minute. Can't I have a cup of coffee?" Then he reminded her, "I bought you a cup of coffee."

"And now you want your ten cents back, I suppose, is that it? Well, come on up." And under her breath she muttered, "I hope you choke on it."

"I'll try," he said accommodatingly, and followed her inside the hotel.

Upstairs, she turned on the element in the serving pantry, drew water and put it on, then came outside again. She flung herself down on the sofa with a moan of unfeigned exhaustion, without even taking off her coat.

"No wonder people break under those things. I mean guilty people."

He came away from the window and sat companionably down without being asked. "Know something? The innocent break quicker than the guilty. They haven't the desperate necessity to cling to their lies."

"Why did he reach out and shake hands with me? The captain, I mean. They don't usually do that with people who are brought in for questioning, do they?"

"He could tell you were a better type," he said glibly.

"No, he wanted to get a look at my hands."

"You're on the ball," he said with a sly smile of admission.

She reached for one of her cigarettes in the guest holder, and deliberately refrained from offering one to him. Then when he held a match for her, she didn't seem to see that either.

"Hate the sight of me, don't you?" he said calmly. "But if the woman who lost her life had been your sister, that would have been different. That would've been my job, my duty. I would've been too lenient if I didn't break everyone's arm in at least three places."

"Well, she wasn't my sister. Thank God for that." She got up and went in to take the boiling water off for the coffee. "How do you take it?" she asked crossly.

"Any way it comes."

I'd like to put some lighter fluid in it, she thought malevolently.

He chuckled as she came back to him with the two cups. "I bet I know what you were thinking just then."

"Even my very thoughts are under cross-examination."

"Oh, don't take it so big," he said wearily. "A girl without a sense of humor is a bore." He drank half his cup down at one swallow. He could do that because he had a very large mouth (in both senses of the word, she hastened to insist upon to herself).

"How'd you come to get mixed up with such a type as that, anyway?" he asked, looking down into his coffee as though trying to make up his mind whether there was enough of it left to make up one decent mouthful.

"I've been over all that twice already. I thought I could get ahead in my songwriting asp—"

"Oh, knock it off," he cut in knowingly. "You're no more interested in songwriting than my"—he changed whatever word he'd been about to use, and finished it—"my armhole. I bet you can't even put two consecutive notes together. The stuff you showed her you probably cribbed from something somebody else composed and published. I picked up one of those masterpieces of yours over there. One of the cops detailed to standby duty happened to know how to play the piano. I tell you the truth, the rings made by the liquor glasses on the score sheets sounded much better than your notes. I know it's a funny thing to do, play the piano with a corpse still on the premises, but if that didn't wake her up we could be sure she was dead for real. Half the guys were holding their hands over their ears and begging him to quit before he even got to the end of it."

"Go ahead," she said with lethal suavity. "Anything else?"

He saw her glance down momentarily at what she was holding in her hands. "Don't throw that. It can give a nasty burn."

She put the steamy cup aside, as if to make sure she wouldn't lose control and let it fly at him after all.

"No, the way I figure you," he went on, sobering, "you're one of these do-gooders. You feel guilty about some real or imaginary wrong you think you've done, and you're trying to work it off in this way, by taking up with beauts like this Nelson."

Although she scarcely moved at all, the sensation she experienced was that of receiving a stunning impact that kited her all the way back against a wall.

He'd only set eyes on her for the first time about four hours ago, and yet he already knew her that well! She kept shaking her head slightly to herself. A glaze of tears even formed in her eyes, without dropping. Tears of amazement, of humility. To think someone had read her that right.

She wondered if they realized, the fellow members of his squad, what they had working for them in this man in the way of instinct, intuitiveness, and ability to read human nature. All just as important to a detective, maybe more so, than technical know-how and cat-and-mouse stalking. He was a natural at his trade.

And yet this same man, she already knew to a certain extent, off duty could be noisy, frivolous, partial to lowbrow practical jokes, juvenile almost to the point of asininity or inanity.

But it takes many components, she realized, to make up a complete man.

He'd gone back to talking about the case again. "That stunt of pulling the shower curtain across to try to cover up the fact she was in the tub was very stupid," he said reflectively. "The minute I spotted that I knew there had been violence committed. A person taking a shower pulls the curtain across to keep the water from getting on the floor, but a person taking a bath never does."

"The shower curtain—" wasn't pulled across the tub. She caught herself just in time. In the breath space between two words. The shower curtain—"could have been pulled across by her herself if she felt a draft, for instance." Just a double space between two words instead of a single one.

But he was a detective. Was he a detective. "I knew you were up there," he said cheerfully. "I had a pretty good hunch you were, all along, anyway. But this cinches it. Because I heard what it was you *didn't* say just now."

"So it's still going on!" she flared. "Is that what you came up here for?"

He got to his feet. "Why not? Just to satisfy myself. I couldn't get it out of you while you were on guard. I figured maybe I might if you were relaxed and with your guard down."

She looked after him, and he had the door open and was about to leave—without her.

"Does the fact that you think I was over there tonight put me back into the case?" she asked him.

"There isn't any more case," he answered, "to put you back

into. The case is closed. It was closed just as I was leaving the precinct house. That's what delayed me."

"But who is it—who was it?" she tried to call out after him.

But he shut the door behind him and left.

The radio didn't carry it until about twenty hours later. It first came on on the 8:00 P.M. news break, and from then on was repeated every half hour until it had ridden out the night. In other words they, Homicide, must have deliberately withheld the news until they were sure beyond any doubt or chance of a slip-up. Smitts had already told her the case was closed when he left her door at 12:30 the night before. But that was off the record, so to speak.

It was this angle of it that froze her, frightened her stiff, much more than the news in itself. The murder item had been on the news all day long, but without the definitive arrest. She kept listening and listening, switching from station to station, and it was always the same, just with a change of tired, beat-up adjectives. "The glamorous café singer" was found dead in her tub. "The beautiful café star" was found dead in her bath. "The exotic café performer" was found slain. "Night-life-celebrity" discovered lifeless in bath.

"A tramp got croaked, " Madeline finished it off for them, with a touch of the toughness she'd learned from Dell herself.

She didn't eat all day. Didn't leave the room all day, because the radio was there. Why had he told her that? Had he been kidding? But why should he want to kid her? She had an impression that he didn't kid about squadroom cases, especially not with outsiders. Well, then, what were they waiting for, what was holding them up?

Twelve times she'd heard that a dog had ridden the earth's orbit in a capsule, and couldn't have cared less. Twelve times what Senator Somebody had said was repeated verbatim, and it

hadn't even been good the first time. Twelve times the exact
location of Hurricane Hilda was pinpointed. Twelve times Cuba,
the Congo, Algeria, Vietnam, and all the pharmacopoeia of the
sick and suffering sixties were trotted out on display and then
trotted back in again. And twelve times poor Adelaide Nelson
was drowned in her bathtub, until the old saw about belaboring
a dead horse became almost literal.

The newscasts were like flying saucers circling around her,
going away, then coming back again.

Then suddenly it came. Came, went, and was over with.

"An arrest has been made in the Adelaide Nelson slaying. A
man named Jack d'Angelo has been brought in and is undergoing questioning."

She cried it out loud, it was wrenched from her with such
shattering violence. "My God! They've got the wrong man!
Shiller was the one I sent the note to!"

Thirty minutes went by. She didn't leave the side of the set.
Almost picked it up and shook it, like a recalcitrant clock, to get
the words out of it more quickly. They'd changed a couple of
words in it this time. "…and has been undergoing questioning
the greater part of the day."

And then, the following time, "The police are confident they
have the right man."

And then, the next time, "He has been formally charged and
bound over…"

And then, the time after that, "…one of the quickest in the
records of the Police Department. Less than twenty-four hours
after the body was found."

"Too quick," she thought, shuddering. "Too quick."

The phone was in her hand.

"Forty-fifth Precinct," a man's voice said.

"Do you have a man there named—uh—well, I guess it
would be Smith?"

The voice chuckled, probably in fondness or because it was tired answering nothing but dry duty calls all day long. "Oh, Himself. The quiet one. The mouse. John Francis Xavier Smith. Yeah, he's known around these parts."

She didn't find the camaraderie at all engaging. After all, to be a professional detective, to trap human beings, trick them, trip them up, send them on to be publicly murdered (instead of privately), was for her money simply a hyperthyroid enlargement of the trait of cruelty and penchant for bullying that are to be found latent in almost all adult males. Only, a professional plainclothesman got a salary for doing it. And even a pension, when he got older.

As she stood there at the phone, waiting to tell them they had the wrong man, she was completely on the side of the man on the other end of the line, on the other end of the line from the law, the one against the millions. Only three crimes were worse than the punishment that was meted out; only three crimes deserved it. A crime against a child, the rape of an innocent woman, and a crime against the whole community which threatened it with extinction (espionage in wartime). The rest were pale replicas of the awful majesty of the law, when it set the day and it set the hour, and it said, "You shall die."

Smitts's house was out in a low-wage suburban development, nothing fancy about it but neat and clean as a whistle. It turned out not to be his, actually, but she hadn't been told that.

He came to the door and let her in.

"You were able to find it all right, I see."

The partner was in the living room when she stepped in there. They had two copper beer cans with neat digs in their tops, two more without, and two glasses going. But they weren't drunk and it wasn't a party, she could tell; they were just relaxing. Some mysterious woman's touch had placed postage-stamp

140 CORNELL WOOLRICH & LAWRENCE BLOCK

saltine crackers and diminutive wedges of orange cheese on a large thick blue-patterned plate. No man would have cut the bites that small. Both were in shirt sleeves and tieless. "We meet again, Miss Chalmers," the partner said, but rather luke-warmly, as though he preferred spending his off-time among people of his own choosing.

She came out with it without wasting any further time. "The reason I had to see you so badly, the reason I insisted on coming out here, is—you've got to listen to me, you've got to believe me—you're holding the wrong man in the Nelson case."

It took a minute to sink in.

"Oh," he said then.

He looked at his partner.

Then he looked back at her again.

"Oh, we are?" he said this time. He slung one rock-solid hip onto the edge of the large round table. He folded his arms speculatively. "How do you figure that?" he asked her.

A woman's voice suddenly interrupted, saving her from what would have been a ticklish question to answer, without bringing the knife-in-the-back note into it.

"Smitts," it called down from the head of the stairs, "Evie's ready for her good-night kiss now."

He got up, went outside, and went trooping up the stairs, giving the whole fairly flimsy house the shaking of its life. The chain pulls on the lamps jittered. The very floorboards she was standing on seemed to pulsate a little. Even the water level in the small greenish fishbowl began to oscillate, climbing a little on this side, dipping on that.

"I didn't know he was married," she said artlessly. Or artfully artlessly might be better.

"He ain't," the teammate said. "He lives with his sister and brother-in-law. This is their house. They'd be happy to have him along for the ride, they think that much of him, but he insists on paying for his lodging. That's the kind of guy Smitts is. The kid's crazier about him than her own parents."

She snickered a little. "That nickname. For a big bruiser like him."

"He got it the first day he went to kindergarten and it's stuck to him ever since. He couldn't say his own name right when they asked him what it was."

The return trip downstairs was equally dynamic to the ascent, possibly even more so. A thin thread of plaster sifted off one corner of the ceiling like talcum powder. The fish in the bowl looked startled and changed directions abruptly.

"Is he always that noisy?" she asked, wincing.

The teammate gave her a hurt look. "You can't expect him to go around tippytoeing in ballet slippers."

"No, but he *could* tone it down a little," she suggested.

His partner's loyalty wouldn't dim, not by one kilowatt.

"At least you always know where he is," he defended sturdily. "He ain't one of these sneaks."

He came in making a remark at a tangent for his partner alone. "That kid gets cuter every day." Then to her, "Where were we? Oh, about the man being the wrong man."

"Well, you're holding d'Angelo, aren't you?"

"We're booking d'Angelo, is right."

"Well, but there was another man in her life." (And if he asks me how I knew, I'll simply have to admit I withheld information and take whatever they dish out to me on that count.)

But he didn't. "Shiller the investment broker? We know all about him. We questioned him right at the very beginning and we released him on his own recognizance. He had a complete and perfect alibi. He was host to a dinner party of forty celebrating his wife's birthday at one of the swellest restaurants in town. Every society photographer on the beat there snapping him."

"But—but—" she sputtered.

"D'Angelo's the wrong man?" he queried with a grin.

"He is. He's got to be," she cried vehemently.

He gave her not only the old one-two but a one-two-three-four. Left, right, right, left, leaving her groggy and down for the count. "Then what are the strokes from her nails doing on the backs of both his hands, and on his lower forearms?

"Why do the particles of skin embedded under her finger-nails match up by lab analysis with samples taken from his?

"Why did he call us up, voluntarily, wait for us at a certain place, namely his home, voluntarily, give himself up to us when we got there, voluntarily, and accompany us back to headquarters, voluntarily?

"And lastly and mostly and mainly, why did he dictate and sign, unforced and of his own free will, a full confession?

"That he killed her, not because he hated her, but because he loved her. Loved her too much to be able to go on living with his own jealousy. Above all, loved her too much to be able to go on living without her after he *had* killed her.

"D'ja ever read *Othello*? That's it, in today's world.

"He might have had a hundred cheap little loves in his gangster days, but the real thing only hit him at last late in his life, real enough to live for, real enough to die for."

He sighed, almost as though he understood a thing like that, and how could he, how could anyone except the one who did the loving, lived the loving? Loved what was crass brass to others, loved it as precious imperishable gold.

The mystery of the human heart, that no detective can ever solve.

She sank down dazedly into the nearest chair at hand, still only half comprehending, and the title of the song she had seen on Dell's piano passed through her mind like a faraway echo. "Heaven Drops Its Curtain Down upon My Heart."

＊

As she reentered her hotel and walked past the desk, the clerk greeted her and held out a letter toward her. She took it and stared at it with that momentary feeling of unreality which is apt to overcome anyone when they are confronted by their own handwriting. It was addressed: "Walter Shiller Esq., Warren, Shiller, Davis and Norton." In the upper right-hand corner there was a small glossy patch where the stamp, possibly dried out by too long a confinement in the vending machine, had loosened and dropped off. Beside the glossy patch, a petulant magenta-ink post office rubber stamp chided: "Returned for failure to pay postage."

"It came back several days ago," the clerk apologized. "I called up to ask you if you wanted us to put a stamp on it and remail it for you, but you were out. I guess I put it in your box and forgot about it. We've been very busy the last few days—"

He stopped short and stared, as she pressed the envelope to her lips, passionately, voraciously, over and over, like a love note from a lover, like a refund from the Internal Revenue Service.

"I thought you wanted it to go," he remarked uncertainly.

"So did I," she said. "So did I. Oh, how wrong can you be?"

"Miss Chalmers, please," he protested mournfully as she tore it into a hundred little pieces and scattered it all about her, "think of the poor porter who has to clean up here later on."

Upstairs at her desk afterward, she took out the cheap little pocket notebook with the line-ruled pages, and where it said,

1. *To get even with a woman.*

ran a line through it.

Somebody else really did the job, not I, though, was her inescapable reflection.

IV

"And now to kill a man."

How simple the words were. How easy to say, or think. And yet how frightful, how fearsome, to put into effect, to carry out. And once carried out, how impossible ever again to undo, to restore as it was before.

To turn someone like that—she let her gaze slowly travel around the hotel dining room, encompassing it and taking in each man in it in turn, but only the men (for it was a man who was to die, not a woman. Though women died too, they were no different):

One was smiling at the girl in front of him, interestedly drinking in her quick flow of words, nodding approvingly, admiringly, eyes glued to her unswervingly in the first head-on impact of youthful love.

One was looking at his watch as her eyes passed over him and telling the other three people at the table (probably) that it was time to start for the theater.

One was sitting alone, but quite complacently, an empty stemglass with a tiny white onion in it before him, thinking of something that pleased him very much, judging by the almost fatuous expression on his face.

One, just coming back after being called outside to answer a phone, was anything but complacent. His face was flushed with sulkiness and wounded vanity, and after he'd reseated himself to wait some more, he drummed anger-expressing fingers on the table.

One was breaking a roll open, preparing it for buttering.

One had his hand inside his pocket to get out money, and with the other one was good-naturedly waving off his friend's attempt to pay.

One was holding a vivaciously twinkling lighter across the table to the cigarette of his woman companion.

—to turn someone like that, or that, or that, into something that didn't move anymore. And soon rotted away. That didn't smile at some girl anymore, or look at a watch anymore. Or flick on a lighter anymore. Or take money out of his pocket.

Well, what was so terrible about it? God in His infinite wisdom—or infinite indifference—did that every day, stopped lives by the score and by the hundreds. Blind Nature did it too, in a multitude of ways, if any distinction could be made between the two.

Yes, but she wasn't God, and she wasn't Nature. That was what was terrible about it.

Death took only an instant, a second. It couldn't by its nature take more than that. Even a lengthy dying was still life up until that final second. To destroy in less than a second, then, what it had taken twenty-five, thirty, forty years to grow and shape. To efface, to wipe out, what some mother had nurtured and cherished. What some younger woman had loved and joined her life to. To blank out the collected knowledge inside that mind, the specialties, the talents, the knacks, the lacks; never again to be reassembled in just that identical collectivity and ratio and proportion and degree. Unique, each single mind, out of all the millions of others. Irreplaceable. The memories, the experiences, the disappointments, the hates, the loves, the plans, the hopes.

All this—in just an instant, erased, extinguished, annihilated.

And yet it had to be. It was to be. It would be.

She wanted her own peace of mind back. She was entitled to it. She couldn't live without it, life would be unendurable.

She took up an unused table knife and slowly drew an invisible line along the tablecloth.

This is his path, slowly coming toward mine. Nearer as the days go by, nearer each hour and each day.

She drew another line toward the first one, but stopped it short before they encountered one another.

This is my path, slowly going toward his. Inevitably, they will come together. After they meet, mine will keep going on again. His won't. His will have stopped.

The shadow of a man's head and shoulders dimmed the whiteness of the table a little, and the waiter asked her if there was anything more.

She shook her head inattentively without looking up at him, and watched the faint outline efface itself from the cloth again.

Like that, life left you, went away from you. Like a faint shadowing slipping off the blankness of some empty tablecloth. Just like that.

It is at one and the same time both the easiest and yet the hardest thing in the world for a girl to meet a certain designated man, who is a stranger to her and within whose orbit she does not naturally fall: that is, with whom she does not share mutual friends nor gravitate within the same business or professional background as he does. It is easy if her long-range motive is marriage or her short-range one simply a love affair. Or for that matter, even just a quick sex-kick. Because then all she does is place herself in his way, go somewhere where she knows he'll be and where he can't help see her, and let the rest follow automatically from there. Either let him pick her up, or else pick him up and let him think he did.

But if her motive is something else again, if there is not the slightest possibility of love on her part, and even less on his, so that even the phony promise of love-yet-to-come cannot be used as an inducement or come-on in helping to break the ice, and if they have no mutual friends, no complementary backgrounds, then the difficulty becomes almost insurmountable.

Madeline's motive was murder, no more, no less. She was honest enough to admit to herself that that was all it could be called in the final analysis, no matter how she tried to gloss it over by calling it a deed of retribution, or atonement, or vindication, or whatever. It was death by violence, at her hands, and that was murder.

There had to be a relationship to precede this act. She couldn't just shoot him down at sight. One very good reason being she didn't *know* him by sight. All she'd seen was his smile, in one torn photograph. She had to know he was the right one, she had to make sure. Since love was barred, and there was no business or professional empathy, the only possible relationship had to be friendship. No matter how false, but still a friendship.

And that was where the problem came in. A woman cannot suddenly meet and commence a friendship with a strange man, just like that.

Even apart from that, the logistics of getting within reach of him, she had a minor problem of identification on her hands. She had very little to go by. Charlotte herself had never set eyes on him in her life. She, Madeline, had no physical description beyond the single, brief black-and-white glimpse of his lips. Starr's letters to her mother had been filled with emotional descriptives, but never physical ones. He might be stocky, he might be slender, might be short, might be tall. She had to cut him out of a whole worldful of men.

Only two facts about him had filtered through Charlotte to

her, both coming at second hand from Starr. And those two facts were the minimum that can be known about anyone: They were his two names, first and last. "Vick" and "Herrick." Not another thing. Not even that much in full, for one of them was probably a nickname. There was a very good possibility that "Vick" stood for "Victor," but not an out-and-out certainty.

She didn't even know what his occupation was, his method of earning a living. Starr had never told Charlotte, oddly enough, and so Charlotte had been unable to tell Madeline. Dell herself had only used the word "work," which could have meant anything. "Sometimes he used to go straight from work to pick her up."

Madeline took stock. She had this much, then: "Vick Herrick." And one thing in addition, gathered by indirection. Dell had admitted he was younger than she when she married him. Since Dell herself had been at the most still in her early thirties, he must be in his late twenties, even today.

Not much to go by. Very little. Vick Herrick, age twenty-eight, -nine, or thirty. No face, no height, no hair coloring. To be singled out, isolated, from a huge population complex.

For days on end, the very hopelessness of the task held her immobile, kept her from doing anything at all. So afraid of failure that she was afraid even to start in. Finally she had to say to herself, "Get up your nerve. Don't let it throw you like this. Even if you fail, it's better than just to sit doing nothing. It's too late to turn back now anymore, so the only place you can go is ahead." She took a deep breath, and without knowing just where to begin, began anyway.

The obvious thing of course was to consult the telephone directory. That wouldn't facilitate her striking up a friendship with him, but it might at least indicate *whom* to strike it up with. When she had hit upon a way of going about it.

She was surprised at the number of Herricks she encountered. She had thought it a fairly uncommon name. But she counted eighteen of them. However, of these there were only three listed with given names starting with a V, so the problem wasn't as bad as it seemed. One was a female, Vivian; other two just had initials after the "Herrick." She eliminated Vivian at once, and that left her with just two to concentrate on. At least within the metropolitan city limits. There was nothing of course to exclude his being a suburbanite, one of that teeming horde that siphoned in each morning and out again each night. In which case the task would be so magnified it might take the better part of a year. She closed her eyes with a shudder to ward off the dismal prospect.

She had her two V. Herricks, then; one on Lane Street, one on St. Joseph. Now to make contact.

She decided a spurious phone call, to try to elicit information was not only impractical, it might even be risky and defeat its own purpose. People do not readily drop their guard, open up their lives, to the voice of a stranger on the telephone. And how could she claim to be anything else? To make an impostor out of herself, pass herself off as somebody he already knew or who already knew him, was out of the question. She didn't know whom to impersonate, in the first place, and the imposture would probably fall flat on its face after the second sentence had been spoken.

A personal visit, a face-to-face confrontation or sizing up was the only feasible modus operandi.

This much granted, now she was stymied by having to find a plausible excuse. A personal visit, a call, had to have one. She couldn't just go up to his doorbell and ring it.

Additional days went by while she pondered this. Each new idea that came to her seemed fine, the very thing, at first sight.

Then as she examined it, flaws would appear, more and more of them. Until it was as full of holes as a fishnet.

More than once, pacing the floor, trailing question marks of cigarette smoke, she would say to herself, "If I were only a man." How much easier that would have made it. She could have passed herself off as a gas-meter inspector, a plumber, an electrician, a telephone repairman, a building inspector. Even rented a bike and borrowed a carton and pretended to be a grocery-store deliveryman who'd rung the wrong bell by mistake. Any number of things like that, just to gain access and size him up, if nothing more. But who ever heard of a girl filling such duties?

And then, as so often happens in this unpredictable world, when she least expected it, and from the quarter it was least likely to have come from, the inspiration was dropped into her lap. Or rather placed in her hand. Ready-made, complete, and practically foolproof.

One night she went down to dinner in the hotel dining room, as she did most nights. But this one night she discovered she'd left her handbag upstairs in the apartment, which she did not do other nights. There was no great predicament involved —the meal was always charged to her bill, and so could the tip be if it had to—except for one thing. Her room key was in the handbag, so she found she'd locked herself out. Here again there was no difficulty, the hotel always kept duplicates at the desk for just such an eventuality.

She therefore stopped at the desk, a thing she rarely had occasion to do, for she never received any mail or messages, and to her surprise the desk man put an unsealed envelope with her name and room number written out on it into her hand.

It was a form appeal for contributions to a multiple-sclerosis fund, and looking up at the mail rack she could see that a similar envelope had been placed in every single letter slot. They all showed evenly white, as though a diagonally slanted blizzard had struck them.

On the back flap, partly printed out and the rest filled in in handwriting, was the notation: "Kindly return this with your contribution to your floor monitor, Mrs. Richard Fairfield, 710."

Madeline had what she'd been looking for, and she recognized it at sight. She took it upstairs with her, let herself in with the emergency key, took twenty-five dollars out of the repossessed handbag, and put it inside the donation form. Then, conceding that it was extremely important for her purposes to get into Mrs. Fairfield's good graces and win her confidence as fully as possible, she added a second twenty-five to the first, making her total contribution a generous and impressive fifty dollars.

She left the envelope unsealed, so there would be the least possible obstacle to Mrs. Fairfield's almost immediate discovery of her munificence, preferably while she was still present. Then she patted her hair a little and went down the hall to 710. She tipped the knocker, and in a moment a strangely composite type of person was standing before her. She was both youthfully old and oldly youthful, a peculiar blend of overage flapper and vivacious dowager. She hadn't jelled right; one hadn't been able to submerge the other. Artfully waved silver-blue hair. Triple ropes of pearls the size of Chiclets, which couldn't have been anything but genuine, they were too large. Some sort of trailing garb with lots of satin and lots of lace. She was even carrying a cigarette in a short jade holder, a thing Madeline hadn't seen anyone do since her own childhood in the fourth Roosevelt Administration. She was completely unlifelike, she seemed to have stepped out of a cartoon in *The New Yorker*. Madeline almost wanted to look down around the floor under her in search of a signature.

"Mrs. Fairfield?" Madeline said smilingly. "I took the liberty of bringing this to you myself, because I—"

"Miss Chalmers," Mrs. Fairfield said, reading the name on the envelope. "How d'do. Very kind of you."

Madeline's strategy had proved well advised. It now paid off handsomely. Mrs. Fairfield had managed to deftly project and compute the bills in the folder without seeming to do so at all, just by a trick of the fingernails, much in the way a practiced card player scans his cards by the merest tips of their corners while he holds them close in to him.

Madeline suddenly found herself high in favor, high beyond mere cordiality, high almost to the point of unbridled enthusiasm. Mrs. Fairfield gave her a dazzling electric smile with teeth that must have cost a fortune. "Won't you come in for a few moments and chat?" she invited.

"If I'm not taking up your time," Madeline said apologetically, but moving forward even as she was saying it.

"I'm expecting my husband to take me to a violin recital," Mrs. Fairfield informed her as they seated themselves, "but he's late. He always seems to be late at times like this." Then she added archly, "Sometimes I wonder about that."

Madeline wasn't interested in the surroundings, she wasn't there for that, so she took no notice of them. But she inescapably received a blurred off-center impression of ornateness all around her, and at least one detail came through clearly: a large oil painting on the wall of Mrs. Fairfield herself, some twenty-five or thirty years ago. Irreproachably beautiful, but irreparably dated by the peculiar flat hairstyling of the early thirties, always worn with a part far over to the side of the head, the way men wore them. Madeline recognized it from movies she'd seen.

Mrs. Fairfield had seen her gaze up at the wall. "My husband insisted I sit for that," she remarked complacently. Then she went on to explain, rather piquantly, "Not this one. One of the earlier ones. I forget just which."

She wants me to know she's been married more than once, Madeline thought, so that it won't fail to point up how attractive to men she once was. But anyone can be married more than once, she reflected. All it takes is a disagreeable disposition.

"I've seen you from a distance once or twice, coming and going," Mrs. Fairfield confided. "I asked everyone, 'Who is that lovely young girl?' No one seemed to know. No one could tell me anything about you—"

"There isn't anything to tell," Madeline murmured.

"—Always alone. Never a young man with you. Why, when I was your age, I could hardly put my foot down without fear of stepping on one of them."

She wants to give me the mental picture that they were always on their knees all around her, groveling.

"They don't interest me too much," Madeline said dryly. "They seem to be always there, a part of the background. I take them for granted."

A look of genuine horror passed fleetingly across Mrs. Fairfield's marshmallow-white face. She promptly dropped the topic, which was what Madeline had wanted in the first place, anyway.

"I don't suppose most people deliver their contributions in person," she said.

"I assume you wanted to be very certain I received it."

"That's only part of the reason," Madeline said. "It struck me that I might be able to do something for the cause besides what cash I can afford to contribute."

"How do you mean?"

"I thought I could solicit donations. I'm sure not every building in the city is fortunate enough to have a volunteer passing out envelopes and collecting contributions. I could go around to other buildings, tell people a little about multiple sclerosis, and see if they'd care to make a donation."

"That's grueling," the woman said. "If you just leave envelopes you never hear from the people again. And if you press for a donation on the spot, you get turned down time after time. All in all, it can be a terrible waste of time."

"It's my time," Madeline said evenly. "I don't mind wasting it, not if it's in a good cause."

"I don't know. I'm not authorized to deputize you as a building representative or anything of the sort—"

"Just give me some literature and contribution envelopes," she suggested. "I don't have to have any official standing. Any contributions I receive I'll hand over directly to you and you can turn them in with whatever else you collect."

The woman thought for a moment. Then, abruptly, she shook her head. "I'll list you as a volunteer," she said. "It may be slightly irregular, but it will be all right."

An hour later, a sheaf of donation envelopes in her purse, she stood on the sidewalk in front of the address listed for V. Herrick, on Lane Street.

It was a frugal, little apartment building, no frills or luxuries, somewhat run-down in appearance but still clinging to an overall aspect of respectability. It was of newer vintage than the old walk-ups of the early 1900s—she could see a self-service elevator no wider than a filing cabinet standing open at the end of the hall—but it was anything but modern. It probably dated, she surmised, from the immediate pre-Pearl Harbor period, when all such construction was jerry-built, due to the shortage of funds and the low level of rents. It had probably just gotten in

156   CORNELL WOOLRICH & LAWRENCE BLOCK

under the wire before controls went on, all private building was
frozen, and the hordes of war workers came pouring in from all
over the country, to beg, bribe, and fight for every square inch
of floor space that was to be had. And today—who wanted it?

The Herrick door was indicated as the first one on her left as
she entered the ground-floor hall. There was a peculiar vibra-
tion such as a riveting machine might make somewhere about,
but she couldn't identify what the source of it was. She took out
the donation forms, took in a deep but not very heroic breath,
and knocked. Nothing happened. She knocked again. Nothing
happened again. There was a roaring sound, then it died down
again.

She noticed a small push button at the side of the door. It
had escaped her until now because some unsung but remarkably conscientious (or remarkably sloppy) painter had painted
it over the same sage-green color he'd used on all the rest of
the woodwork around it.

She didn't hear any sound when she thumbed it in, but evidently it still worked, because in a matter of not more than a
minute or so the door opened, and the torrential tumult of
hundreds of shouting voices came banging out at Madeline's
eardrums, almost bowling her over by the sheer impact and
unexpectedness of it alone. Somewhere in the middle of it all a
man was screaming away, as if he were being torn apart by wild
horses: "—into the bleachers back of left field! Bob Allen,
twenty-three! A left-hander from Texas!"

And closer at hand, another man yelped shrilly: "Bejeezis,
don't ever tell me they're no good!"

The woman looking out at Madeline was somewhat slipshod,
but had amiability written all over her broad, good-natured
face. She had evidently grown used to immeasurable decibels
of noise and it no longer had any effect on her placidity. She

was holding an orange-pop bottle in one hand and a bottle opener poised in the other. Madeline read the word "Yes?" from her pleasantly up-cornered lips.

"Would you be interested in contributing something to the multiple-sclerosis fund?" Madeline rattled off. "Any amount you care to give will be appreciated."

"I can't hear you," the woman shouted.

"The multiple-sclerosis fund!" Madeline yelled back.

"I still can't hear you!" the woman screeched.

Madeline let her arms sag limply. "I can't yell any louder. I've used up all my voice."

"Wait a minute," the woman said. Or at least lip-formed. She turned her head around. "Vince!"

"Ball one," came back hollowly in answer.

"Vince, I'm talking to you! There's somebody at the door. Tone that thing down a minute, so I can find out what she wants."

This time an injured but stentorian baritone managed to penetrate the sound barrier. "Top of the ninth, five-all, two men on base, and she asks me to tone it down!"

But Madeline didn't wait for any more. She quietly but firmly closed the door again, from the outside, and went away.

It was a basement furnished room, and even as she stepped down from the sidewalk into the enclosed areaway it fronted on, a sense of foreboding overcame her. She even halted a moment and made a half turn as if to get back onto the sidewalk again. Then she overrode her hesitancy and crossed to the arched brownstone doorway set in under the high stoop, and rang. She could hear the faint ring deep inside the house somewhere. If personal risk was going to deter her, she told herself, then she shouldn't have embarked on this odyssey in the first place. There was bound to be risk now and then along the way. Risk was to be expected. There had been risk attached to the Dell Nelson business and she'd come through that all right.

A dim bulb lit up behind the iron-barred basement door, and a man came into view.

She didn't like the barred effect the door created between them. It suggested prison, confinement, restraint, something she wasn't able to quite put her finger upon. Danger, that was it. It suggested some sort of latent danger, as if you were facing someone kept apart from you for his own good.

His face wasn't what troubled her. There was nothing in it to suggest malevolence. It had deep lines in it, at the brow and around the eyes, not the lines of age but of punishing experience. But its overall aspect was a grim stoicism that took what it got, asked no quarter, and sought no retaliation.

He was anything but trim of appearance. He had on a rumpled shirt open at the neck, a pullover sweater that badly needed dry cleaning, and a pair of dingy slacks that needed pressing. He hadn't shaved today, even if he had yesterday. His hair was light brown and tumbled. His eyes were a darker brown, and looked as though they'd seen a lot of things they wished they hadn't.

The lips…she could hardly say anything for certain, but she thought they *could* have been the right lips.

Something inside her told her that if he wasn't the one she was looking for, he came closer to being it than anyone else she'd come across yet.

"Yeah?" he said.

"Do you want to contribute to the multiple-sclerosis fund?"

"Why don't they get up a fund for me sometimes?" he said, dourly. "I could use one too."

"Well—" she faltered. "That's not the point. The point is—"

He reached out and opened the grillwork door. "Do you want to come in and tell me about it?"

It was an invitation that even a seventeen-year-old novice would have backed away from in mistrust. It wasn't even put forward artfully or adroitly. It made no promises of immunity, not even false ones meant to be broken. She even saw him glance past her shoulder, as if to see whether there was anyone else around out there.

And yet somehow the very baldness of his technique had the reverse effect of not driving her away, of arousing her interest. This was the very sort of man that might have inspired a wife to want him dead. Maybe something like this had happened to Starr. To others, that is to say, while he was married to Starr and she had to stand by looking on. He had every earmark of the professional rapist.

"You're Mr. Herrick?"

"Mr. Herrick, right."

"We keep lists of the people we call on back at our headquarters, Mr. Herrick. I have you down for my last call of the day," she said pointedly. "So if I don't report back afterward—"

"What makes you think you won't report back afterward?"

"Nothing—so far."

They eyed one another steadily for a moment, each one trying to dominate. Then his eyes lost, and slid edgewise. They came right back again, but hers had had their victory. With that, she stepped past him and turned into the basement hallway. Without looking around she knew he had put out his hand to reclose the iron gate. "Would you mind leaving that open," she said, "while I'm in here?"

He gave a sniff of laughter. "You won't have to leave in that much of a hurry."

The room was about what she'd expected it to be. A sagging cot against the wall, which he slept on. A couple of wood-backed chairs, of unsure stability. A table with a smoldering cigarette gnawing its way into its rim to join the dozens of other indented burns that ringed it around. A gas ring hooked to a jet and parked on a shelf. A number of copper beer cans in two positions, upright and prone. Meaning full and empty. A calendar on the wall, but it was the wrong year and the last leaf had never been torn off: December 1960. Yesterday's newspaper and the day before yesterday's newspaper, neither of them yet thrown out. Last month's magazine (*For Men Only*), ditto. On the wall opposite the calendar, a photograph of a soldier in a flowerpot helmet, with a girl leaning her head against his shoulder.

Not much else.

Lives, she realized, are lived in such rooms. Some lives.

There was one other thing, though, of undetermined connotation, which caught her eye. There was a standpipe over in one corner, running through from floor to ceiling. Alongside it was a small steam radiator with a flat piece of tin nailed over it. On this lay a monkey wrench. She noticed a curious thing about the standpipe, which she couldn't identify at first. It seemed to have a metal ring or "collar" encircling it at one point, and from this hung a short chain, at the end of which there was another ring or band. But this one was open at one end, and was not encircling the standpipe but was hanging down flat alongside it.

Suddenly it dawned on her what the complicated design was. It was a pair of handcuffs, fastened by one cuff to the pipe. And the other one, the open one, what was that for? Something made her go a little cold inside.

"How much do you want me to give?" he said, putting his

hand to the baggy pocket of a moldy sweater hanging from a nail. This one was a coat-sweater with sleeves, but they had big holes at the elbows that seemed to peel outward.

"Give whatever you feel you can afford," she said. Then, because it was a good opportunity, she rang the question in. "Are you married?"

"Not this minute."

It was beginning to shape up more and more, she told herself.

He handed her a five-dollar bill. "Here," he said grudgingly, and repeated the ancient wisecrack: "Don't say I never gave you anything."

"But are you sure you can spare this?" She couldn't resist glancing around a second time at the squalid room.

He caught her doing it. "Don't let it worry you," he said. "Money's one thing I've got plenty of. Enough to get by on, anyway. I draw a Veterans' Disability Pension."

"Oh," she said, and looked at him. He seemed untouched.

"I was wounded in the war. Kara something-or-other, I think it was called. It was an island."

"Tarawa," she said impatiently. "You were there but you don't know the name. We learned about it in high school."

"We were dying, not studying geography," he rebuked her mildly. "I can still see it, though," he went on. "Just a little patch of hell stuck out there in the ocean. Never knew why the Japs wanted it, or why we wanted to take it away from them. I can get sick thinking of all the boys who died for islands that were never any use to anybody, and never will be." His eyes challenged her. "A lot of boys died," he said.

"I know."

"And they were the lucky ones," he said. "Do you know that too?"

"What do you mean?"

"I mean there's worse things than dying, but I don't expect you to believe that."

She thought of Starr, dying, and of herself, with a leftover life to live. "I believe it," she said, softly.

He didn't seem to have heard her. "Tarawa," he said. "Guys left their arms there. Or their legs. Or came away blind or deaf or with their brains scrambled. They were lucky too. Not as lucky as the dead ones, but luckier than some."

"How can you say that?"

"Because I wasn't so lucky."

She stared at him. "You've got your arms and legs," she said. "And your hearing and your eyesight. What makes you the unluckiest man at Tarawa?"

"Do you know the difference between a bull and an ox?"

"Not exactly. An ox is bigger, isn't it? And stronger, I guess."

He laughed sourly. "You must be a city girl," he said. "A farm girl would have the picture by now. How about a ram and a wether? A rooster and a capon?"

"I—"

"Or a stallion and a gelding. How about that?"

"You don't mean—"

"Don't I? We were on patrol. From out of nowhere, a Jap threw a grenade at us. My buddy dove for it to throw it back. It went off in his hand and killed him. The lucky bastard."

"And—"

"And I got to keep my arms and my legs and my sight and my hearing. All I lost was what makes a man a man."

"My God," she breathed.

"When I came back, my wife walked out on me. I didn't blame her. She would've stood by me in anything else, if I was on crutches, if I was blind. She was a good wife. But she was entitled to a husband."

She looked over at the picture on the wall. The soldier in his helmet, the girl looking up worshipfully from his shoulder. It couldn't have been Starr, then. Tarawa had been in 1943. But maybe Starr had come along afterward, unsuspecting. Who knows what this terrible tourniquet had turned into later on?

"At first it wasn't so bad for a little while. I went out on dates like I had before I got married. Plenty of dates. Plenty of girls. Some wanted to marry. Some were ready to settle for less. But there always comes a time in an evening when the two of you are alone by yourselves. I used to tell all kinds of lies to cover myself up." He laughed mirthlessly. "I even told one girl I was contagious."

"What'd she say?"

"She told me she didn't mind, not to let it stop me, because she was contagious herself."

He went over to the vicinity of the washbasin and picked up a flat brown-glass bottle from somewhere near it, she didn't quite see where. "I don't suppose I can offer you a drink?" he said uncertainly.

"That might only lead to trouble."

"Trouble?"

"Trouble for me. And trouble for me spells trouble for you too," she told him coolly. "You know that, don't you?"

Even his answer was the perfect answer—for her line of inquiry. "I ought to by now," he said with a heavy sigh.

He tipped the bottle up, pulled the cork with his teeth, held it fast there, let some liquor run into his mouth alongside of it, then reinserted the cork, still with his teeth only. She'd never seen that done before.

"It started in gradually, the bad part of it. I found myself starting to hit them, to get a little rough, to throw them around and swing at them. One or two even stood for it, but not too long. Most ran away. Then the stray slaps and knocks became regular beatings. I beat one girl up very badly one night. I had to throw cold water on her before she came around. I put some money in her hand, all I had on me, and kissed her and beat it away. She never preferred charges against me, but she used to duck out of sight if she saw me on the street after that."

She gave him a look of antipathy. "You hated them because of what had happened to you. Is that why you roughed them up?"

"No, no. You've got it turned around. I only did it because I loved them. I couldn't show them I loved them like other guys can. And you have to *show* it, you have to express it, it has to come out, it can't be kept back. I could only show it by violence at the end of my hands. Those were my caresses. It was the only way I could find my peace and satisfaction. I had no other way of going through to the end."

This is the one, she told herself inexorably. He's the one— knew Starr.

"But I knew it wouldn't stop there. I knew sooner or later I was going to kill one of them."

"And have you?"

His answer was bloodcurdling in its simplicity. "Not yet."

"Why don't you have yourself placed under treatment before that? Before that happens?"

"There *is* no treatment for this. Maybe you didn't understand me right. This isn't something mental, that a headshrinker can work on. I went through all those tests in the beginning, and they found me normal. This is a physical dismemberment. As physical as a busted arm would be. Only, a busted arm can be put back in business again. This can't.

"What year is this?" he asked at a tangent.

"Sixty-one."

"That don't mean my memory's failing," he defended himself. "It's just that I lose track every now and then. I was nineteen when I was on Tarawa. That means I'm still only thirty-seven today. At thirty-seven you still get restless every week or so. You wouldn't know it, but you do."

She lowered her head, strangely touched for a moment.

"You want to go out for a stroll, be a part of the world again, the world you once knew. You see other fellows with their girls. You want a girl too. Nothing dirty about it, unhealthy about it. It's as normal, as natural, as that. But that's when the trouble comes in."

He poked his thumb over his shoulder. "Do you see that pipe back there?"

"I noticed it when I first came in."

"I've set up a system. You know, like a fire-protection system. The superintendent of this building is a Norwegian, his name is Jansen, husky as an ox. He has the apartment right over this one. He used to live down here in the basement, but when I came in he turned this one over to me and moved upstairs. You see, he likes me. His son and I were buddies in the war. Well, one night we were having a few beers around the corner, and I told him about it: how I was afraid I was going to end up in serious trouble if things kept on going the way they were; maybe even do away with someone altogether.

"So we rigged up this signal between us. When I start getting restless, and know that I'm about to go out and roam around, I hit that pipe a wallop with that monkey wrench over there, and he comes down here and keeps me from going. Sits down and plays cards with me, and we have a few drinks, and when I start to get sleepy he locks the door from the outside and goes back upstairs. Next day I'm all over it."

"What're the handcuffs for?" she asked batedly.

"Once in a while I won't listen to reason."

He started to light a cigarette, then interrupted the act, flame before lips, to tell her: "So if I start to crowd you too much, remember to pick up that monkey wrench there and hit the steam pipe with it with all your might."

"That won't be necessary," she said a little tautly, "because I'm leaving now."

She got up from the rickety chair she'd seated herself on (without noticing) a long while before, turned her back on him, went over to the door, and turned the knob.

The knob turned willingly enough, but the door wouldn't open.

"What'd you do, lock this?" she said sharply. "Don't try anything like that! You'd better open it, if you know what's—"

Her last glimpse of him had had him standing on the opposite side of the table from her, a considerable distance, hands rounded toward chin, matchlight streaking his face like yellow crayon. Suddenly, before she even had time to turn her head and finish the denunciation facing him, she felt his arm go around her waist. Then the other one crossed over her shoulder, interlacing with the first. His face pressed hard against hers from over the opposite shoulder. She could feel the tough, often-shaved skin, stiff as cardboard, and he planted a trail of kisses down her cheek until he found her mouth.

Fear didn't come at first, only anger and outrage did. But when she found she couldn't move, not even enough to squirm or struggle, that the embrace was like iron, like steel, almost traumatic in its intensity, then fear did come, in a cold, sick rush, like nausea of the mind. She kept cautioning herself: Don't panic, don't lose your head, that's the worst thing you could do. And then: Go limp, let yourself go limp, and his instinctive reaction may be to relax the embrace.

She let her knees dip, and though the rest of her body was held too compressed to slide down after them, she let him carry her full weight, and it worked. His arms slackened in reflex, and she was able to duck down under them and up again on the outside.

He was too close to the door, had it boxed in, so she fled back again the other way, behind the large round center table where he'd originally been himself.

She spoke in a breathless voice, as though she were whispering in confidence. "Don't! Cut it out!"

"You overstayed your margin of safety."

"I'm going to have you arrested for this!"

Again he came after her. She tried to overturn the table toward him, but it had too wide a base to tilt easily. Then she remembered what he'd told her about the wrench, fled over into the corner, picked it up, and swung it in a long, shattering arc against the standpipe. The sound of it was brazen in its intensity, and it seemed to go echoing up through the house high over their heads, playing back upon itself section by section.

She only had time for the one blow, he came in at her too fast. She threw it at him and it hit him, but only on the protective arm he'd thrown up before his head. Again he penned her in his arms, but this time forward, not from in back, and she could feel the heat of his breath stirring her hair like some kind of an ill wind. She tried to kick him in the ankle with the sharp point of one of her shoes, and did, but the blow couldn't have hurt much, he hardly flinched, it had been too foreshortened.

He lied, she thought frantically. He said the man would come.

"A little love is all I want," he was coaxing. "Just a little love—"

She saw the cigarette that he'd lit just before the thing

began, still balanced there on the rim of the table. She strained one arm toward it behind his back, but it fell a finger-length short, for she could only use the forearm because the upper arm was pinned under his. She pushed forward against him unexpectedly, instead of pulling away as she had been doing. He wasn't expecting the impulse and had to take a couple of steps back to hold his equilibrium. Her flexing fingers snatched up the cigarette, and she jabbed it into the drum of his ear, coal-forward.

He didn't cry out, but he recoiled like a bounced ball and let go of her. He bent his head over to one side as though his neck had been broken, and kept pounding at his ear with one hand, and stamped his heel on the floor twice.

Then before she knew what was coming, he swung the flat of his hand around at her and gave her a terrific slap that covered one whole half of her face from eyebrow to jawline. The pain of it wasn't as bad as the force, or at least she had no time to experience it; she went back onto the cot, shoulders prone, rolled over once in a complete body turn, and landed on the floor at the foot of it, but with one arm out to break her fall.

She saw him pick up the monkey wrench from the floor where she'd thrown it before, and for a moment thought he was going to attack her with it, but before she could have moved or done anything to defend herself, other than just draw her legs defensively in underneath her, he turned and went the other way with it, and banged the standpipe, not just once but three or four times in urgent succession.

Then he flung it away from him, and settled onto a chair, head bowed down and held in both hands. Not from pain, from remorse.

The room was quiet by the time the half-running footsteps came along the passage outside and a key started to work in the door. Neither of them had moved. They were both emotionally exhausted. They weren't even looking at each other anymore.

A heavily built man with a shock of yellow-white hair came in. He had a massive neck, arms, and shoulders, and a sizable paunch under his blue denim work shirt. He had on a pair of peculiarly shaped glasses—they were either square or octagonal—that gave him an oddly benign, homespun appearance.

"What happened down here?" he demanded. "Vern, what have you been up to down here?"

"It's over," the man on the chair said apathetically.

The older man came over and stood looking down at Madeline. "What did he do to you?" he said. "The whole side of your face is red."

"He slapped me," she said, and began to cry from pent-up tension. "No man ever slapped me before in my life. Even my own father never slapped me."

"What took you so long?" the man on the chair said accusingly.

"I was up on the roof, doing a yob," the superintendent said.

He helped Madeline to her feet and brushed off the back of her dress with a heavy but well-meaning hand. "Sh-h, sh-h," he said consolingly, as if he were talking to a child. "It's all right now. Do you want a drink of water? I get you a drink of water."

She stopped crying abruptly. "I don't want a drink of water!" she said angrily. "I want to get out of here."

"Well, go," he told her matter-of-factly. "The door's open. Nobody stops you."

She went over and stood by it, but without leaving.

Jansen had turned his attention to Herrick, took no further notice of her.

"Get up," he said brusquely. "Get up and come over here." But she detected a paternal note in the brusqueness.

"I'm all right now," Herrick said docilely, looking up at him.

"Yust the same, you do like I say," Jansen insisted. "You come and sit over here." He took the chair Herrick had just been on, and moved it over against the standpipe. Then he brought a table up against it, not the large round one in the middle of the room but a small unpainted one that had been against the wall. He opened a shallow drawer in it and took out a greasy deck of cards. "We play a few hands," he said, and he brought up another chair for himself and sat down across the table from Herrick. Then he took a small drawstring sack of pipe tobacco out of his breast pocket and placed that on the table also.

"We better put that on a few minutes," he said. "Yust to be on the safe side."

Herrick sheepishly extended his wrist, and Jansen snapped the open cuff around it. Then he began to deal the cards.

Madeline had watched the proceedings with incredulous eyes. "He's vicious!" she burst out. "He oughtn't to be allowed at large, a man like that. He's a menace. A maniac."

Jansen turned on her as fiercely as though she were the offender, not the man.

"He's not a maniac," he said severely.

"No? Well, what do you call it when he beats women—"

"He's just unfortunate, that's all. Well, go to the police, if that's what you want to do. Go and have him taken in, if it make you feel better."

She bit her lip. "For personal reasons of my own, which don't happen to have anything to do with this, I prefer not to. But he won't get off so easy if he ever tries it again, with somebody else, let me tell you."

"You're as much to blame as he is," he told her. "You didn't have to come into his room. You know better than that. You're not a child."

"Why are you so ready to defend him?"

This time he threw down his entire hand with vehemence. "He saved my son's life. He covered him with his own body when my son lay there helpless, unable to move, his leg caught in a booby trap. He didn't stop to ask questions then, did he? He didn't stop to argue if it was right or if it was wrong, did he? Why should I now? Today, thanks to him, Harald is a successful businessman in San Francisco. He has a lovely wife, three beautiful children, a fine house, a car. All because of this 'maniac,' as you call him. I'm a poor man, I work hard, but I have scruples—"

He probably meant to say morals, she surmised.

"I only know one thing. When you owe, you repay. When good is done you, you do good back."

Herrick had kept his eyes lowered throughout the whole discussion.

"How many drunken husbands come home and beat their wives? How many jealous lovers knock their sweethearts around?"

"That doesn't make it right, though," she said defensively, but in a minor key.

"No, that doesn't make it right. He and I both know that. That's why we made up this signal between us."

"And what about the time, the one time too many, when his control slips, he doesn't signal, he gets away from you? That time will surely come. You know it will. And some girl will pay with her life."

He didn't answer that. He just looked down.

"Will you hide him then?" she insisted. "Will you still protect him then?"

"We'll know what to do, if that time ever comes. We've talked about it. We've agreed. We'll handle it—between us two. Yust us two."

She saw an odd look pass between them, which she couldn't interpret. Something about it chilled her.

They took up their cards and started playing, but she still lingered there by the door, unable to tear herself away, though they seemed to have become oblivious of her.

"What was that you called him," she said to Jansen, "when you first came into the room?" The passage of violence that had occurred between Herrick and herself made her self-conscious about addressing him directly.

"His name is Vernon," the older man said.

"What was his wife's name, the one that left him?"

"He only had one wife," Jansen answered. "Marika. She was Polish."

Madeline went "Hhhhhh" on a long, deflating note of disappointment.

"I don't blame her," Herrick said. "She did the right thing. She was only twenty then. It was better to walk out like that, make a clean break, than stay by me and cheat right and left right under my nose."

He played a card.

"I'm sorry what happened," he said to Madeline without looking at her. "I apologize."

"That's all right," she murmured almost inaudibly. "I understand how it was."

He suddenly lifted his head and looked directly over at her. "Good night," he said timorously.

"Good night," she answered. "Thanks for your contribution."

It only occurred to her afterward what an anticlimactic remark that was, coming after what had taken place between them.

❖

Some sort of inner integrity prevented Madeline from discarding the unused contribution folders she still had left. After all, they had been given to her in good faith, no matter what her own purpose had been. She therefore slipped a couple of dollars into each one, wrote the names of fictitious donors on the outsides, and prepared to return them without, if possible, encountering the committeewoman a second time. An encounter that held very little appeal for her.

Her timing was faulty. By one of the flukes which are impossible to guard against, just as she straightened up from sliding the envelopes underneath the door, Mrs. Fairfield appeared at the upper end of the corridor, coming from the elevators, and caught her in the act.

"How are you making out with your legwork?" she greeted Madeline jauntily.

"I just now finished up," Madeline said.

"Come in a minute and we'll tally up."

"I'm afraid I have to run," Madeline demurred.

"But I have to enter the amount and give you credit."

"You take the credit yourself, I don't mind."

"But we're not allowed to do that!" Mrs. Fairfield gasped, as horrified as though she'd been asked to participate in an embezzlement.

By this time she had the door open and one persuasive hand under Madeline's elbow, so Madeline followed her in with a private sigh of frustration, prepared to submit with as good grace as possible to a retelling of her hostess's past triumphs, in the man-killing and marital fields.

Mrs. Fairfield, seating herself at the desk to do a little lightweight bookkeeping, asked her if she wanted additional contribution forms. Madeline no-thanked her, explained she'd used up all the spare time she had, and a shudder flickered through her as she thought of last night's incident on St. Joseph Street.

Mrs. Fairfield had more than her fair share of narcissism, as all women have who have once been beautiful. "I've just had some new pictures taken," she said, indicating a sheaf of large oblong folders stacked on the desk. "I suppose you think it's silly at my age."

Madeline tractably said what she knew Mrs. Fairfield wanted to hear her say. "You're not old enough to stop having your picture taken."

"Friends of mine kept asking me—" Mrs. Fairfield got up and brought two of them over to show Madeline.

"I like this one best," she said. "But I want your opinion. Which one do you think does me the most justice?"

"This," said Madeline in a stifled voice. But her eyes weren't on the subject's face. They were on the signature in sepia ink that ran diagonally across the lower right-hand corner: "Vick's Photo Studio."

"Vick," she said. "Is that the photographer's first name or his last name?"

"His first name," the woman said. "Although that's an unusual way to spell it, isn't it? With a K."

"I had a friend once who spelled it that way," Madeline said. "I don't suppose you remember the photographer's last name."

"I'm afraid I don't." The woman frowned in thought. "But I'm sure I received a receipt, and I'm sure I kept it. Let me see if I can find it."

And, a few minutes later, Madeline was holding the receipt in her hand. Vick's Photo Studio, with the street address and phone number. And, at the bottom, the signature: Vick Herrick.

❖

It had all the appointments of a business office, she thought curiously as she stepped in from the hall. There was a small reception room first, with a desk, a girl at the desk, paperwork for her to do on the desk. Even an intercom.

"I'm Miss Chalmers," Madeline said. "I phoned in for an appointment."

"Oh, yes," the girl remembered. "You asked for the last appointment of the day, if possible. Well, I have you down for it. Won't you have a seat? Mr. Herrick will be ready for you in just a few minutes."

He had framed samples of his work displayed on the walls. They did him credit, she thought, looking them over. He was more than an expert craftsman at his work, he was an artist. Each was more arresting than the last.

He was almost a surrealist in portrait photography, she told herself. There was one haunting study of a young girl that, once you had looked at it, you couldn't keep your eyes off from then on. He had achieved the impossible by violating all the laws of photography. The light was *behind* the subject, not in front of it. A dazzlingly bright light, almost explosive, almost like a chemical reaction. He must have had a large bare-faced bulb hanging concealed in back of her head. You could almost see the rays streaking out from it, like sun rays when the sun is embedded in a tangle of cloud. As a result, the face itself was in shadow, of course, only a contour, a silhouette. Then he had taken some reflective surface, possibly a narrow strip of mirror, and centered it on the face from in front, so that the eyes were lighted up in misty suffusion, a narrow line ran down the center of the nose, and the curve of the underlip was faintly traced. No more than that. It was like a sketch of a face done in chalk on a blackboard. It was like a negative, where all the white area shows black. And yet all the girl's delicacy of feature managed to come through, and with it something of the loneliness and awe of youth. It was a cameo of grace, a camera chiaroscuro.

"Who is that?" Madeline asked, open-mouthed.

"Everyone who comes in here asks that," the girl smiled. Then she added, "Can't you guess? It took real love to create a piece of work like that, not just skill with a camera. It's his wife."

Are those the same eyes that closed against my heart? Madeline wondered. Is that the face I saw die out? The eyes, she thought now that she knew, seemed to have a knowledge of approaching death, seemed to be looking at it from a great distance, waiting, waiting...

"It could easily take a prize in any show," the girl was saying, "but he won't exhibit it. I've heard people offer to buy it, and he just gives them a look—"

"Is that what she was like?" asked Madeline. Meaning, in full life, before she was struck down.

"I never saw her," the girl said.

"Wasn't it made right here, at the studio?"

"He must have done it at home. Or somewhere else. He brought it in one day. They're separated now, you know."

"Oh," said Madeline, realizing—she doesn't know Starr is dead.

"Or so I understand." Then she confided, with that typical feminine freemasonry that springs up whenever affairs of the heart are under discussion. "I came to work one morning and I found him asleep in the chair here. That one there, facing it. He'd never gone home all night. Thousands of cigarette butts. A small empty bottle. He had the shade of the lamp tilted so that it shone directly on it. All night long..."

She shook her head compassionately.

"I pretended I didn't notice anything. Which was a hard

thing to do. He never did it again, though. Did it at home, I suppose."

Madeline looked down pensively.

The girl said, "He'll be ready for you any minute now. Would you like to freshen up before you go in? There's a little powder room behind that door there. You'll find everything you need in there, I think."

Madeline got up and went in.

There was a long dressing table, backed by a mirror of matching length. A number of bottles on it, hair glosses and the like.

She took off her watch and put it down on the table. Then she combed her hair over a little. Then she pulled two or three Kleenex tissues out of their slotted mirrored holder and put them down over the watch. She got up and went toward the door. She glanced back, and you could still partly see the watch. She went back and rearranged the tissues so that they hid it more fully, covered it completely over. Then she stepped out.

She had the last appointment of the day. No one else would be coming in here. Only the girl, to lock up and put out the lights. Madeline hoped she was honest. At any rate, she already had a watch of her own, Madeline had noticed it on her, so there was that much of a safeguard.

"You can go right in," the girl said. The door to the studio proper was standing open now.

Madeline stepped in past it, and there was a man in there standing looking at her.

For the first time they saw one another. For the first time their eyes met and looked at one another. For the first time in the world. The killer and the one to be killed.

She only received an overall impression, a summary of him, at first. Two-dimensional, without depth. There was no time for

anything else, her senses were too preoccupied with the physical immediacy of the meeting to be able to stand aside and
study him in detail. Comely of face, unhandsome but agreeable. Well-proportioned bone structure, no slackness of jaw or
anything like that, but otherwise undistinguished. Was this the
jaw, the lips, from the photograph? Hair a very light brown, but
still not quite blond, with a crisp crinkle to it. Eyebrows a little
darker, eyes darker still. Intelligence in them, also some sensi-
tivity. About five-ten, not heavily built but symmetrical, on the
spare side. And when he spoke, in another moment, a light
voice, but not a high one, no localized dialect overtones, just
basic well-bred eastern-seaboard United States.

To sum up: someone you could quite easily have taken to—if
you didn't have to kill him.

"You're very pretty, Miss Chalmers," was his opening remark.

It was said with professional objectivity, not personal interest,
that much she could tell.

"You probably know it already," he added, "so there's no sense
in my telling you."

"One knows," she said quite simply. "If not, one's a fool. Or a
liar."

He gave her a quick look, as though he liked that. Found it
refreshing.

"Is that your wife out there?" she asked. "She's very beautiful too."

"The girl already told you who it was," he said quietly.

She accepted the dig unruffledly. "I wanted to make sure."

He answered her previous remark. "Yes, she is," he agreed.
"Starr is very beautiful."

Now at last, she told herself exultantly, and clenched her fist
in mental imagery and brought it down. Now at long, long final
last. No more mistakes, no more false alarms. No more noisy

baseball fans, no more pathetic war derelicts. The right one at last. The man that Starr had married, here before her.

And he'd said *is*—Starr *is* very beautiful. Was it possible he didn't know she was dead either? Madeline thought back to the newspapers and radio news from the time of Starr's death, her killing appearing in none of them. How *would* he know?

"I think I'd like to have you sit here," he said, shifting a shell-backed chair. "I'm just going to take the face and throat."

He moved around her, shifting and adjusting various screens and reflectors, every move a sure one, knowing just what he wanted to do.

"Just relax. You can cross your legs if you want to. I want to make a few preliminary tests with the lights first."

"It's my hands that I don't know what to do with," she admitted.

"Do anything you want with them. They won't be in the picture. Here. Here's something that I sometimes use." He thrust a common ordinary lead pencil into her hand. "Do anything with it. Fiddle with it. Just so long as it keeps your hands from becoming clenched and tight. That can have an effect on the shoulder line and even the neck, sometimes."

He turned on something, and the reflectors threw a dazzling light all over her, bright as magnesium.

"Try not to blink. You'll get used to it in a moment." He toned it down a little.

He knows his job, inside and out, she thought.

"I'm glad to see you don't wear jewelry," he said. "Jewelry distracts, takes the eye away from the face, which should be the focus of the picture."

She thought of the watch. She hoped the girl didn't go into the powder room too soon, before she managed to get out of the studio.

"Turn a little bit this way. Do you see that seam running up and down between the two walls over there? Keep your eyes on that. No, that's too blank. Think of something a little puzzling. Can you? A little baffling, mystifying."

"Puzzling?"

"I can get a very nice eyebrow line, a certain lift to the brows, that way, that I can't get in any other way. I had a sitter in here one day who told me she was very poor at arithmetic. I had her do the higher multiplication tables, you know, times-thirteen, times-fourteen, and I got the most beautiful quirk into her eyebrows. It made her whole face. Most brows are too straight."

She thought: It's hard to kill a man whom you don't hate. Just hate by proxy.

"That was a remarkable expression!" he exclaimed with satisfaction. "One of the most remarkable I've ever seen!"

"When are you going to take me?" she asked.

"I just did," he said blandly. "That expression was too good to pass up. You're going to have quite a photograph on your hands."

He took her several times more, with various changes of angle, and then it was over.

"Thank you," she said. She held out her hand, more to test out his grip than anything else.

His grip was sincere and warm and firm.

The grip of an honest, straightforward man.

The first phone call practically raced her back to the hotel. It was sounding as she keyed the door open. She made no move to go over and answer it; instead she carefully reclosed the door, took off her hat, settled herself comfortably in a corner of the sofa, all as oblivious as if she were stone-deaf and didn't hear it. It finally rang itself out.

It rang again about a quarter hour later. They must have

waited that long to give her additional time to get home. Again she didn't go near it. She wanted him out of the studio before she answered. Again it dwindled down, like a spent alarm clock.

The third time it rang sooner, inside of about ten minutes. This time she went over to it and answered. It was now close to six. He couldn't possibly still be at the studio this late, watch or no watch.

"Miss Chalmers?" It was his voice, not the girl's.

"Yes?" she said as guilelessly as though she didn't know who it was.

"This is Mr. Herrick, the photographer. Are you by any chance missing a watch?"

"Yes, I am," she lied superbly. "I only just now noticed it was gone as I came in the door. I thought I might have lost it in the taxi—"

"We found one in the dressing room," he said. "No offense, but could I ask you to describe it, please?"

"It's silver, round, with a circle of tiny stones around the dial. It's a Bulova. It's mounted on a twisted black cord instead of the usual strap or band."

"That's the one," he said. "I have it. Miss Stevens found it right after you'd left."

"Oh, bless her heart!" she exclaimed fervently. "What a relief. I don't know how to thank you. My mother gave it to me as a birthday gift." Which latter part was true, anyway; it had been her grandmother's first.

"I have it with me right now," he said. Then explained, "I'm downstairs in the hotel. Shall I turn it over to the desk?"

"No, no," she cried, in such alarm that he must have taken it to be an excess of gratitude. "Please come up, if only for a moment. You must let me thank you personally."

"Fine." He hung up.

She had him on her own territory now. The gambit had worked beautifully, without a hitch, from beginning to end.

It was still light outside the windows, but she turned on a certain lamp, so that if he sat within its radius as she proposed to arrange that he do, the light would fall on his face and she could watch his expression more closely. He was not the only expert in lighting effects, she said to herself arrogantly. Only, his were created for appeal, hers for espionage.

He knocked, she opened the door, and he came in.

He handed her the watch, and she did a thorough acting job over it, uttering little cries, even holding it pressed for a moment to her heart. Then she put it back on her wrist.

"I don't know how I came to do that."

"We don't have a safe at the studio, don't keep anything of too much value down there, and I didn't want to just leave it in a desk drawer overnight. I decided to take it home with me and call you in the morning, but I knew you might worry about it all night, so I took a chance and had the taxi stop off here first on the way home."

"Sit down and visit." She guided him with just a shadow of a gesture to exactly where she had wanted to have him sit. "Let me buy you a drink, to show my appreciation."

"Please don't trouble," he demurred.

But she was already at the phone. "Don't deny me that privilege, I'll feel hurt. What would you like to have?"

"Scotch and plain water."

"What Scotch?"

"Chivas Regal."

"Room service," she said. And then concluded with, "A double and a single."

"I have another customer who lives in this building," he remarked when she'd rejoined him.

"I know her," she said.

They both laughed a little in common understanding, but good-naturedly, not unkindly, without having to say anything further.

"I'm not keeping you from anything, am I?" she asked. "Your wife isn't expecting you, is she?"

"We're not together anymore," he said expressionlessly.

"I'm sorry."

"That makes two of us," he said.

It wasn't news to her, of course, but now that she'd worked it so that he'd seemed to tell her himself, they could go on from there without further hindrance.

Nothing memorable was said, but then it was too early in the game for that, anyway.

She learned little things about him, tiny facets, nothing more. He drank slowly, and he left an inch of liquor in the glass. That meant he didn't qualify as a heavy drinker nor even as a moderate one, he qualified as a light sociability drinker. He was not a nervous nor a restless type of person. At one point what must have been an oversized truck backfired with a thunderous detonation immediately outside the window somewhere. She jarred an inch above her seat in recoil. He never moved at all, just gave her a humorously rueful smile. Also, soon after he sat down, she noticed that he crossed his legs, the left one over the right. At the very end, when they were both ready to get up and go, they were still that way, the left one over the right. He was placid, restful to have around.

She watched the play of his hands a great deal. They were sensitive, dexterous hands, good for the work he did. The nails were cut square across the top. A home job, obviously; he wasn't one of these male popinjays that go in for manicures. But they were faultlessly clean. She could detect no cruelty or meanness in his hands. And yet could one be sure? They were only hands, no matter what was said, and not the mind that ruled them. She wondered if they'd ever clenched and struck a blow in anger and in hate at Starr.

He still wore Starr's gold wedding ring, one of the pair they must have exchanged.

Somehow she knew then, though she could not have told why, that no, he'd never struck a blow in anger or in hate at Starr.

He seemed to feel comfortable with her, made no drastic attempt to get up and go. She purposely procrastinated, prolonged the interlude until all the light outside had faded away and it was almost too late for him to go anywhere else for his dinner.

Then craftily she went inside to the phone and asked for two menus to be sent up, without letting him near her.

"What're you doing?" he said to her, when the waiter showed up at the door.

"I'm ordering dinner for us," she said sleekly.

He half rose to his feet in protest, but she could see that he was flattered. "I can't let you do that—!" And then, "Well, only if you'll let me buy it—"

"I live here," she said firmly. "The next one will be your buy."

In the end they compromised, went downstairs and sat at the corner table she usually occupied, and she signed the tab and he paid the tip.

Once dinner was taken care of, it was easy to get him back upstairs again. He could not have left her right after the meal without being guilty of the classic "eat-and-run" offense.

And he had a very strong sense of social responsibility, she could tell that much about him already.

Once upstairs and with a symbolic rather than utilized cognac

in front of each of them, they found themselves on more intimate terms than before. The dinner and the predinner drink
had mellowed him, and she found it easy, with an adroit question or two for a lead, to get him started talking about himself.
Not the private inner self that Starr had known, of course. She
didn't dare reach for that. It was too soon, it would only have
evaded her. But the self of his outer life, his work, his experiences.

"How did you get started in photography?"

"It was born in me," he told her candidly. "I couldn't have
been anything else."

At ten or eleven his father had given him a camera as a
birthday gift, one of the elementary Kodaks of those days.
Nearly all boys are given cameras at one time or another, and to
nearly all boys it becomes a hobby for a while, just like collecting stamps or coins or things of that sort. And then it passes
and is forgotten.

But from the minute he first put his hands on it, something
happened.

"I knew right then what I was going to be. I knew right then
what I wanted to be, had to be. I was holding my whole life's
work in my hands."

He quickly learned the mechanics of the thing, the developing of his own prints. Most boys do, anyway, and it cost too
much to take them down to the corner drugstore, even at those
days' thrifty prices.

But there was much more than that to it. It was as though
there had been pent up in him until now this force, this drive,
this reservoir of creative ability, and this outlet came along and
released it, acted as catalyst to it, so that it poured forth un-
slackening from then on, for the rest of his days.

From the beginning he wasn't interested in snapping his

friends' grinning faces, or their pups, or their little sisters. Or the school team in their baseball togs.

Odd shots and angles. That was all that ever interested him. He was always looking for new and different angles. That intrusion of self between the lens and the object that transmutes a mere mechanical process into art.

There was a lamppost across the street and down a little way that he could see from his bedroom window. But from there it was nothing at all. In the summer it cast a soft hazy light, almost blurred by the humidity. In the fall it had dried leaves swirling about its base. But in the winter it was best of all, with snowflakes softly sifting down past it, lighting up for a minute like sparks, then going out again in the dark.

He wanted to get it from *below*, from directly underneath, nothing else would do.

So he waited patiently, and finally just what he wanted came along: a whopping big snowfall, about three feet deep. He sneaked out of the house about midnight, when there was no one much on the streets anymore. He lay flat on his back in the snow under it, focusing straight up. It was two o'clock in the morning before he finally got the shot he wanted, the one perfect shot, and the imprints his body had made in the snow were like the spokes of a wheel going all around the base of the lamppost.

His mother rubbed his back with alcohol for the better part of an hour, but he went down with a light case of pleurisy the next day anyway. The only thing that kept his father from whaling him was that he was so sick. But the one punishment that would have really been a punishment they didn't inflict. They never withheld his camera from him. They must have sensed somehow what it would have meant to have it taken away from him.

Then another time he wanted to get a shot of lightning flashing in the sky. This too he wanted to take from directly underneath, as if it were coming down on him. Again he lay on his back, this time in a meadow in the park in the middle of a walloping summer shower, his camera tucked under his chin and a tarpaulin wrapped around the two of them. Most of the flashes bleached the entire sky, they were worthless to the lens, there was no darkness left to differentiate from. Several times it must have struck nearby, he could feel the ground reverberate under him, but he was too taken up to have any time for fear. He must have used up three rolls of film, trying to get what he was after. But, as in the other instance, he finally did get it. Lightning that could be printed and made to last forever.

"Like a live wire, like a filament—you know what I mean?—corkscrewing across the sky." Then he added wistfully, "I still have it, somewhere."

And that was the way it went, all those young years of his. A man wielding a blowtorch, in a puddle of sparks, a fountain blown awry by the breeze, an iron demolition ball at the moment of impact as it sundered a wall, a man riding a crane as seen through the black frame of the opening at the end of a pier. He'd hang around such potentialities by the hour, until he had his shot made. Even drunks sleeping it off in doorways didn't escape his visual voracity. He kept a patient vigil beside one one late afternoon until a certain slanting ray of sunlight had caught and kindled the empty bottle he held cherished in his arms, and that in turn sent a reflected highlight up into the sleeping face above it. Like someone hovering over the afterglow of the fire that has consumed him. The story the picture told was implicit, but only he had known how to add the one little touch that gave it full expression.

Once he almost lost his life, lying full-length under a parked car making a series of montages of the feet of pedestrians coursing along the sidewalk, when the owner unexpectedly got in and started it.

At the end of his basic schooling, he went to vocational high school and took a course in photography, but there already wasn't very much they could teach him. Just a little more up-to-dateness in the equipment used and in the processing methods, that was all. He could have taught his teachers how to take an unforgettable picture. But at least it gave him the necessary credentials.

He found the going very hard at first. He got a few jobs as assistant in other people's photo studios, but the pay wasn't enough to get along on, and the interesting part of the work, the creative part, wasn't thrown his way. Sometimes he was little better than an errand boy, bringing back coffee, sweeping the floor, emptying out trays of solution.

He had to take odd jobs, whatever he could find, to tide himself over. Then one summer he managed to get hired on as a stagehand at a summer-stock theater in the country. He'd gone up there originally to work as a waiter at the resort hotel. One week the man who had charge of lighting the plays (they used to do one a week) was hurt in a car crash coming out from the city and stood them up. Herrick talked them into letting him pinch-hit for the absentee, and he turned out such an eye-fluttering job (the play was a natural for trick lighting exercises, anyway: *Berkeley Square*) that they kept him on from then on.

When the season ended, he went to New York, armed with a letter of introduction from the summer-playhouse manager, to tackle the theater there. After heartbreaking months he managed to get a job, and then after he'd worked like a dog over his lights and gelatin slides and dissolves and all the rest of it, the play promptly closed down after its second performance. Presently he landed another, and it went on like that.

One or two of the reviews even had a line of praise in them for the lighting effects, which is a very unusual thing. But you can't eat lines of praise, and his name was never mentioned, anyway, so who cared?

"It still wasn't my kind of work. It was a dead end. And the layoff between shows was awfully long sometimes."

Then one night the leading lady of the current particular show he'd lighted caught him in the act of taking candid shots of her from the wings as she came off. She got him to show her the finished prints the next day, and she was so impressed when she looked them over, she offered to buy them from him. He gave them to her instead. One thing led to another, and in the course of conversation he told her what his dream was. She ended up by staking him to it, advancing him enough money to open his own studio and start out by himself.

"Everyone in the case, of course, thought there was something else behind it. She was a woman about forty and she was known to have a weakness for much younger men. But there was nothing like that in back of it at all. As a matter of fact she was very much in love with somebody else right at the very time. But she was a great humanitarian, and she believed enough in my talent and ability to want to help me. That was all there was to it. And I made a point of seeing to it that she got back every penny of that loan by the time I was through."

She knew he had; that was his characteristic.

"She was my first sitter. And she let me display one of the portraits I made of her under glass alongside the street entrance to the studio. The publicity helped. She didn't need it; I did."

He left at about eleven. Not much had been accomplished, but at least a start had been made. The groundwork had been laid. They were "Vick" and "Madeline" to one another now. And he owed her a dinner. That was important, because he had an abnormally acute sense of reciprocal obligation, she had detected that about him already. What he owed, he repaid.

At any rate, the ball had started rolling.

He called a week later, toward the end of the week.

"Vick Herrick."

"Hello, Vick."

"I've been given two tickets to a show, and if you're not doing anything tonight, I was wondering if you'd care to take it in with me."

"I would," she said immediately.

"Have dinner with me first and—"

"No," she said, just as immediately. "Give me a rain check on the dinner part." She wanted to keep the obligation going, so she would have that much of a lien on seeing him a third time.

"You won't let me buy you dinner?" he said, crestfallen.

"Next time around I will, not tonight. But I will take in the show with you, and you can buy me a cup of coffee afterward. I like to sit up late and talk."

"All right, I'll pick you up at the hotel."

"I can meet you at the theater, if you want."

"No, it's one of these off-trail playhouses, you might have a hard time finding it. I'll stop by for you at eight."

She waited for him just inside the lobby entrance, in order to save time and trouble. Since this wasn't a romance, there was no reason for playing coy or hard to get and making him come inside, call up to her room, and all the rest of the court-ship trimmings.

She recognized him through the cab window as it drove up, went outside, and joined him just as he opened the door and stepped out.

"How's that for timing?" she asked cheerfully.

"To a tee," he grinned. "You're the kind of person I'd like to have along when I have to make a train in a hurry."

The backtracking lights outside stippled their faces as the cab got underway again.

"Get your pictures all right?"

"Vick, they're simply incredible. How do you do it?"

"It's my métier, as the French say. By the way, you never did tell me—just what were you thinking when you got that marvelous hike into your brows?"

She laughed. "You know something? If I were to tell you, you'd be the one with a hike in your brows."

"I don't guarantee this thing we're going to," he said. "It was done in New York two years ago, at one of the little off-Broadway theaters. Even then, I don't think professionals were in it. So tonight you might say we're going to see a road company of an amateur production."

"It doesn't matter," she said leniently. "It'll be an experience, at least."

It was. It was called *The Connection*, and it had something to do with narcotic addiction. Other than that, what it was about was completely undecipherable. The stage was set in the center of the audience the way a boxing ring is. It was furnished with two or three wood-backed chairs and that was all. Two or three men stood in one corner of it talking. Occasionally one or the other of them would move about a little, then rejoin the others. And that was the extent of the dramatic action.

Madeline wasn't too put out about it; she was there on behalf of dramatic action of her own, and not to watch that of others. What did jar her occasionally was to glimpse other faces in the audience looking her way through the actors' legs whenever they made a move or took a stand. It destroyed all chances the play might have had of weaving an illusion.

At one point they both turned simultaneously and looked at one another.

"I can hear them perfectly," she said under her breath. "Their delivery is good. But I can't make out what they're talking about."

"I was just going to say the same thing to you," he chuckled. "I think a lot of it is users' slang, that's why. Drug users, you know."

They stayed on for a rather valiant length of time at that, but finally gave up the struggle and left when it showed no signs of stopping.

"I don't know how we would have known when it was over, anyway," she remarked on their way out. "They had no curtain."

"One way of telling it wasn't going on anymore might have been by the general perking up in the surrounding atmosphere. I really owe you an apology."

"No, you don't at all. It's part of the scene around us today. A tiny part, but still a part. Maybe drug addicts do stand around like that and just wait; I've never known any of them. Still, I'm glad we took it in."

"It was very avant-garde, I suppose. But why couldn't it be that and at the same time lucid? They never are."

"I don't care for any of that stuff," she told him decidedly. "I must have been born a hundred years too late."

It was true. She was a formalist. She had been born old-fashioned. She wanted plot in her plays (à la Shakespeare); she wanted a melody in her music (à la Verdi, à la Strauss); she wanted a reproduction of the natural image in her paintings, her art (à la Rembrandt, Titian, Raphael). Those men were good enough for her.

She wasn't interested in kindergarten-age children's crayon daubings when done by grown-ups. Or reefer dreams improvised out of a slide trombone without any notes to back them up. Or sculpture done with chicken wire. Or people on a stage who talked but didn't move.

For her it had to be laid on the line, circle-perfect, rounded out, no gaps left to be filled in.

And it must have been something of this feeling for completion, for symmetry, that lay at the bottom of her compulsion to finish out Starr's life for her. The original guilt complex wasn't solely responsible for it any longer; that would have worn thin by this time.

A modernist would have walked away with a laugh. *I* should finish up somebody else's life for them? I got my own, and one at a time's enough.

But the nineteenth century would have understood. The nineteenth century with its idealism.

They found a little espresso coffee place, dim as a flickering match flame but a good place to talk in. They sat way over in a corner in the gloom, barely able to see one another's eyes. A girl with her back against the wall lazily picked at a mandolin, but she never seemed to finish more than the first bar of anything she started.

"Tell me about your wife," she said, the way you drop a small pebble into a smooth sleek pool of water and wait to see the ripples slowly widen around it.

But no ripples came; it suddenly solidified, seemed to harden over. The way his eyes did too. And the ease of talk was gone for a moment.

It's too soon, she realized. He won't tell me yet. Maybe he never will.

"Tell you what about her?" he said guardedly.

"I only meant—her looks," she corrected. "It's hard to tell from that picture at the studio, she's so much in shadow."

"Oh," he relented. And he thought for a minute. And he probably saw her face in the flame of the candle she could see him staring at. It reflected itself doubly in his eyes, once in each pupil, like two small tapers shining at an altar of recollection.

"She's stunningly beautiful," he murmured reverently.

Madeline had held her in her arms when she was dying, had looked into her face, had seen it. True, she was in pain, she was in shock, life was flowing out of her. But even with that allowed for, she had not been stunningly beautiful. Attractive, yes; pleasing to look upon; the structure and the proportions of her face did that for her. Above all, youth did that for her. But she had *not* been stunningly beautiful. Yet to him she was, she had been.

Therefore: *He had really loved her.*

No further doubt was needed, no question remained about that. He had loved her with the true eyes of love, which for each man see one thing, one thing only, and pass by all the rest and all the others.

She took that home with her and thought about it. Whatever it was he had done to her, it hadn't been done from lack of love, but in the fullness of love.

Returning home one night after she had been out with him— their evenings spent together numbered upwards of six or eight by this time—she took off her things, put a wrap over her, and sat down at the desk to think things out, to analyze what she had of him so far.

She knew the externals of his life by now almost as well as one person can ever know those of another. Even had he been her husband. His boyhood hobby with the camera, his early knocking around before he found himself, his final success and fulfillment in his chosen work, he had told her all about that. But the injury to Starr lay somewhere in the inner, private life that he had not told her about.

Whatever it had been, it had been within the framework of his love for her, of that there could be no doubt. It had been an offense, an outrage, of love, and not of hatred or ill-will. This should have simplified it greatly. How innumerable are the harmful acts you can commit against someone you dislike; how few those against someone you love. But it didn't.

She picked up a pencil, finally, and a piece of paper, and tried to draw up a list of possibilities, to help her thinking powers along. She had a great predilection for using a pencil to help crystallize her thinking. She would have made a good draftsman.

Alcohol: Completely ruled out. He had none of the telltale signs about him, which are so easy to read. He drank even more slowly than she did herself. He invariably left the bottom of his glass still holding liquor in it. He hadn't attained the status of even moderate social drinking. He was an occasional social drinker, the first stage above complete abstention.

Narcotics: There she was on obscure ground. He had none of the traces, but she was no expert at divining them, either. She thought momentarily of the play he had taken her to see. Was there some sort of an inkling there? But then she dismissed it as unfair, it had been simply a coincidence. Or rather, since there was nothing for it to coincide with, a random occurrence. In any case, arguing that he had been an addict himself, what then would have been the attraction in going to see such a play? He would have known the life so well, why go to see a reproduction of it? He would have been more likely to shy away from it, if only to spare his own guilty conscience. Finally, she recalled, he had seemed as unfamiliar with the specialized slang used in the play as she was herself. And there was no reason to think this was an act.

A criminal record, or some past criminal offense: This didn't seem to fit him at all. True, she wasn't naive enough to expect criminals or lawbreakers to go around looking like criminals, or to carry a sandwich board on their chests reading: "I am a criminal." And true again, she had heard it said that often as not some of the worst people in this category were, at home with their families, gentle, devoted, considerate, even more so than the average run of husbands and fathers. But when all this had been duly allowed for, the fact remained he didn't fit into the picture at all and the picture didn't fit him.

The simple, tightly knitted little story of his life he had told her need not have been true, of course. He could not have been expected to reveal some serious criminal act or criminal way of life to her on such short notice. But it was so plausible, so artless, so uncontrived from beginning to end that it didn't seem likely he had left anything out. In other words, it was too monotonous to be anything but true. If it had been rigged, it would have at least been more colorful. And there wasn't a chink, a gap in it, in which to insert, to wedge, some major off-law experience. Almost, you might say, there was no room in it. It was as though every day, pretty nearly every minute, had been accounted for in that brief, unmemorable, but somehow *simpático* saga of his thirty years that he had given her.

She knew this man pretty well by now. There wasn't violence in him or she would already have glimpsed it, no matter how hard he tried to keep it from showing. That is to say, violence on the grand scale, beyond a mere swear word and punch of a fist. He'd never lived by violence, and he'd never done violence. And above all else, he lacked that sharp acuteness that is needful to criminality. He was a simple man. He was good at his work, but personally he was simple, uninvolved, uncomplicated. Just a run-of-the-mill Joe, with camera fingers, loaded with good nature and goodwill and deathlessly loyal in his love.

That was the way she saw him, and nothing could convince her she was wrong.

All the possibilities she had listed had one thing in common, she couldn't help noting. They were negative offenses. That is, offenses against himself, not against Starr. Any woman, any wife, would have done one of two things in such a case. Either stuck by him and tried to help him, or if she saw that was hopeless, simply washed her hands and walked out on him. But not turn around and want him killed. Even get ready to kill him herself. There wasn't anything in any of those hypothetical malefactions that warranted that.

She found the list had vanished.

She crumpled the little leaf of paper and threw it away. She tugged the chain pull on the hooded desk lamp, and the pool of light in front of her eyes went out.

I can't stand this uncertainty anymore, she thought, raking her fingers through her hair and dragging it down in front of her face. I'll have to be a blind instrument of justice then, in every sense of the word, and do it still without knowing. Anything, anything, to get it over with and get rid of it!

The very next time we're together, I'll do it. I'll have to do it then, or I may never do it at all.

Finally, the day had come. She knew it from the time she first opened her eyes early in the morning. On the one hand, there was no actual reason for it to be that day, and not the one that had just preceded it or the one that would immediately follow it; it was wholly arbitrary. Yet on the other hand, there was every reason. She had nerved herself to a certain pitch which she might not be able to hold longer than for just a few hours, and once lost or even partially relaxed, might never be able to regain. She needed this certain pitch, she could not do the thing without it. For she was not a professional killer nor yet a passionate one. She could kill neither in cold blood nor in hot. Both extremes were foreign to her nature. She could only kill as she was about to kill now: for an ideal, as an obligation, to fulfill a vow. As one lighted a taper at an altar: in expiation.

And only this once, never again.

He was a man. Of that there could be no doubt. He had been married to Starr, Starr had been his wife. He was the one she wanted killed, he and no other. And Starr–Madeline would be the goddess of the machine, who earned it out for her.

Let whatever he had done to her, whatever had made her want him killed, be buried with him, then, go down into the grave with the two of them and never be known. Maybe it was better that way. Who knew what the thing was? Why let it live on, dirtying the world? Why take it with her into some cell and nurse the morbid knowledge of it for the next twenty years or even her whole lifetime? Somehow in all her calculations—no, that wasn't the word, she didn't calculate in this—in all her willingness to accept punishment, to undergo penalty, she had never visualized herself being given a death sentence. Not that this would have deterred her. But it was always a lengthy prison term that she foresaw being meted out to her.

This was the day, then. It had come.

She hadn't even left her bed yet. The slats of the Venetian blinds, or rather the interstices between them, drew thin pencil strokes of yellow on the wall opposite the window, and on the floor, and on the counterpane on her bed, and even partly up one of her bare arms. She even had the impression that one of these stripes of light must be lying flat across the bridge of her nose, because of a dazzle effect she got in both eyes. She thought it was charming; like being in a golden cage.

She got up and went over to the blinds and tugged the cord that controlled them. They went up supplely, with only a slight rustling sound, and the day became a full foursquare panel, not just streaked glimmers on a wall. It was surging with sunlight, and in it the city looked like something brand-new, that had just come into being. Every brick spotless, every paving block freshly laid. She leaned out, and a taxi with an orange roof polished as a mirror went scuttling by under her eyes, like some kind of an amiable, off-color beetle scampering for cover.

How strange, she thought, we're both in this city together at this very moment, though at a distance. We're both breathing, we're both looking at things, even though we're apart. Yet, by tonight, or by the early hours of the morning, he'll be dead. Then he won't be in this city anymore, just I will be, alone. Where will his breaths be then, where will they have gone? Where will the sights reflected on the irises of his eyes be then, where will they have gone?

I don't know, for I didn't order death, fashion it. I only know that he'll be gone into it.

She turned away from the window, and as she passed the discomposed bed she'd just now been sleeping in, glanced at it reflectively. Last night, she thought, we both slept, he and I, and our sleeps were alike. Today we both woke up from our sleeps. Tonight we'll both sleep again, he and I, but our sleeps this time will be different. Tomorrow again I'll wake up, as I did today. Tomorrow he won't; for him there'll be no tomorrow.

Sleep, that little bit of death embedded in life. No, she corrected herself. Sleep is not death. Not at all like it. People are wrong when they say or think that. "Dead to the world," meaning a sound sleep. Completely wrong. For the body goes on functioning. It breathes, the blood flows, the heart beats. Sometimes the body even moves, turns itself over. The dreams of the daytime world color sleep; night after night they are there, even though they may not be recalled the next day.

No, the French Revolutionaries who inscribed "Death is eternal sleep" on tombstones were mistaken. There is no point of similarity between the two, not any at all. Even the position of the eyes is different, for in sleep they are closed, but in death, paradoxically, they remain open. It is human hands that have to close them.

No, sleep is not death. Sleep is submerged life.

She shook her head in self-annoyance. Why do I torture myself so? Just do it, and have done with it! Not *think* about it, *think* about it, *think* about it, all the time.

But I have to think about it. The other things I did for her were minor, subsidiary. This is the main thing. This is the important one. This is the one she wanted most.

She took a brief shower, without using soap. She took an average of two a day, one in the morning, one in the evening, and only used soap about every second one; it was actually superfluous more often than that, she was inclined to believe. Possibly even unbeneficial to the skin.

She dressed and made a cup of instant coffee. She told herself unwillingly, I suppose I ought to eat something. She was always telling herself this, in the mornings, and always trying to evade doing so. She finally compelled herself, against her own inclination, to slip a slice of wheat bread into the toaster, and plug it in.

Then she ate standing up, biting at the toast in one hand, taking swallows of the coffee in the other. She put the cup down finally, left part of the rind of the bread, and acted as if she were glad it was over. She was.

The city was awake now. She lit a cigarette and went back to the window and stood there looking out again. The day was so normal, so everyday looking. You couldn't tell it held death in it.

A mouse-colored French poodle on leash to a young girl stopped to investigate a tree, decided against it, went on to the next. A deliveryman came along pedaling a bicycle with a built-in box for carrying groceries.

A trim-looking truck went by, the legend "U.S. Mail" on it, the lower half blue, the upper half white, a thin band, no more than a stripe, of red separating them. They should have put the red on top, she thought idly; the expression was "red, white, and blue," not "white, red, and blue." Still, she supposed, maybe they decided a red roof wouldn't look good on a truck.

Somewhere in the immediate vicinity, but out of sight, an apartment-house doorman kept blowing on his whistle, trying to conjure up a cab for his waiting tenant. There was something unutterably lonely and plaintive about the sound.

A defective "Don't Walk" sign stayed red when it should have turned green and caused a minor amount of traffic confusion down at the next crossing. Then it finally meshed and turned green, but by now all the others had turned red again.

Two nuns floated majestically along, heading a long double-file procession of small schoolchildren.

A jet coursed by overhead, turning the sky into a tom-tom, heading for some faraway romantic place. Anchorage, Tokyo, Manila.

A couple of pigeons, outmoded, flew up from a cornice defiantly then turned around and came down on it again, their challenge ignored.

A Sanitation Department street-washing vehicle came trundling clumsily along, held its water along a stretch of curb where there were no pedestrians, then let fly target-accurate as it came abreast of a man and woman walking together. They both jumped aside and started to brush at themselves, ruefully but uncomplainingly.

A stocky workman was standing by an open manhole, with a bright orange circular guardrail ringed about it, and a red flag on a stick projecting from this, talking to someone else unseen down inside it. It made a little eddy in the otherwise smooth flow of the traffic.

In the building across the way from Madeline's hotel, but at the same floor level she was, a window washer attached his safety belt to the two brackets flanking the window, and then seated himself backward on the ledge, closed the sash down tightly across his thighs, and began to go over the pane with a wet sponge.

What a way to earn a living, Madeline thought deprecatingly. And he may even have a wife and child at home. Why shouldn't he have, just as well as everyone else?

But for every job there is in the world, no matter how unrewarding, there's always someone there to fill it. Or else the world couldn't go on.

Standing there, she decided she'd call him at noon, just before he took his lunch break.

Just as the decision crystallized in her mind, there was a knock at the door. She sighed, crossed the room, and opened the door.

It was the maid. They exchanged good-mornings, and then the maid said, "Isn't it a lovely day!"

"It certainly is," Madeline agreed. And then the thought of his death came back again. Not that it had ever been very far away. He's having nice weather to die in, she reflected.

"Aren't you going out and get some of that beautiful sunshine?" the maid wanted to know.

"I'm going out later on," Madeline told her. "I'm going out

this afternoon." She wondered what the maid would think or say if she were to tell her, I'm going out to kill a man. Probably grin ephemerally as at a joke you don't understand and go right on with her work.

"You don't have to bother with that," Madeline said as the maid picked up the coffee cup to rinse it out.

"It's no trouble, let me do it," the maid said accommodatingly. "I like to leave your place spic and span." Madeline was a good tipper.

And that was the last exchange of the day between them.

The morning had gone. The morning of Herrick's last day on earth.

She looked at her wristwatch. Three and a half to twelve. She went into the bedroom once more and sat down on the bed again, now neatly made up.

The death call.

She waited two and a half minutes. Then she picked up the phone and gave the apartment hotel operator his business number. She was as calm as though she were asking for a time check or valet service.

She gave his name to a girl. Then she heard his voice. Every word it said meant it had used up one word more and had that many fewer left to use before it grew silent forever. Still, isn't that true of all of us? she thought.

"This is Madeline," she said, and smiled a little at him in greeting though he couldn't see her.

"Funny, I was thinking of you only a little while ago," he said.

"I was thinking of you too," she admitted.

"Do you believe in mental telepathy?"

"It's impossible not to," she said soberly, "when something comes up like what we're saying right now."

"Come down and have lunch with me," he invited. "The whole town is playing hooky from school. A day as fine as this isn't for working in, it's for idling in."

"No," she said quickly, "I can't. I have some things I want to do this afternoon."

"Have lunch with me first, and then you can do them later," he suggested.

"No," she said, "but I'll tell you what I'll do."

"What?" he said eagerly.

"I'll have dinner with you tonight, if you're free."

Eagerness had become enthusiasm. "Fine," he said heartily. "That'll be just fine. Where'll we make it and where'll I meet you?"

"Have you got facilities over in your place?" she said at a sudden tangent.

"Facilities?"

"Facilities for making a meal."

"Oh, yes, sure. Why, would you rather eat up in my place?"

"Yes," she said. "I'd like that better than a restaurant. I'm just in the mood for that. The only obstacle is—"

"What?" he said.

"I can't cook worth a nickel."

He laughed in relief. "I can," he said. "Want me to, rather than have it sent in?"

"By all means," she said gaily. "That's what I'm fishing for, a home-cooked meal for once in my life."

"You've got it," he said. "Now, what would you like? Name your menu. I'll phone in the order, and it'll be all delivered and ready to go to work on by the time you arrive."

"Well," she said, looking thoughtfully along the wall. "I'm not a fancy eater, and I'm not a large one. I like plain fare."

"All right, " he said. "I've got paper and pencil here. Let's start at the beginning. What do you want for a before-dinner drink?"

"Sherry," she said decidedly. "Always and only. I don't go for mixed drinks. In that, I'm with the Europeans."

"Brand?"

"Domecq. La Ina, if you have it. It's one of the driest in the world."

"I do have it," he said. "Like it myself. Next?"

"No soup, no nothin'. Just a one-course meal. I know most men are fond of red meat, and I am myself, in moderation. How about a steak?"

"You're a girl after my own heart."

"But not one of these oversized sirloins," she said quickly. "Why don't you get us each a little individual club steak? They're small and tender."

"I know a great sauce," he enthused.

"Put mushrooms into it."

"They go with it. Mushrooms and sauterne."

"No trimmings, no salad."

"Dessert?"

"No dessert. I hate sweet desserts. They're for children."

"I do too."

"Or, I'll tell you what. Roquefort on thin saltine crackers, and then black coffee laced with cognac. And that's it."

"You've got good sense in food," he complimented her. "And good taste in it."

"Thank you," she said quite matter-of-factly. Then she asked him, "What time shall I drop by?"

"Oh, anytime after five-thirty. I'm not going to start in until after you're there. Half the fun is having someone around you when you're doing it."

"All right," she said with grave politeness. "I'll be there. You can count on it."

"'Bye for now," he said.

"'Bye for now," she repeated.

She didn't smile vindictively when she'd hung up, or look grim, or anything melodramatic like that. She had a pensive, wistful look in her eyes, almost as if she felt sorry for the guy. She gave a soft sigh, underneath her breath. Then she shrugged one shoulder very slightly, as if realizing the whole thing was beyond her control.

She left the apartment at about one-thirty, and had a midday snack at the fountain in the hotel drugstore. This was only a degree less frugal than her preceding repast had been: a tomato sandwich and a malted milk.

Then she got on a bus and, avoiding the larger department stores, where the clothes had a tendency to lack individuality, sought out a small specialty shop on a side street that she had been to once or twice before.

"Something in black," she mentioned.

About the fourth one struck her interest. She went into the dressing room, put it on, and came outside again.

"You two go very well together," the brisk manager-saleswoman told her.

"I can see that," Madeline agreed. "That's why I picked it out. The only thing is this—" She put her hand over a small metallic ornament. "Can't you take it off? I don't like gewgaws on my clothes."

"Oh, but that makes it look too much like mourning," the other protested. "You're not going to a funeral."

Aren't I? thought Madeline, eying her inscrutably. Aren't I?

"It'll have to come off," she said flatly, "if you want me to take the dress."

The woman brought a small pair of scissors and severed it.

Madeline paid for the dress and had it boxed.

It was now a little after three, and she still had better than two hours to kill.

She went back to the hotel, had a bellman take the dress up to her room for her, and she herself went into the hotel beauty salon. This was more for the sake of using up the excess time that she had on her hands than because she was interested in having her hair done. As a matter of fact, for a girl in her own particular age bracket, she patronized such places remarkably seldom; not more than once or twice a year.

"Can you take care of me?" she asked the girl at the desk. "I don't have an appointment."

"I have a customer who's late again for her appointment, as usual," the girl remarked resentfully. A resentment that was not, however, intended for Madeline, it was apparent. "You can have her time. If she does show up, she can just wait until after you're through. It may teach her to be more punctual after this." Then she added, no doubt as a special concession, "Would you like Mr. Leonard to take care of you?"

"No," Madeline said. "I'd rather have a girl do my hair."

"I'll call Miss Claudia," the receptionist said.

Following an enamel-smooth redhead into a booth, Madeline wondered, as she had once or twice before, why in this particular profession the names of the personnel were always prefixed by a "miss," whereas in all others employees of equal rank simply called one another by their given names. One of the traditions of the trade, she supposed.

"What would you like to have done?" the girl asked Madeline, running a professionally appraising eye over her hairdo.

"I'm not too well up on the new styles," Madeline let her know. "I've worn my own this way since I was sixteen, but I know it must be outdated by now, because I no longer see it on anyone else, the way I used to at the start."

The girl handed her a brochure of glossy photographs. "Perhaps you may find something in there you like." She pointed one out. "We get a lot of requests for this." It looked like a beehive. It was massive, rising to a point high above the head.

"It must be a lot of trouble to keep it looking right," Madeline remarked dubiously

"It is," the girl admitted. "But it's very dramatic."

Madeline laughed outright. "I don't think I'd care to go around with dramatic-looking hair, whatever that is."

They finally arrived at a compromise. Madeline kept her original flat downswept style, but it was modernized by being shortened to the ear tips and combed several different ways at once on top.

"Not bad," she conceded when the job had been completed.

"Not bad?" the girl almost yelped. "Why, you look marvelous. You'll be a killer tonight," she promised.

Then she faltered and stopped. "Why, what a strange smile," she said lamely. "I never saw a smile quite like that before."

She was still staring after Madeline with more than just professional interest as she walked out, knowing she'd come across something, but not knowing exactly what it was.

Madeline went up to her room and began at last the final preparations for the meeting. The death meeting. She put on the new black dress, and wondered as she did so if she would ever again be able to bring herself to wear it after tonight. Probably not. She decided she would give it to the nice maid, when she came in in the morning. She pulled her valise out of the closet, unlocked it, and got out the revolver that Charlotte Bartlett had given her so long ago. Almost in another lifetime, it seemed. She checked it, not that she was an expert on firearms, in fact hardly knew the first thing about them, but simply to make sure that it was fully loaded. It couldn't fail to be, of course; it had been fully loaded when she first put it into the valise, and who had gone near it since? It was. It was a cylinder-type weapon, and as she "broke" it at the heft she could see that all six of the little bores were solidly plugged by the little brass bases of the bullets.

As for the ability to sight and hit with it—in which, again, she was completely amateur—how could she fail, at almost point-blank range? Two people together in a room, one of them motionless. Only the width of a dinner table or the length of a settee between them.

She closed it up and put it lengthwise, upside down, into the bottom of her handbag. That way her hand could reach down and bring it out in a single unbroken movement, without reversing. Also it balanced better, resting on its back with its handle up.

As she completed fastening the handbag—it was an underarm, envelope type, without a strap—a sudden surge of chilling fear coursed through her, tingling as ice water. The telephone was going. Not that she had anything to fear from it in itself; it was simply the sequence in which it had occurred, following immediately upon what she had just been doing with the gun. It felt as though the tripper were hitting her on the heart each time, instead of striking the bell.

It must be he. She didn't know anyone else. And if it were he, then he was calling to postpone or cancel the date. That would be the only possible reason. She stood there like a statue, refused to move. If she didn't answer, then he couldn't reach her to tell her not to come. She would go, anyway, just as she had intended to all along.

She gave it a minute even after it stopped, to make sure the line had been vacated. Then she went over to it and asked the operator, "That call you had for me just now, was that a man's voice? I was prevented from answering."

"That call wasn't for you," the operator said. "I'm sorry, I plugged in the wrong room number."

Madeline let out a long, deep breath as she hung up.

She still had a little loose time on her hands. She drew a glass of water in the serving-pantry, brought it out, and sat down with it in a chair, slowly sipping at it.

Finally she got up, went back into the other room, and got her handbag with the gun in it. As she surveyed herself in the mirror, ready to leave, a sudden sense of unreality came over her. This isn't so. This isn't true. Am I going out of here within the next couple of minutes on my way to kill a man?

She bent forward more closely, only inches away from the glass. Are those the eyes of a killer? Those soft, almost childlike things, pale blue disks swimming in crystalline moisture, pale brown lashes all around them like a feathery fringe. *Those*, the eyes of death?

She turned and ran out like someone possessed, as though the sight of her own face had frightened her. She didn't even turn to close the door after her, but gave it a backhand sweep as she went by it that closed it of its own momentum a few seconds after.

Even riding down in the elevator, the operator turned and darted her a quick little glance, as if he sensed some sort of stress emanating from her.

She got into a taxi and gave the address of Herrick's apartment.

In less than fifteen minutes they were at a halt in front of the place.

The driver waited a moment entering the pick-up point and destination in his logbook. Then he turned around and said to her, "Isn't this where you wanted to go?"

She nodded affirmatively, without answering. What she wanted to say to him was, "Please turn around and take me back where we started from," but she forced herself not to.

He waited another minute, his elbow slung on top of the front seat. Then he asked, still patient, still tractable, "Didn't you bring any money with you? That what it is?"

Still without speaking, she opened her handbag, gave him some money, and opened the door. She shuddered as she got out.

But, upstairs before his door, she put her finger firmly enough on the button. She was now past the point of no return. There would be no more hesitancies, no more backing away.

He came to the door and they greeted one another with casual congeniality, even down to shaking hands.

"Hello, Madeline."

"Hello, Vick."

She said the usual things a woman visitor does when she looks over a man's apartment for the first time. "Very nice. I didn't realize you had as nice a place as this."

"It came to me just the way it is, nothing added, nothing taken away. A friend of mine had it, and when he got married he and his girl moved out to the country, so he turned this place over to me. I'm paying the old rent, too. It's a steal."

"Have you been here long?"

"Two and a half years."

Then she'd been here with him. This was where she'd lived. She asked it, anyway. There was no reason not to.

"Did your wife live here with you?"

"Yes, Starr and I spent our marriage here." She saw the old pain cross his face again. The pain, the wanting, that wouldn't die.

He brought out the sherry and sprang the cork and poured it. The wine wasn't chilled but the empty glasses were. He'd learned that trick, which she knew of herself.

He offered her a cigarette. She had her own but she took one of his, to be agreeable. It turned out they smoked the same brand. They laughed a little about it.

"Would you like some music?" he offered. "Or would you rather not?"

"I would, I think it would be nice."

"What would you like?"

She considered. "'One Fine Day,' from *Madame Butterfly*; 'Musetta's Waltz,' from *La Bohème*; 'The Stars Are Shining,' from *Tosca*; maybe 'Villa,' from *The Merry Widow*; the tango 'Jealousy'; 'April in Portugal.' Like that. I like music to follow a melody, I don't like ricky-tick music."

"I have them all. I'll keep it down," he said. "So that we can talk comfortably."

He racked records, flicked the lever, and the needle arm swung out, then in, then down, like something with an intelligence of its own. Then he came back and sat down opposite her on the sofa. The sofa that was to be his bier.

They sat half turned toward one another, easily, negligently, and they chatted.

"I like you very much, Madeline," he said at one point.

She knew exactly how he meant it. It wasn't a declaration of love. You don't lean back on an elbow, with your legs crossed, and say I like you very much, and mean it for love. He had his love already. He liked her as a person. She was compatible.

She didn't know just what to say to that, so she quite simply said the obvious thing: "Thank you. It's always nice to be told that."

After the second glass of sherry, he got up and began his preparations.

The food was excellent. He might not have been an all-around cook (as he had told her he wasn't), but the few dishes he knew how to do, he knew how to do well.

But her concern wasn't with the food.

The setting was charming. Only it had the wrong people in it.

The setting would have been perfect for two lovers. Or even appealing for just two friends. The comfortable, livable, unostentatious yet well-done apartment, the bright-spirited table, the unobtrusive music, the intimacy of a highly attractive woman and a personable man. But they weren't lovers, they weren't friends, they were the slayer and the one who was to be slain.

She glanced around once, in the middle of something he was saying, at the handbag lying there on the sofa across the room where she had left it, with the gun in it, then turned back to him again.

No, it was all wrong to do it this way. To come here and take his food and hospitality, and then to shoot him between the eyes. It was abominable, it was cowardly, it was the worst kind of treachery. And yet what other way was there for her to do it? There was no other way. To lie in wait and shoot him from some doorway as he stepped from a taxi to his entrance? To go up and ring his bell and shoot him as he came to the door, unaware and unprepared? That was for sneak assassinations, such as the underworld carried out, or jealous women, or former business associates with an obsessive grudge. She wasn't an assassin, and this wasn't that kind of killing; This was a killing in fulfillment of a sacred pledge. There was no other way to do it but this, in the open, to his face, letting him know if possible what it was for before he died.

"I thought you looked a little white, just then," he said.

She smiled without denying it.

"But now you don't again."

He filtered the Hennessy into the coffees, then held them both in his hands.

"Shall we take our coffee over there?" he said, tipping his head toward the sofa. "Starr and I always did, whenever we ate home. Which wasn't often."

She got up and went over to it, and they both reseated themselves again where they'd been before, one at each end of it. At a distance of about five feet. There really was no reason for them to be any closer.

But I still don't know, she thought. I must try to get that out of him. I still don't know why she left him.

"Doesn't it hurt you?" she asked him quite bluntly.

"Doesn't what?"

"Doesn't it remind you?"

"Oh, the coffee. No, little things like that don't matter. There's nothing the same about it. The cups aren't the same. The girl sharing them with me isn't the same. The only thing that's the same is the man." Then the pain came and went. "The only thing that hurts is the one big thing—that she left me."

I have him going now. I have him going.

The rack of records finally came to an end. There was a definitive little click, almost like a snub. He turned his head around toward it, then gave her an inquiring look.

"No more," she said curtly, and sliced her hand at it edgewise almost fiercely. Damn that ill-timed machine, she thought.

"Was it very sudden, her leaving you?" She had been straining forward a little toward him. She became aware of it herself, and forced herself to lean back more.

"Terribly sudden. Awfully sudden." He killed all the rest of his coffee in one swallow, more for the brandy than for the coffee, she surmised.

"Sometimes that's kinder, sometimes it's not."

"It's never kind, in love."

And I'm not being kind, am I, doing this to you? But I've got to know. Oh, I've got to know—why I'm killing you.

"Take another drink," she said, with perfidious sympathy— which was only partly perfidious. "When you take a drink, it makes it easier to talk. When you talk, it makes it easier to bear."

He looked at her in acknowledgment. "I've never told it to anybody. You see, there wasn't anybody *to* tell."

"There is now," she said lullingly.

He poured Hennessy into a snifter, about a quarter of the way up the sides. Then he rolled it back and forth between his hands.

She took a chance. It might not come if she just sat and waited. "Was there a quarrel—just before?"

"There wasn't time for a quarrel."

"Oh," she said.

"It started out as some kind of an attack. I didn't know it was going to end up by her leaving me. I didn't know until weeks later."

"But you said—"

It was coming now. It had started. It had started and nothing could stop it. Like when you turn on a faucet and the handle breaks off. Or start a rock slide down a slope of shale.

He pointed to a place nearer the opposite wall than to them. "She fell down on the carpet right there. See where I'm pointing? She fell down very suddenly. Fell like a stone." And as if to re-assure her, he said, "It's not the same carpet. Don't be alarmed. I had it changed."

"Illness?"

"I didn't know at first, I couldn't tell. She was conscious, her eyes stayed open. But she couldn't talk, or wouldn't. She kept thrashing around on the floor, as if she were having a convul-sion. Saliva kept flowing out of her mouth, in spurts. It shone silvery, in little foamy patches. That's why I had the carpet changed, later on. And she started to bite at it. She pulled little tufts out of it with her teeth."

Sweat was pouring down his own face now.

Starr? This was the same Starr who died in my own arms so quietly, so unassumingly, later on? "Not temporary insan—?"

"No," he said quickly, before she had time to finish. "I couldn't do anything with her. She became worse each time I tried to go near her. When I'd try to pick her up in my arms, she'd thrash violently. Unmanageably. A spasm would go through her, almost like a patient undergoing electric-shock therapy."

He swallowed some of his drink. He looked as though it were pulling all the lining off his throat as it went down.

"I had to phone for an ambulance finally. The intern examined her right there on the floor where she was lying. He said it was shock. Acute shock. Emotional shock. He said he'd seen it in soldiers, during the Korean War. He gave her a needle to quiet her, and, of course, they took her to the hospital."

Now he took another drink, a worse one, a more hurtful one.

She took a chance and opened her handbag narrowly, just about the width of the edge of her hand, and dipped inside and pulled out a handkerchief. It had a little cologne on it, but that couldn't be helped. She threw it over toward him, and he picked it up and mopped his soaking forehead with it, and then pressed it between the palms of his hands.

"As she went out that door on the stretcher, that was the last time I ever saw her. I never saw her again to this day. She never came back here from that night on."

"But how is it you didn't go with her? Doesn't a husband usually go with his wife, when she's taken ill like that?"

"She wouldn't let me. She carried on so terribly. You see the needle didn't take effect quickly enough, and she must have heard me say I'd ride over with her in the ambulance. She started to moan and plead to them not to let me come near her, she didn't want me to come near her. Finally the intern took me aside and said it might be better if I didn't, the idea seemed to have an exciting effect on her. To wait awhile and give her time to quiet down. He said he didn't think it was anything to worry about, it was just a nerve crisis of some kind.

"So I walked the floor, walked the floor, all night long."

He stopped suddenly. He gave her a peculiar look and said, "Why am I telling you all this?"

"I don't know," Madeline said quietly. "There are times when everybody has to tell somebody things—and I'm the one this time." Then she added, "Finish it. You've already told me so much, it doesn't matter if you go ahead. I'd like to hear the rest."

"The rest is very little," he said. "I gave them time to get her there, and then I called the hospital. They'd checked her in— I'd arranged for a private room—and they told me she was asleep.

"I stayed on my feet all night. I went around the very first thing the next day, and they told me she was resting quietly, but I must have patience, I couldn't see her yet, she still wasn't in any condition to be disturbed.

"I went back in the evening. There was a new nurse on duty, but she told me the same thing.

"Well, for the first three, maybe four, days I could understand it and I could accept it." He clenched his fist, and then splayed the fingers open again in all directions. "But for three weeks—three weeks—three weeks"—he said it three times— "I visited that hospital twice a day. Forty-two visits. And somewhere along in those weeks I finally caught on. It might have been hospital regulations in the beginning but it was her own doing that was keeping me out by this time. She must have refused to see me and ordered them not to admit me. I couldn't even reach her by phone. The nurse always answered each time, and wouldn't let me talk to her. I tried writing. The letters came back unopened inside typed hospital envelopes."

"And then?"

"And then. The forty-second time I went around there was the evening of the twenty-first day. I got a different message that time. The nurse told me she'd checked out that morning, without leaving any forwarding address. They didn't know where she'd gone."

He fell silent for a minute, and she thought it was over.

But it wasn't. Suddenly he went on, "The nurse was very worldly-wise, you know how nurses are. She looked at me very closely and she said, 'I don't know what happened between the two of you, Mr. Herrick. She didn't tell me, and I don't want to know, it's not my business. But don't you think it's better for her sake if you keep away from her from now on, don't try to go after her, don't try to find her. That young girl we had in here all those weeks wasn't fooling, wasn't acting a part. She's a real sick girl.' And she took a very small envelope out of her desk drawer, one of those little things they use for holding pills and capsules, and handed it to me. It was sealed and nothing was written on it. I didn't open it until I'd taken it home with me."

"What was in it?" she asked when the halt had become noticeable.

"Do you really want me to tell you what was in it? You don't leave me anything, do you?"

She gestured imperturbably with one turned-up hand.

"My wedding ring was in it. Hers. The one I'd bought her. And another thing, a terrible thing. I don't think any husband ever got a thing like that, from the wife who was walking away from him."

And again he couldn't seem to bring it out, but this time she didn't ask.

"A scrap of toilet tissue. That had been soiled. It was folded all around the ring. The ring was embedded in it."

She backed her hand to her mouth, in reflex dismay.

After that he didn't talk anymore. What more was there to say, after what he'd told her at the very last?

Now was the time for her to talk, and after she'd talked, for him to die.

"I met Starr once," she said tonelessly, casually.

She could tell he didn't think he'd heard her right. "You what? What was that you said?"

"I met Starr once."

"After she left me?"

"After she left, yes."

Hope was lighting up his face, even this soon. It was like a flame. He was handsome with hope, dazzle-eyed with it.

"No, no," she said quickly, and motioned to him forbiddingly. "Don't hope. Don't. It'll hurt twice as much after, if you do."

His face died again, went out again.

God, how he loves her, she thought. But what did he *do* to her—?

His mouth was hanging open, mutely begging, silently pleading.

"Yes, I'm going to tell you. I'm going to tell you about it, all about it. Just as you told me your story, from your end, I'm going to tell you my story, from my end. Isn't it funny how the two of us come together, and piece the two pieces together, and then we have the whole story."

"Hurry," he panted, almost like a man dying of thirst.

"It was last May, a year ago. I was going to kill myself."

"Why?"

"Do you want to know something? It's hard to remember why. Because life had no meaning, I guess. Because—just because. I had a gun, the only thing my father left me when he drank himself to death. I put the gun to my head and actually pulled the trigger and the gun didn't go off."

"A miracle," he breathed.

"That's what I thought. I felt reborn. I leaped up, ready to dance and sing with joy. I threw the gun down. And—"

"Yes?"

"It went off. The shot passed through the window. Are you sure you want to hear this? Are you sure?"

"Don't torture me."

"That's when I met Starr. She was the one the bullet hit. She died in my arms."

She stopped. There wasn't any more to tell him.

She wondered if he'd cry, or moan, or what he'd do. She'd think a little less of him if he did—she didn't like whimpering men—yet what right had she to set a pattern for his grief?

He didn't move at all for several minutes. Just sat there numbed, dazed.

Then he picked up the brandy snifter. She thought he was going to drain its contents in a gulp.

Instead he stood up, shock-sudden, all six feet of him, and hurled it. The liquor made an amber rainbow of falling drops all across the room and the glass exploded into a hundred pieces against the wall.

He roared at the top of his voice, something without words to it, something guttural and horrible and made of pain. And then he balled a fist, and bared his teeth like an animal snarling at a master who had just kicked him, and looked straight up overhead at the ceiling. But she knew he wasn't seeing the ceiling.

"As for you—!"

She went over to him quickly and sealed his mouth with her hand.

"Don't," she cautioned him, almost superstitiously. "Not that. Haven't you been punished enough? Are you begging for more? Don't turn on your God because of something you've done yourself."

"He's not my—"

She quickly put her hand back again. Then he slumped, and all the defiance went out of him. He turned and went back to the sofa, and sagged into it bonelessly, soddenly.

"Something I've done myself," he kept repeating listlessly, the words she'd just used. "Something I've done myself."

"It must have been," she said finally, in a low, almost inaudible voice. "Why would the girl leave you like that, why send you back your ring defiled? I'll tell you something else, Vick. She wanted you killed, Starr wanted you killed. If she'd lived, she could have known no peace until you were killed. What was it? What was it you did to her?"

She watched him, studied him. She could see a change coming over his face. A look that hadn't been there before. Not the pain of loving and losing Starr. Not the grief-rage of hearing of her death. No, something else.

She tried to translate it, and she thought she did.

While the thing he loved was alive yet, in the same world with him yet, even though they were apart, nothing could slake his thirst for her, fever, addiction, use whichever word you want. Nothing else counted, nothing else mattered, nothing else existed. There was no right, there was no wrong, there was no good, there was no bad.

Now she no longer lived, was gone from the world.

The flame that had fed on her body, even though it was only in his mind and nowhere else, now had nothing more to feed on. And when flames have nothing more to feed on, they go down, down, down. A flame can't stay alive on a memory.

She could see it expiring in him as he was sitting there. Horror was coming on. It was written on his face, and his eyes were big and round and flickering with horror. Now the blazing flame that must have kept things, unspeakable things, at a distance, beyond the pale, like a burning, slowly turning sword, was gone. Now the skeletons and the worms, the maggots and the vermin, all the things that were fearsome and unclean and foul, crept slowly in toward him, ringing him around, closing in, feeding on him, covering him.

And he, in their center, was in a hell such as this world never knew of, nor even the hell that was the hell beyond this world.

She could see it on his face. It was almost too awful to watch. She looked down into her lap, batedly, fearfully.

She could hear her own words still echoing, ringing faintly in the room around her, though it seemed long ago that they'd been spoken. "What was it? What was it you did to her?"

And suddenly he answered, and everything was over.

"Because I was her own brother!"

In the hollow stillness that followed came the sound of far-away voices from the past, drumming in her ears like knells of doom; came the memory of things that had been said, and things that she had read.

She heard Charlotte Bartlett's voice again, in the distance: "We had a little baby boy first, before Starr. Then we lost him. He just disappeared from the face of the earth. One minute he was playing in front of the door. The next minute there wasn't a sign of him."

Starr herself, in a letter to her mother: "…That little-boy look, that husband look. I threw my arms around him and hung from his neck with my feet lifted clear of the ground, and kissed him about eighteen times."

Dell, baring her heart in reminiscence: "I could tell when

he'd been with her. The telltale little signs that give a man away. Tired, all vitality spent. A hollowness in the cheeks and at the temples that was gone again inside twenty-four hours. To come back once more inside forty-eight."

Even the nurse at the hospital, as given at second hand by himself: "She's a real sick girl. I don't know what you've done to her, but keep away from her!"

She jolted to her feet, and her face wasn't just white, it was yellow with illness.

"Where's the bathroom? Hurry up—!" she said in a strangled voice.

"In there—the door with the mirror—"

The mirror flashed back the lights of the room as she flung the door open, then an instant later flashed again like a panel of running water as she came out almost immediately afterward.

"False alarm," she said sardonically, to no one in particular. "I must have a stronger stomach than I—"

She looked around for the Hennessy, found it, and poured herself some without asking him to help her. She poured it into a small shot glass, downed it at a throw. She needed it.

She sat down on the sofa without looking toward him. There was silence between them for a long time after that. He seemed to have forgotten she was even there. She couldn't forget that he was.

"How long after you were married did you find it out?" she asked suddenly.

He shook his head doggedly. "I knew it before."

If anything new could have been rung in on the gamut of emotions she'd already experienced in this one evening, this did it now. She felt a mixture of disgust and dismay, and an overall incredulity. "You knew it, and you went ahead and married her!" she choked.

"I was in love with her. I even left my wife for her." Then he corrected, as an afterthought, "My first wife."

"Don't put it that way," she said, grimacing in horror.

For the first time since the thing had come out into the open, he turned and looked directly at her. Her own eyes turned and fled off into a far corner, straining to get away from his look, refusing to endure him. "I never loved somebody like I loved her. Couldn't you see it, the way I looked when you said her name? Couldn't you tell it, the way I spoke when I said it?

"I knew when I married her. She didn't. I married her with my eyes wide open. What was the difference, by then?"

"What was the *difference*?" she gasped.

"We'd already been sleeping with each other while I was still living with Dell. The marriage didn't bring on anything new. I didn't want a paramour. I loved her like a man loves the woman he wants to marry—and does marry.

"It's not so terrible. It's just the idea that frightens you and sounds so terrible."

"It's accursed," she cut in sharply. "It's unclean. It's forbidden," but he paid no attention.

"We were complete strangers," he said, raising his voice in his own defense. "Even if we'd spent a year together as children—even a half year, a month. But we'd never set eyes on each other in our lives before, until the day we met and started to fall in love. No one was as complete strangers as we two were. The only thing that was the same was the blood. And what does the blood know, how can it tell? Cousins often marry cousins. In ancient Egypt the law in the ruling family was for brother to marry sister. It was traditional. It's only because it's taboo now that it shocks so."

"That was paganism. This is Christianity. And by that I mean as well Judaism, Islam, call it what you will; it's condemned by all of them alike. It's taboo for a reason," she said coldly, "and it's not meant to be disobeyed."

"You see this beautiful face," he said dreamily. "You love this beautiful face. You love this beautiful person. Then you find out that for a little while, at the start of life, you nursed at the breast of the same woman who nursed her afterward. But if you already love as deeply as you do it's too late to make a difference anymore. It doesn't seem to matter, it fans your love even more. Now you love not only her, you love the added closeness that brings you that much nearer to her each time. Your sense of owning, of possessing, is strengthened that much more."

"You're not trying to convince me," she said dully. "You're trying to convince yourself. It's written on your face, the guilt, the fear—"

"Yes, because now she's gone. She's not here anymore to keep the guilt, the fear, at a distance, make me forget."

"You can't bury your conscience, you can't kill it completely. You've destroyed yourself. Now you won't be able to bear living, and you'll be terrified of dying. Or you should be."

He hung his head in admission.

"How did you first find out?"

He spoke with his head still downturned, without looking up at her. "Quite simply, nothing complicated about it. My mother died about seven, eight years ago. The night before she passed, I was sitting there beside her bed, and she told me there was something she wanted to get off her mind before she went, she'd feel better about it if she did. It sounds like one of those old melodramas, I know, but it really happened this way.

"She was jilted, as a young girl, after the guy got her pregnant. The child, when it came, was stillborn. This preyed on her mind and, I guess, turned her queer for a while.

"She talked about walking through a certain street one day,

and seeing this small child playing there in front of a house. She named the street and even gave the number of the house. She said she couldn't help herself. Before she realized she was doing it, she was leading the child by the hand down the street.

"Around the corner she got into a taxi with it, and had the taxi drive her to a false address, completely away from where she really lived. Then from there she rode a bus back to her own place.

"They lived in one of these old-fashioned private houses, just she and her mother, and so they were at least safe from the prying eyes of neighbors in adjoining flats. I don't know how they got away with it, but they did. I suppose they kept me indoors and away from the windows for the remainder of their stay there. It was easier to get away with things like that in the thirties than it would be in the sixties. The mother was in a wheelchair and couldn't have done much to oppose the thing even if she'd wanted to. But she was all for it, because it made her daughter happy and in a very short while she herself had grown very attached to me.

"As soon as it was safe to do so, in about a year's time, after most of the furor had subsided, they took the precaution of selling the house and moving out to a place in the country.

"Then when my father appeared on the scene—I should say the man she married—and proposed to her, she told him all about the old-time seduction, but not the other thing, and let him think that I was the child in question. He married her, anyway, and he was not only a good husband but a good father to me all his life.

"It's as simple as that.

"Then after I met Starr, about a month after we first started making love to each other, she was lying next to me talking to me one night. You know how people tell everything about themselves at times like that. She mentioned her father's drinking, and said she thought it was caused by her mother's resentment because he'd tricked her into having her, Starr, when she didn't want to have any more children. And she went on to tell about this little brother of hers who'd disappeared before she was born and never'd been seen again. Quite casually, she mentioned the street and the house number where they'd been living when it happened. I didn't even ask her to. It was the same street, the same house, my mother had referred to.

"I knew I was that same child."

"Didn't you show anything? Couldn't she tell you were surprised?"

"We were in the dark. She couldn't see my face."

"And you never told her." It wasn't a question.

"Never to the end."

"Then how did she find out?"

"It must have been my first wife, Dell. I never found out for sure, but it couldn't have been anyone else but Dell.

"Starr and I had been making love, that one night. Later I was drowsing, half asleep. It seemed like far off—you know how things sound when you're half asleep like that—far off I seemed to hear the phone ring. It was right there next to the bed, but I was too groggy to answer it, so I guess she must have. If only I'd picked it up instead, maybe we'd still be together today, the two of us. I didn't hear her saying much. Just one thing came through clearly. She must have raised her voice or something at that point. Just one thing is all I heard. 'You must be crazy!' The next thing, I could feel her shaking me and shaking me, as though she were half distracted. I couldn't snap out of it, I couldn't open my eyes. I heard her say, 'Were you adopted? Were you an adopted child? Were you?' She kept on shaking me, until I mumbled yes. All I wanted was for her to stop shaking me, let me go back to sleep. But she kept asking me, 'From where? From where?' I spoke with my eyes still closed, my brain in a fog, just the name of the state, that's all. Not even the town. But it was enough. It was enough.

"Suddenly the lights flashed on. That opened my eyes finally, I was awake at last. And she was running from the room, running from the room. I can't tell you how she was running from the room. As if—as if pursued by the very hounds of hell. I jumped up and went after her. I caught up to her here, in this room we're in now. I asked her what the matter was, and I put out my hand and touched her. At the mere touch of my hand, she fell down on the floor like I told you, in this shock state."

This was no petty harm, she thought, no little meanness, no small unhappiness. This was an enormity. It was no wonder that Starr wanted him dead. He deserved to die.

She took up the handbag, held it upright in her lap, a hand at each corner of its frame. She wondered if he had any idea what was in it. How could he? But he would, very soon now.

"Aren't you asking yourself why I came here tonight?"

"That was a thousand years ago," he said listlessly, "before I knew she was dead. I remember now, you came here to have dinner." He looked at the table they'd used. "We did have dinner. A thousand years ago."

"But is that all I'd come here for, a dinner? I can get a dinner anywhere. Why should I come here to you? We're not in love. We're not even close friends."

"Then why did you?"

"I told you she died in my arms. Now do you understand?"

He looked at her strangely, as though in a sudden flash of premonition he did. But he didn't admit that he did. And he didn't show any fear.

"I retraced her steps," she told him. "Those steps she took away from you. Would you like to know where they carried her, toward what?"

"I'd like to know anything about her there is," he said as insatiably as ever. "Anything about her is what I want to know, to hear, to be told. It brings her back again for a little while, in all her flame, all her glow, all her glory."

"Her glory was shame and darkness, the glory that you gave her," she spat out at him. "The hospital might have cured the shock symptoms, but she was a sick girl the day she walked out of there, sick in mind and sick in soul. She walked in shadows. She hid away, tried to hide away, from those shadows, in a cheap furnished room. I've been in it. I can see her there now, as she must have been. The shades pulled all the way down, all day long; hiding from life, trying to keep it out. Trembling on the bed at times, even though she wasn't cold. Waking up at night from a fever-sleep and screaming out her horror and despair.

"She saw there was only one way to dispel those shadows, only one way to cleanse them out of her heart. Only one way to achieve purification. She had been brought up in a religion which forbade administration of the last rites or burial in consecrated ground to suicides. That way out was barred to her, then, or she surely would have taken it. But she was too frightened by what she'd been through to be able to face death without consolation, lie for all eternity an outcast, unhallowed and unprayed for. So she chose another crime, another sin, instead, perhaps as being the lesser of the two, who knows? The more redeemable. And that was the blotting out, the extirpation, of the source of the impurity that had engulfed her. That was the only way she could find peace.

"She left the room, gave up the room for the time being, and went back to her mother's. To try to pull herself together a little, and also to make her preparations."

She saw his brows twitch involuntarily.

"She bought a gun," she said. "I have it. Its license is in her name."

She saw his face go momentarily to the handbag, and then back to her face again.

He knows, she said to herself. He knows.

There was no fear. And neither was there any will to self-preservation, any crafty, calculating look of planning how best to evade or outwit it. She didn't receive that impression. It was more like somebody waiting with as much patience as they could for something good, some benefit, to come to them.

"It's, in many ways, far easier for a girl to obtain a permit for a gun than it is for a man. At least if she is known to the license department, has been a lifelong resident of the community, and is known to have a good reputation. She can plead molesta-tion, real or fancied, fear of being followed or accosted on her way home late at night; fear of breaking and entry, if she occu-pies an apartment alone or, as in Starr's case, with just an elderly woman; crackpot or obscene phone calls; any number of things like that.

"I don't know if Starr did that. I do know she got her license and got the gun. She bought it quite openly at a sporting-goods store.

"When she was on the point of coming back here again, her mother, who'd guessed enough to feel uneasy about the whole thing, sneaked it out of her locked bag and hid it. She turned it over to me, when I retraced Starr's path, step by step."

This time he kept from looking at the handbag, but she could tell by his eyes he wanted to.

"Starr actually only discovered she was without the gun when she was once more back in the same furnished room she'd occupied the first time. I suppose she would have simply gone about the business of trying to get another one here in the city, which wouldn't have been quite as easy a matter. But before she could do anything at all, she walked past the ground-floor windows of my house quite at random—and she didn't need a gun anymore. I was the means of killing her."

She saw him put a hand around his throat and hold it tightly, as though it hurt him there to breathe.

"I pledged myself to carry out whatever she wanted most out of life. The wreckage of life that was all there was left to her.

"Above all else, she wanted your death."

At this, he slowly inclined his head in a sort of fatalistic acquiescence, as if to say: If she wanted it thus, thus let it be.

"And I'm pledged to carry that out for her. For I took her life away, and I must do the things, in her place, that I kept her from doing."

She opened the handbag at long last and took out the gun. He winced a little, very briefly, as you do when you know pain is coming. Necessary, benevolent pain. Then he turned more fully toward her, as if to give her a better surface at which to shoot, and he took a deep breath. It almost sounded like relief.

He didn't speak another word from then on, for all the rest of the time she was there in the room.

Although the way it lay, on its side, it was pointing straight at him, she didn't raise it in her hand.

He started to lean a little toward her. Not in an attempt to close the gap between them, in order to snatch at it or try to deflect it. For he kept his arms where they'd been—they were now slightly to the rear of him—and he leaned forward with his upper body only. He was like a man slowly preparing for a dive, a dive down into death. He even tilted his face upward a little, as if trying to help her, trying to cooperate. And his eyes were pleading, begging, she couldn't mistake what they were saying to her. Asking for this gift that she alone could give him. The gift of death. The gift of clean, fast death, and then no more horror, no more fear, no more anything but nothing.

The tip of his tongue even crept out for an instant over at the far corner of his mouth, and touched the edge of his lips, as if in barely restrained anticipation.

Then he dropped the lids over his eyes and he just waited, breathing a little fast but breathing hopefully. Not cringing. Waiting bated for the accolade of deliverance. "You are free." God's greatest gift to man: death.

"But I'm not going to do it," she said, with no more inflection than they'd used at the dinner table earlier. "I can't. I see that now. This isn't my affair. Why should I interfere? Who gave me that right and who gave me that obligation? I have my own happiness, my own peace, to think of. I've caused one death, taken one life, already. Why should I add a second to it? Will that make it easier for my conscience to bear the first? No. Why should I liquidate my debt to Starr, only to find myself with a new one on my hands, to you? And after you, who next? On and on and on, like the links of an endless chain. And if she could look at you now as I'm looking at you, perhaps she wouldn't want you dead after all. For the greater punishment for you by far is not to be dead. I think for you, life is death. And death would be—just escape. So Starr gets her fulfillment after all.

"My hand won't be the one to meddle with your destiny."

His eyes had flown open, stunned, reproachful, long ago.

She'd gotten to her feet, and as she did so, the gun slid off her lap and into the inside corner of the sofa. She made no move to reclaim it. If she saw it at all, it had lost all meaning for her; her faculties were too absorbed in the metaphysical problem that engaged them both, inanimate objects around her had no bearing or existence.

He didn't seem to notice it either. It was into her face that he kept looking, with his haunted, pleading eyes, so strained they were like white scars slashed across his face. Nothing else existed. To the end they were fixed on her, begging without a word.

She opened the door, and from it looked back at him. "Good-bye," she said quietly. "May God have mercy on your soul. Your poor, poor soul."

She closed the door, and shut the sight of him out.

She ran and ran and ran, through endless corridors of the night—as Starr had once run the unattainable distance between his bed and his front door—ran for miles and ran for hours, through countless turnings and this-ways and that-ways, and ups and downs, and meshing of cabs and braking of cabs, and the supporting arms of doormen and of elevator men around her, until at last the running stopped and she lay still, holding a palmful of little white pellets in one hand, a small half-empty bottle in the other.

When she opened her eyes in the morning after a tranquilizer-induced sleep, somehow she knew right away. He wasn't in the world with her anymore. He was dead.

She was so sure, so certain, that she almost didn't bother to ascertain. When she'd dressed, she went over to the window as she had yesterday and stood looking out. How long ago yesterday seemed.

She looked up at the sky and the clouds skimming by across it like little puff balls of white cotton, some of them unraveling with their own speed. Was it a better world without him? Was it a worse world? It was neither, she knew. It was an oblivious world, it didn't even know he was gone. One living soul less, that was all.

She happened to glance at the watch on her wrist, and it was twenty-eight before the hour. Just in time for the half-hourly news break. She'd probably missed the lead item, but that was sure to have been political, most likely the Congo. She turned the knob of the little transistor, which had the advantage of not taking time to warm up. The radio came on abruptly in the middle of an item, a drug-related shooting on the West Side. She listened to the full newscast without hearing anything of personal significance.

Then they were playing music again. She left the radio on but paid no attention to what she was hearing. She had the impulse to turn off the radio and switch off the lamp, and she remembered when she'd done that once before, ultimately taking her father's gun and pressing it to her temple.

If only it had gone off when she squeezed the trigger. She remembered Vernon Herrick, his eyes wild as he told her about his injury on Tarawa. He was right—sometimes the ones who died were the lucky ones.

> *You and I, together all alone,*
> *In a little country of our own,*
> *Where the population's only two—*

She started. Was she hallucinating? Or was it her song, playing on the radio?

The tune was unfamiliar, nothing she had heard before. But the lyric was hers, the one lyrical fragment Dell had commented favorably on. The rest of the lyric was as unfamiliar to her as the melody. She heard the song all the way through, entranced by it, and at the end her bit of lyric returned as the song's climax.

You and I, together all alone,
In a little country of our own,
Where the population's only two.

It was easy to guess what must have happened. Dell, more impressed by the words than she'd cared to admit, had passed them on to a professional songwriter. And he'd incorporated them in a song, stealing them without a qualm, and now a singer had recorded the song and it was getting air play. It might even become a hit.

The irony of it, she thought. That a song with that particular lyric should become popular at just this stage of her life.

Because here she was, just as she'd been at the beginning. All alone, on a desert island of her own.

Where the population's only one.

She was scanning the radio dial, trying to find another news report—or, failing that, perhaps the song again, on another station—when there was a knock on the door.

The police, she thought.

Her mind flew back to the scene in Vick's apartment, her fingerprints on the dinner dishes, the silverware. The chilled wine glass. The coffee cup. Would they believe that she'd had nothing to do with his suicide? Or would she finally receive the punishment she was due, not for the death she'd actually caused but for one she hadn't, one for which she had been at most a posthumous intermediary?

She turned the radio down to a whisper, approached the door. "Who is it?" she called.

The response was muffled. She couldn't make it out.

"Who is it?"

The voice rose, spoke louder. A voice she had never thought to hear again. "Please, Madeline. Please open the door."

She turned the lock and the knob. Vick Herrick stood on the threshold, wearing the same clothes he'd been in last night, the skin of his face pale and sallow. He hadn't slept, she could see that. No tranquilizers had helped him survive the long night. But survive it he somehow had.

He held a black velvet handbag clutched before him at his chest. Black velvet beaded with a design of flowers. One of Starr's, one that she had left behind when she had left him, one that he had kept. Preserved. And found again when he had something precious to carry in it.

Something of hers.

Madeline stepped back and he entered her room.

She said to him, "You couldn't…?"

Suddenly he was weeping, shaking his head forcefully as wetness streaked his cheeks. "I had to see you again. Even if it's to be for the last time. Because—" he choked back a sob deep in his throat "—because you brought her back to me. As horrible as it was, as painful as it was, I felt Starr there with us last night. Not just her memory. Her. She was there with us, and no power in all the world could make me end my own life when somewhere in this city her presence remained."

The weight of that phrase—my own life—hung between them like a thundercloud in a lowering sky. He couldn't end his *own* life.

He held the velvet clutch out toward her, but Madeline kept her hands down by her sides. She stepped back, and he stepped forward, like a man leading his beloved in a dance. At her hip Madeline felt the wooden edge of a table and she leaned on it for support.

"I can't do it for you, Vick. I can't and I won't."

"You must," he said, urging the velvet bag on her. She thought she could see the weight it held, its black, beaded sides swelling softly around its deadly burden. "You must." And again: "You must," but this time with something added, "You must, Starr."

Madeline froze. I am not, she wanted to cry, I never was, I never took her place, no, not that way. I swore to live *for* her but not *as* her—

With his free hand, Vick reached out and took one of hers, lifted it, pressed the soft velvet into it, and through the thin layer of fabric she felt it inside, the long barrel and then the heavier, wider part fused to it at its root where the bullets lay, waiting to spring forward.

Her breath escaped in a small explosion and she tried to pull her hand away, but he closed her fingers around the deadly tool, and when she snatched her hand back at last, it came as well, in her suddenly tightened grip.

"I won't! I won't!" she cried, and slammed the thing down on the table beside her. And she meant to say more: "It's Starr's," she would have said, "not mine." Or, "It's yours, as your life is, to keep or to throw away, but you cannot put it on me."

She would have said these things, or other things perhaps. But instead her mouth hung open and, as he tipped his chin to look downwards, so did his.

In the small hotel room, the sound of the gunshot was enormous.

A hole, torn, in the velvet. Its edges singed.

An echoing sound, like the echo of a cymbal crash in a symphony hall, before the thunderous applause that follows.

But there would be no applause here, in this hotel room, on this street, in this city—there would be no applause, only thunder, only the radio's thin whisper as the echoes died.

And then the other sounds:

The slap of footsteps, running in the corridor. Knuckles

landing roughly on the outside of her door. Voices calling.

And down below in the street, in the distance at first but then nearer, nearer, always nearer, a siren.

Vick was on his side now, his head resting against the carpet. Madeline sank down beside him.

He was trying to speak, but in this swelling sea of sounds, no sound remained to him. She saw his lips form the word. She knew what word it was.

Starr.

And on his lips—was it only her imagination?—she imagined she saw the slight curve of a smile. The smile from the torn photograph, restored again.

The radio played on. The music. The song. Her song. Their song.

> *You and I, together all alone,*
> *In a little country of our own,*
> *Where the population's only two.*

SONGS of INNOCENCE

by **RICHARD ALEAS**

Three years ago, detective John Blake solved a mystery that changed his life forever—and left a woman he loved dead. Now Blake is back, to investigate the apparent suicide of Dorothy Louise Burke, a beautiful college student with a double life. The secrets Blake uncovers could blow the lid off New York City's sex trade...if they don't kill him first.

Richard Aleas' first novel, LITTLE GIRL LOST, was among the most celebrated crime novels of the year, nominated for both the Edgar and Shamus Awards. *But nothing in John Blake's first case could prepare you for the shocking conclusion of his second...*

PRAISE FOR SONGS OF INNOCENCE:

"An instant classic."
— Washington Post

"The best thing Hard Case is publishing right now."
— San Francisco Chronicle

"His powerful conclusion will drop jaws."
— Publishers Weekly

"So sharp [it'll] slice your finger as you flip the pages."
— Playboy

**Available now from your favorite bookseller.
For more information, visit
www.HardCaseCrime.com**